GROCERY GIRL

BOOK 1

VIRGINIA'DELE SMITH

BOOKS ARE UBIQUITOUS

BOOKS ARE UBIQUITOUS

Published by Books are Ubiquitous, Inc.
Tulsa, Oklahoma in the United States of America
www.booksareubiquitous.com
contact@booksareubiquitous.com
Books are Ubiquitous is a federally registered trademark.

This book is a work of fiction.

Names, characters, places, and incidents either are the product of the author's imagination or are used fictitiously. Any resemblance to actual persons, living or dead, business establishments, events, or locales is entirely coincidental.

ISBN: 978-1-957036-04-5

To my Angel Girl, Maci Maree.

When I envision a strong, brilliant, compassionate,
and gorgeous young woman,
I see you.

There is no such thing as a coincidence.
Gibbs's rule #9, NCIS

Green Hills, Oklahoma, was no longer so small that every single person knew all the others, but it was still small enough for Maree to notice the new addition to fire engine #33.

She bought fruit at the Get'n'Go grocery store every Monday morning. And almost every week, a fire truck from station #2 was parked in front of the building while she was there. She knew the firefighters cooked the majority of their meals at the firehouse, and she had learned from a cashier that each shift created their own menus and shopped for ingredients at the beginning of their twenty-four hours on.

They were always polite, high-fiving kids and saying hello to customers throughout the store. Other than noticing that and being impressed with their friendliness when no doubt they were in a rush to get in and out, Maree had never paid them much attention.

She was on her own grocery-gathering mission and tended to go about her shopping with a singular focus. Her Monday morning ritual stemmed from cherished childhood memories of her mom providing fresh fruit for a youth shelter every week. Maree could close her eyes and be transported back to those days. How special she'd felt as a preschooler accompanying her mother on what Momma always called their "most important business" with her trademark wink and a stunning smile that radiated warmth in Maree's heart.

Maree was young enough to go every week, but the very best shopping adventures occurred when her older siblings, Max and M'Kenzee, went with them during school breaks and summer vacations.

Each Monday morning, Momma would wake up all three kids, feed them some breakfast, and scuttle them into the car to take them on her weekly errand. If the kids groaned with exaggeration about not being allowed to sleep late during vacation, she'd tease that they were "blessed to spend time with their adoring mother." If they faux-complained about going to the grocery store, she'd point out the "beautiful bounty to behold all around." And if they dramatically dragged their feet going into the shelter, she'd quietly remind them that "any old building becomes a home when we put a little love into it."

Maree thought Max and M'Kenzee were clever and funny. She would quietly giggle watching them give Momma a hard time, fussing and moaning as if she was torturing them. Of course, they were just pretending. Every one of them knew how much they loved going on this mission. All three of them, and in fact, everyone Maree ever saw in Momma's presence, seemed to bloom under the glow of her attention like a flower opening its face to absorb the sun and blossoming to its fullest potential.

Momma made those fruit deliveries year-round and without fail. If they were going to be out of town for some reason — maybe away on a family trip — she always arranged for someone to do the shopping and drop off the fruit in her place. There was something steady and stable about knowing exactly what Momma would be doing following school drop-off on the first day of every week. She was consistent and true, dependable, and always there for those in need.

But then came the greatest tragedy of Maree's life, and like it was just yesterday, she remembered waking up in a cold sweat the first Monday after her parents died. She couldn't stop crying because she knew that just as she was lost and staggering without her, those kids at the shelter would be missing Momma. She begged everyone to drive her to the store. The friends and neighbors and social workers stepping in to help take care of the three orphans wanted only to placate her; no one listened past her tears. She cried to Max and M'Kenzee that they needed to take care of the fruit, that it was "most important business" just as Momma had always said, but both of her siblings were lost in their own sadness and grief. Everyone said the exact same thing, even though they knew it was nothing more than a lie meant to reassure: "Everything will be okay."

It was not okay with Maree. Not then, and not in the years to follow. As soon as she was on her own in college, she found a shelter that could benefit from a box of fresh fruit every week and reinstated the tradition. She did it in honor of Momma and their Monday mornings together.

When she moved to Green Hills right after her college graduation two years ago, she was not able to find a shelter or church that would accept her donations. The people she spoke with appreciated the offer and loved the idea, but Green Hills was a small town with philanthropic citizens who liked to take care of one another without much fuss. Everywhere she went, she heard that there simply wasn't enough need, that too much would go unused and be thrown out.

She had mentioned her goal — and her struggles attaining it — to her landlord at Marshall Mansion, the bed-and-breakfast where she had lived until she'd found a place of her own. Without a moment's hesitation, Miss Sadie said she'd be blessed to receive that fruit each week, to share with her boarders and passers-through.

Miss Sadie could afford her own fruit, but Maree needed to be needed. Miss Sadie and Maree could both see that as plain as day. With Max and M'Kenzee both pursuing careers across the country, feeling engaged in her new community was vital to fighting off the loneliness that crept up on Maree from time to time. Maree believed that God created human beings to connect with and count on one another, that people were wired to be together. She longed for those connections. Above all else, she needed to maintain this very special memory of her momma, who seemed so terribly far away after all the years since her death.

Like clockwork, every Monday morning Maree hit the grocery store around 9 a.m., selected several dozen pieces of fruit that looked the best, and drove the bags out to Miss Sadie. She never did her own shopping at the same time; she treasured this particular trip too much to water it down with distractions. On top of that, the one time she'd asked her mother why they bought only the fruit for the shelter when they had groceries on their own list, Momma had replied, "Our needs can wait; today is about others." That lesson lived close to Maree's heart, as a guide to life as much as a guarded and precious memory.

Then, one bright, shining Monday morning, while sunbeams filtered into the produce section through the wall of glass at the front of the store, Maree was humming an old Loretta Lynn classic to herself, soaking up the beauty of a perfect day, and basking in her weekly routine. She was sorting through the apricots and delighting in their perfectly sweet smell when the firefighters entered the store.

To say that they made an entrance was *quite* an understatement!

With heads held high and purpose in their steps, the firefighters exuded strength and quiet confidence. They wore turnout pants and suspenders over gray cotton t-shirts with the letters GHFD prominently and boldly stamped across their muscular chests, black leather station boots, and heavy belts with radios and tools hanging low on their hips. It was only natural to take notice when the group walked in.

Like everyone else in the Get'n'Go, Maree glanced up as they walked through the sliding glass doors that Monday morning, the backlighting of sunbeams making them appear ethereal and Godlike. Were they actually glittering, or was that just her imagination?

And then her gaze locked with a set of uniquely gray eyes.

Maree had never seen *this* firefighter before. Their stare held for a smidge longer than a split second. Then he nodded a brief acknowledgment and kept walking. It took her a blink or two — or maybe ten — to get her wits about her.

He was definitely new in town, because there was no way she would have forgotten having seen him before. Taking a deep, intentional breath and with a little shake of her head, she broke out of the mini-trance, forced herself to refocus, and finished her shopping.

She giggled at herself when she recounted the whole second-and-a-half time lapse of the not-quite interaction to Miss Sadie when she delivered her fruit a half hour later. When Sadie asked what the rest of him looked like, Maree honestly had no idea.

"Miss Sadie," she confessed, "I didn't make it past those eyes."

"Well, that's surely a shame," Miss Sadie crooned. "Now

you'll never know if it's the same fellow when you meet him in town or simply walking down the street."

She was giving Maree a hard time, teasing in good fun, but Maree wasn't worried.

"I'll know him," she replied with dreamy confidence. "I'm certain I'd know those eyes anywhere."

2

*A stunning first impression was not
the same thing as love at first sight.
But surely it was an invitation
to consider the matter.*
Lois McMaster Bujold

*I*t was three weeks later when Maree actually spoke to
the new fireman.

She was not paying great attention to where she was going,
grabbing for a runaway cantaloupe while pushing her basket
toward the checkout station, when she ran into a very stout,
very solid object.

Him.

"Oh! I am so sorry," she exclaimed. Maree looked up in
shock and swallowed a slight giggle. She found it funny — in
that ironic, yet not actually funny way — that after so many
days of hoping she would run into him again at the store, she
had literally run right smack into him. Oops.

He looked flustered and rushed and not amused, and he
held a long list in his hand.

"Are you okay?" she questioned, still amused but starting to worry just a tad.

"What in the world is fresco queso?" he answered with a question of his own.

Now she did laugh. And, craning her neck to look up at him, she could not help but notice the rest of him. Miss Sadie would be so proud.

He was quite tall — she guessed at least six foot two. And he was built — really, *really* well. His hands were still braced on her rogue shopping cart; the skin on the back of each was marked with old scars, yet they did not look damaged or weak. No, his hands were big and tan and undoubtedly strong. They were hands that made her believe this man was very capable. His dark blond hair, cut close on the sides and back, wasn't long on top, but still fell over his forehead, giving him a helpless, little-boy-who-lost-his-dog look when paired with his exasperation over the cheese. The lighter streaks in it gave her the impression he liked to be outdoors, and they acted like a beacon to her itchy fingers, which suddenly, and of their own volition, wanted to reach out and feel the softness; maybe just to brush that one wayward wave back from his brow.

She wanted to laugh even harder, this time at herself and her half-second fantasy. Luckily, she pulled herself together and was able to appear to be a sane, even helpful, human being.

"That's queso fresco," she corrected with an indulgent, soft smile. "And it's right over here." She indicated the cold case between the produce and the deli, taking a step in its direction.

"One or two?" she asked, reaching into the display case. Following her lead, he reached forward at the same time, causing their hands to collide. They grabbed the same package; his hand nearly holding hers.

"Just the one is good." His voice seemed to have dropped half an octave...which caused her stomach to quiver with butterflies. What in the world was wrong with her?

Her lungs were empty of air, and she could barely nod her head as a reply.

Blinking back to life and clearing her throat, she had the good sense to ask, "Anything else on the list?"

"Actually, yes." His voice was almost back to normal, and he sounded relieved by her offer to help as he lifted the crinkled sheet of paper and shifted to her side, standing just behind her so she could read the list and he could look just over her shoulder. "Ever heard of lacinato?" he asked. And then in an exasperated mumble under his breath, "Where do they come up with this stuff?" His question was directed more to himself than to Maree.

"Also called dinosaur kale," she said. "You've probably had it many times and just never knew what it was called."

She started walking over to the wall of greens and veggies, and although he gave a "hmm" that sounded more like a "hmph" of doubt, he followed like an adorable and faithful puppy. *What's with this guy and images of cute canines?*

"With that many eggs on your list and all these veggies, it looks like you might be making a frittata," she said. "Grab a plastic bag right there; these are all wet from the spray." Then she shook out a bunch of long, flat dark-green leaves.

"Who knows," he said, "I—"

"Larsen, let's go," one of the guys hollered from the cashier's stand.

"—guess I better go," he continued, smoothly switching gears midsentence. "Thanks for the help…" He paused this time for her to fill in her name as she dropped the greens into the bag.

"Maree," she provided, looking up into those mystical gray eyes. "Maree Davenport."

"Well, thank you, Maree Davenport." His voice had dropped, having the same effect on her as before. She stood there — butterflies once again fluttering rapidly — without uttering a word as he lightly jogged back over to his crew.

She gathered her wits — once more — and headed to the checkout herself.

The fire truck was pulling away from the front of the store when she exited the automatic glass doors. She looked up at the passenger's window just in time to see him give her half a smile and a wink as they drove off.

"Ah, crap," was the only coherent thought she had for at least five full minutes.

Then, Maree sat in the driver's seat of her car, replaying their conversation in her head. A smile blossomed on her face; she had indeed paid better attention this time.

This time she'd noticed the nice wrapping but also what appeared to be under the surface. From afar, he was the uber-good-looking guy next door: athletic, strong, healthy, and young. But if one made the effort to look closer, it was easy to see that the top layer of All-American perfection concealed a troubled underlayer. He was a bit withdrawn while still attentive and engaged. He was silent and brooding even while politely greeting strangers and fist-bumping kids. A careful observer could see that he was tense and on edge, but he did a great job giving the impression of being laid-back and easygoing. He was an enigma. And who wasn't intrigued by a mystery?

The question Maree didn't think to consider was, were all mysteries meant to be unraveled?

3

Do nothing out of selfish ambition or vain conceit.
Rather, in humility value others above yourselves,
not looking to your own interests
but each of you to the interests of the others.
Philippians 2:3-4

"Maree, you're an angel," Sadie Jones announced with heartfelt admiration while pushing open the rickety screen door, which liked to stick. The locals teased that no one was quite sure about which came first, the house or its mistress, as they were both born and built upon the foundation of the old Marshall Mansion, creaky in the most welcoming ways, and too layered-in to budge.

"You say that every Monday, Miss Sadie."

"And it's true every time I say it, child," she insisted as Maree lugged armloads of grocery bags full of fresh fruit into the most heavenly smelling kitchen one could possibly imagine.

"Cinnamon buns for dessert today?" Maree inhaled deeply with her eyes closed to savor the scent of baking scrumptiousness. "I brought plenty of peaches, which will go perfectly with them! What else is on today's menu, Miss Sadie? You know I can stay and help for a while if you need me," Maree offered. Just as she did every week.

And just like every week, Miss Sadie shooed away her help, pouring hot water into two big mugs and setting her tea caddy on the island. "Don't you worry with that. Janie Lyn is around here somewhere, gathering eggs and whatever else that girl gets a notion to do; she will be wanting to give me a hand," she assured her.

"And speaking of Janie Lyn," Miss Sadie continued, "those cinnamon buns are her doing."

"They smell incredible!" Maree answered.

"You should have seen her tossing things in the mixer, lost in her own world and not a recipe in sight. She was art in motion. We might not know much about her, but I can tell you that she knows her way around a kitchen."

"I'm glad she's here. And I think you need her just as much as she needs you," Maree offered. The unique and quiet young lady who'd arrived at Marshall Mansion a few weeks prior was a welcome addition, kind and hardworking, albeit very much the silent type. She hadn't revealed much of herself, even to Miss Sadie. Sadie had assured Maree that Janie Lyn would do so in her own time.

"At least let me unpack the fruit for you," Maree pleaded.

"No, ma'am. You come sit right here and share a cup of tea with me; tell me all about your week. And notice that I'm wearing the new apron you made me," Sadie preened.

Sadie Jones was eighty if she was a day, yet she never slowed down. She had a gift, an innate ability to make everyone feel most special, most important, and most valued. Maree loved her deeply and found Sadie's story fascinating.

Sadie's dad, Walt Marshall, had begun building the enormous house when he'd brought his young bride, Millie, to Green Hills, Oklahoma, in 1936. Although the state economy had taken massive hits between the Great Depression and the Dust Bowl, Oklahoma had been fighting its way back up from rock bottom. To counter the type of mass "Okie" exodus that John Steinbeck portrayed in *The Grapes of Wrath*, the government had created incentives of cheap land packages to go along with farm and ranch grants. Walt was convinced he could make the most of one of those.

Eager to put down roots and start a ranch of his own, Walt had bought all the land he could afford. He constructed a small, one-room barn to live in while they got settled. Then he established the Marshall Cattle Company and spent every waking moment building his business and completing their home. He'd woken well before sunrise and worked until mid-afternoon placing fence posts, constructing pens, and managing cattle. The rest of the day's light had been used for planing wood, squaring walls, and laying the roof of their new house.

Each evening he'd come in for dinner just as the sun was setting to enjoy the fiery Oklahoma sunsets with Millie, painting a mental picture of the new addition or improvement he'd dreamed up while out there working all day. Walt would bathe, they'd eat supper together, and then he'd collapse into bed to be up well before dawn the next day and do it all over again.

When, after two long years, Millie had been a hair's breadth away from giving up on them ever living in a completed home, as well as giving up on her dream of ever becoming a mom, the Lord provided. Just as Walt had finished painting the front door with the last coat of bright goldenrod-yellow paint that shone like the sun, Sadie Anne Marshall made her entry into this world, like a ray of sunshine herself.

Eighty-plus years later, she was still sleeping in the same bedroom, sweeping the same gorgeously handcrafted pine floors, and cooking in the same kitchen (though it had been updated with top-of-the-line appliances and a touch of remodeling every decade or so).

Sadie's history and deep roots represented a concept that Maree struggled to understand, but she loved it all the same. Maree's own childhood had been a test of resilience since her parents had died just as she was beginning grade school. After that, as wards of the state, Maree, M'Kenzee, and Max were shuffled from home to home, spending stretches of time in foster care centers, but never finding their place, never being part of a permanent family beyond the three of them, and never feeling secure in a forever home.

The closest thing Maree had found to a sense of belonging was in Green Hills, and that had been by accident.

"So, you're spoiling us with peaches today?" Sadie asked as she cut a soft and steaming cinnamon roll into two halves, set each half on a plate, and grabbed two cloth napkins.

"Yes, the peaches looked amazing and smelled perfectly...ummm, peachy," Maree confirmed, cringing at her lack of a better word. "I could just tell that they were extra sweet and juicy. I plan on running back by the Get'n'Go to snag a few dozen for canning, myself. I also got you a cantaloupe, bananas, plums, and grapes. The strawberries were still sad, so those were a no-go, but the blueberries, blackberries, and raspberries are gorgeous," she shared, voice animated and talking with her hands.

Maree knew that she tended to ramble from one exuberance to the next. Sadie had once told Maree that her *joie de vivre* was contagious. That day Sadie had both teased and complimented Maree by saying how much she liked to get Maree started and then let her rattle and prattle on.

"It makes me very happy that you're wearing your new apron and using your new napkins," Maree tacked on as her fruit chatter began to dwindle. She said it in a soft, gentle way to let Sadie know that seeing her indulge in the gifts she'd given to her was a gift for the giver.

"Only because you insist. They are too lovely to risk getting stained or spoiled, but it's Monday, and Mondays are very special," Sadie said.

"Yes, they are," Maree agreed quietly, reflecting on how this moment felt beautifully entwined with those special Mondays with her momma. "And I insist, because beautiful fabric should be touched and seen and enjoyed every day, not stuffed in a drawer as a keepsake. Besides, if those get dirty or raggedy, I know where to get you some more," she finished with a wink.

"Speaking of making some more..." Sadie hedged, which got Maree's attention.

"Yes?" Maree prompted. Whatever Sadie asked, she would find a way to make happen.

"Janie Lyn was studying the seams of my apron, muttering to herself instead of including the rest of us in her thoughts in that way that she tends to do. Perhaps she'd like to try her hand at making one sometime, if you ever need an extra set of hands around the shop."

Sadie had a knack for noticing what others missed, and she was a connoisseur at putting people in the exact places they needed to be.

"I would love that! She's so interesting — she doesn't say much, but she seems to absorb everything, and when she does speak up, I'm continually blown away by her ideas and suggestions," Maree said kindly.

Just then, the subject of conversation walked in carrying a basket of eggs.

"Miss Sadie, Maree," Janie Lyn greeted quietly in her husky Southern accent. She was looking down as she closed the screen door softly and went to the sink to wash the eggs. "The girls left you quite a haul this morning, Miss Sadie; I gathered eleven eggs. I'll just wash them up and set them in the fridge."

"Thank you, Janie Lyn." Miss Sadie smiled. "And then you sit with us for a nice hot cinnamon bun," she instructed, grabbing another plate, teacup, and napkin.

"Mmmmm, this is bound to be a sin," Maree crooned. "Anything that tastes this good can't possibly be anything but pure temptation from the devil himself. Janie Lyn, there is no better cook in Oklahoma than Miss Sadie, but these cinnamon buns might just give her a run for her money."

Janie Lyn blushed, and Sadie glowed with the praise.

Maree wasn't lying. Sadie's baked goods were as legendary as the woman herself. Maree was also very intentional about bragging on Miss Sadie, letting her know through compliments and *oohs* and *ahhs* how treasured the sweet mother hen was by all who knew her.

It was a friendship and a relationship that Maree cherished, one she did not take lightly. Miss Sadie was the only momma that Maree had known since losing her own mother so many years ago.

"Speaking of temptations, little lady, did you see your fireman at the store today?" Maree wasn't surprised by this question — Miss Sadie could also be as tenacious as a dog with a bone.

"First of all, he's not *my* fireman," Maree rebuked over her last bite of scrumptious pastry. "I swear, Janie Lyn, she's incorrigible!" she teased, trying to land an ally while licking a smudge of the sweet icing off her fingers.

But Janie Lyn believed in being Switzerland as well as silent in almost all instances; she was neutral to a fault. She simply smiled at the pair of women, shaking her head in refusal to be wrangled into the debate. Then she set the clean eggs in the refrigerator, washed her hands, poured herself a tall glass of cold milk rather than hot tea, and settled in her seat to devour a cinnamon bun. All without saying a word.

"Furthermore *and* secondly, I was buying fruit at the Get'n'Go just as the firemen were gathering their own groceries at that store *every* Monday morning, long before *he* arrived on the scene," Maree said with a bit of sass.

Sadie and Janie Lyn just looked on, unconvinced.

"And, yes… I saw him today," she conceded with a grin from behind her mug as she sipped her tea to delay the next round of inquiries.

Miss Sadie's insight into her thoughts always amazed Maree. She shouldn't be surprised anymore; it had been just this way since the day they'd met.

The first time Maree limped into Green Hills almost three years ago — literally *limped* into town — she'd had nowhere to go. While driving back to college in Tulsa after teaching a quilting class in Paris, Texas, she was sideswiped on the interstate highway fewer than ten miles from the small, nearly hidden town of Green Hills, Oklahoma. Although she was lucky that she had not been more seriously hurt, Maree did have a knot on her head and a car in need of repairs. The EMTs who responded to the accident encouraged her to see a doctor in Green Hills. The doctor recommended that she rest for a few days and sent her to the Marshall Mansion, where Miss Sadie Jones would have a room for her to rent or borrow.

Achy, fatigued, and emotionally spent, Maree had been amazed by how nice the folks in town were to a complete stranger, and she let them shuffle her through whatever they thought best. She'd simply been too tired and too worn down to do anything else.

"The entire ordeal was God's work," Miss Sadie always said.

Maree stayed for three days, letting Sadie care for her with comfort food, cover her with a warm and welcoming quilt — a very precious quilt that Sadie had made by hand over the past year — and cosset her with love as her bruises ran their course. Meanwhile, Maree dealt with her insurance company, made arrangements to have a replacement car delivered to Green Hills, indulged in long afternoon naps, enjoyed cups and cups of hot tea, and made a friend for life in Miss Sadie Jones.

Maree had also learned that over the last eight decades, the Marshall Mansion had housed many a soul in need. Millie had her baby girl, but she and Walt were never blessed with more children to fill the massive house. Walt, along with men from Oklahoma, Colorado, New Mexico, and Arizona, had been a member of the 45th Infantry Division during World War II. One of more than 24,000 Allied soldiers to lose their lives, Walt was killed in action during the invasion of Sicily in early August 1943. Sadie was not quite five years old, and suddenly Millie was a widow on her own. With strength and determination, Millie did what she knew best: cooked and kept house with welcoming warmth, honest kindness, and a lack of judgment when it came to the challenges others were facing. Ultimately, she turned their home into a bed-and-breakfast to make ends meet.

Somewhere along the way, word got out that rooms could be rented with chores and credit instead of cash-in-hand when someone was down on their luck. Millie was revered for her incredible cooking and her huge heart. Most nights she had a full table of twelve in the dining room for supper as well as a few extras eating their meal in the kitchen and at the breakfast table. Those who could, paid for their plate. Those who could not, well, they pitched in some other way to keep the ranch profitable, the garden tended, and the grounds landscaped. No one went hungry, and everyone had a soft place to sleep indoors.

Maybe it couldn't — or wouldn't — work in every time or place, but here at Marshall Mansion, it did. Life went on like this, happily throughout Sadie's childhood and adolescence. Millie and Sadie were integral to the community and touched many lives during those years.

One traveler, Mr. Samuel Jones, found more than dinner and a room for the night when he was passing through during the spring of 1960.

The moment young Sadie opened the front door with a beaming smile, his heart was pierced, and his life was changed. She was a senior in the business school at the University of Tulsa and home for a few days; he was finishing up the ranch management program at Oklahoma State University.

By the end of that long weekend, they were both equally and thoroughly smitten. Their love blossomed and grew via handwritten letters, anxiously awaited over the time they were apart, long before the days of instant communication and immediate gratification. Perhaps it was that distance, or maybe it was the anticipation of receiving word to learn more about one another that made the heart grow fonder. Regardless of how or why, the two fell hard.

Upon both their graduations, Sam asked for Sadie's promise to be his, always and forever, and they were married on July 4th, just a few months after they'd met. It was a morning wedding, the ceremony kicking off a day of festive celebrations. Millie served enough food for an army, neighbors talked and laughed, and kids chased one another playing yard games. Sadie had thought it was perfect, and she'd sensed her dad's presence and love as though he was there with them. For Sam and Sadie, it had been a beautiful beginning to a cherished and treasured life together.

Sam took over the ranching for Millie, building Marshall Cattle Company to one of the most respected — and most profitable — outfits in the state, as well as in northeast Texas.

Sadie handled the myriad of her mother's "hobbies," which had blossomed into full-blown businesses in their own right. Between the bed-and-breakfast, catering events in town, and selling her canned and baked goods at the general store, Millie had become quite the entrepreneur. As the years went by, Sadie's passion for her mother's work continued to grow and impact the town in powerful ways.

By the time Millie passed away of natural causes, the Marshall Mansion, Marshall Cattle Company, and the Marshall family were all very wealthy — monetarily, for sure, but even more so in abundant blessings.

Like Millie, Sadie struggled to have children. After three miscarriages, tremendous heartache, and an ocean of tears, Sadie and Sam determined that God's calling for them might not be in biological parenthood, but rather parenthood by choice, so they ceased the bed-and-breakfast model and turned Marshall Mansion into a home for youth who needed a place to go, a fresh start, and a mom and dad ready to shower them with love. Sadie ended up with more love and more kids and more treasured memories than she could have asked God to send her.

When Sam started showing signs of memory loss, they slowed down a bit, finding someone to work as the ranch foreman and someone to help with the house.

When he was diagnosed with Alzheimer's disease, they closed the doors to Marshall Mansion and moved into town to stay in assisted living, where Sadie had help with Sam's care, and they could still be together.

Watching that illness steal away her true love was the most painful experience of Sadie's life. In a rare moment of what she termed "self-indulgent" bereavement, Sadie had told Maree that seeing the memories they'd made together disappear from Sam's mind was worse than losing her own daddy as a little girl and the devastation of those miscarriages, combined. His inability to recognize her face after looking upon it with such passion and devotion for fifty-six years was like a knife stabbing into her chest each time she walked into the room, day after day.

"My mind would rationalize that my Sam was still there, that this disease eating away at his brain was the only difference in him. I would tell myself that nothing could break us, nothing could diminish what we had and the world we created together, and then he'd reintroduce himself to me, and my heart would once more shatter into a million tiny pieces," Sadie had explained to Maree.

Hearing Sam and Sadie's story had prompted Maree to learn more about dementia. The more she learned, the more sympathy she felt for Sadie and for any family faced with such a diagnosis. Articles that Maree had read explained that watching Alzheimer's disease take a loved one was like experiencing their death over and over again, because each day was another round of loss. At some point, the caregivers become so physically and emotionally punished that they become a patient themselves, often dying before or immediately after their Alzheimer's-afflicted spouse or parent.

"It's like our life didn't happen at all," Sadie had whispered, heartsick and panicked to believe that such a bond could break. "Maybe I'll wake up one day to find that our marriage was just a beautiful dream and nothing more."

The fatal disease continued to take its toll. Sam lost his ability to communicate, mumbling words and nonsensical sounds at first, and then falling completely mute. He lost the ability to walk, requiring a wheelchair to leave their room and a strong attendant to move him from chair to bed to recliner and back to bed. He lost the ability to chew and swallow, moving from soft solids to pureed mush to not eating at all. In the end, he lost the ability to breathe, as well as the ability for his heart to beat.

Upon Sam's death, Sadie moved back to Marshall Mansion, craving activity and people, needing to be needed again, and desperate for sunshine and happy days to return. She sensed that without air, sunlit spaces, and human engagement, she too would waste away and die.

That was the exact week that Maree Davenport was hit by that car while she was driving down the Indian Nation Turnpike just north of town. Because of that accident, Maree needed a place to go and someone to pamper her with a healthy dose of tender, loving care.

God's work, indeed.

For the first time in a *very* long time, Maree knew where she belonged.

Maree completed her own business degree, just as Sadie had done decades earlier. Then she spent her summer after graduation living with Miss Sadie and setting up her fabric design and quilting studio on Green Hills' Main Street. Every day, she jotted down ideas and plans for her future, and every night, she curled up under that quilt, the one Sadie had told her she'd made while keeping Sam company as day by day, she lost him more and more. Sewing and piecing the blocks had helped calm Sadie. Holding the needle in her fingers, feeling the fabric, soft and soothing in her hands, and gripping the large wooden hoop grounded her at a time when she felt a loss of control over her ability to fix their reality. Running the small needle up and down through the fabric and batting to quilt the three layers together had soothed her. Creating that quilt had been therapy for Sadie; it had served to mend her mind — and her heart — when it was shattering anew every day that Sam declined. There was so much love, so much of Sadie's strength and spirit in that beautiful blanket that it reaffirmed to Maree that she was finally home.

By the end of August, Maree was officially a resident of

Green Hills, her hidden gem in the spectacular landscape of southeast Oklahoma.

And the people around her had become a bonus family — not a replacement for all she had lost, but a very sweet bonus, like icing on a cinnamon bun.

"Well, at least tell us how Maxwell is doing," Sadie said, gracefully changing the subject from the mysterious fireman and winking at Janie Lyn. At the mention of Max Davenport, Janie Lyn's eyes shone with a new gleam.

Maree appreciated Sadie's willingness to change topics, and this was one she could talk about all day with love and adoration.

Max, Maree's older brother by five years, played professional football in Kansas City. He'd also fallen in love on his first visit to Green Hills, but with the land and the entire town, instead of one girl as Sam had done. Within months of Maree's move to Green Hills, Max had purchased one of the great Craftsman-style homes in the historic part of town. The old house was in need of updating, repairs, and a lot of elbow grease when he purchased it, but Max had told Maree that he didn't care, that he'd been drawn to it the moment he pulled up to the curb. During his off-season months, he'd done most of the remodeling work himself; after two years, everyone in town recognized that he was creating quite a masterpiece.

"He's excited to get home during their bye week next month! I'll meet the painters at the house on Saturday so they can finish the upstairs before he arrives. It's going to be incredible — I have no idea how a man who thinks blue jeans and a white undershirt are the epitome of style can have such a great eye when it comes to designing a house, but he absolutely has a gift. I can't wait for you to see it — I know he's planning a nice dinner party in honor of your birthday while he's here."

While Sadie bristled about people bothering over her birthday (it was all for show as she was all-in for a fun day of celebrating), Maree washed their dishes and silverware, handing them to Janie Lyn who dried them and put them back where they belonged in the cupboards and drawers. Then the two finished unbagging the fruit.

Just as they were done tidying up, Landry, another one of Sadie's "kids," entered the kitchen sleepy-eyed, yet smiling at Maree and tugging playfully on Janie Lyn's braid as she headed straight for Miss Sadie.

"Well, good morning," Sadie said with an all-encompassing hug. Landry was in her final year of medical school residency and was living with Sadie while she worked at Green Hills Memorial Hospital. Sadie had told Maree and Janie Lyn that Landry's shift had ended at 7 a.m. and that Landry often ran home to catch a nap for a couple of hours before heading to the library for a study group.

Like Maree, Landry Stark had been on her own in some form or fashion for most of her life. Also like Maree, Landry had attended college on scholarships and worked multiple jobs to avoid taking out student loans. Medical school required financial aid, but she was still determined to live as frugally as possible. And Sadie proved to be a lifeline for Landry, just like she was for Maree, a chosen mom, and a blessing that was life-changing.

"You have a fresh victim to interrogate, so I am off," Maree declared with a wink and a smile, giving hugs to all three ladies. "The cinnamon buns are worth the torture," she told Landry in a stage whisper as the screen door creaked open.

"Janie Lyn, if you're in town, I could use a little help at the studio this week, and maybe an extra set of hands doing a few projects over at Max's house," Maree added nonchalantly and scurried out.

Maree couldn't help but smile as she drove home. Life was good. More than good! She had an amazing family, tossed together and nontraditional, yet beautiful and supportive and loving and kind. They made her heart glow and her soul sing. Without fail, her family, her home, and her work always brought a smile to her face.

And if a certain firefighter crept into her thoughts despite her best efforts to keep him out, she just grinned a little more.

4

The body says what words cannot.
Martha Graham

"Come onnnnn," Landry begged in a pretend whine. She was hopping around the kitchen, getting between Maree and her dinner plate, which prompted Maree to give her "the look" and turn her back to Landry.

Next, Landry looked to Miss Sadie who was silently laughing at the girls and shaking her head.

Landry shifted her pleading toward Janie Lyn, who opened the refrigerator and looked inside for an open jar of plum jam, effectively turning her back on Landry as well. "It will be so fun! And, Janie Lyn, you've never once gone out with us. You haaaaave to go," Landry pleaded.

With the jam in hand, Janie Lyn gave a sympathetic half smile and sidestepped Landry to make her way to the kitchen table.

The three of them — Janie Lyn, Maree, and Miss Sadie — had just filled their plates to enjoy a late afternoon snack of blueberry scones with clotted cream and fresh berries left over from Maree's fruit delivery a couple of days earlier.

It was a calm, peaceful late afternoon snack that Miss Sadie had thrown together when she'd looked up to find that Maree didn't have to rush back to work, Janie Lyn was home early from her volunteer shift in town, and Landry was finished studying for the day. They were in one place without any demands calling them away. Sadie had figured that alone called for an impromptu splurge on something sweet while they were together.

And yet, Landry was being the opposite of calm and peaceful.

"Get a plate and join us," Sadie told her. Landry followed instructions, selecting a small salad plate as well as a matching teacup and saucer from her favorite china pattern in Miss Sadie's dish collection. She continued to list all the reasons why they *must* go out on the town for an evening of fun.

Landry was nothing if not persistent. Hard as she might try though, her current impersonation of a nails-on-a-chalkboard voice was *not* helping her case very much with Maree or Janie Lyn.

It was, however, working wonders on Sadie.

"Go!" Sadie ordered, pointing at the door for emphasis as soon as they were all finished eating. "I'll take care of cleaning up; y'all get on out of here."

"Sorry, I can't... I promised Maree that I'd get fabric kits cut and packaged before Monday," Janie Lyn chimed in.

"That can wai—" Maree tried to argue. They all knew that the project Janie Lyn had offered to help Maree with was not all that pressing and could easily be done next week..

"A promise is a promise," Janie Lyn interrupted, slightly shrugging her shoulders and keeping her gaze down to avoid eye contact as she walked out of the house with a grin and headed to the fabric shop.

"Is she even old enough to get into a bar?" Landry asked in a stage whisper, teasing and faking a pout at the same time.

"Yes," Sadie and Maree answered in unison.

"This child has been nose-in-the-books and pedal-to-the-metal for weeks." Sadie indicated toward Landry by tilting her head. "She's got a free night, and you're taking her somewhere to do something fun," she said to Maree.

And that was that. The decision was made; the girls were going out.

Scooter's was Green Hills' version of a saloon, a bar, and a dance hall all in one, and it was housed in a very large, very fun, very old barn. The concrete floor was covered with dirt, sand, and hay, so every square inch of the building qualified as the dance floor. The handmade mahogany bar ran the length of the side wall, with billiard tables toward the back of the barn, a stage in the front, and cocktail tables scattered in between. Maree imagined every small town in America had a place pretty similar to Scooter's, and she positively adored this little slice of nightlife in Green Hills.

That is why, in all honesty, Maree didn't mind going with Landry. Sadie was absolutely correct in pointing out that Landry had been busting her tail and burning the candle at both ends with classes, labs, clinicals, and volunteering at the hospital around rotations. She deserved a night away from that chaos, and Maree did love Scooter's.

Plus, tonight was karaoke night, always a favorite for Landry and Maree.

The place was already hopping when they arrived. They meandered for a bit, greeting the many people they knew. They'd made a full round of hugs and hellos as they worked their way toward the tall cocktail tables, looking for two empty stools so they could sit down.

The weight of the past few weeks and their overly hectic schedules quickly lifted from their shoulders. They visited with friends, indulged on greasy burgers and fries with cold beers to wash them down, jumped into the line dancing, and embraced the opportunity for lots of laughter as they people-watched and joined in the festivities.

———

*R*hys Larsen and a group of guys he knew through the fire department entered the barn and headed straight for the pool tables. The place was loud and full of personality; the crowd was lively and enthusiastic.

He didn't think that she'd seen him; she'd been deep in conversation with another woman at one of the hightop tables. But Rhys had noticed the girl from the grocery store the second he'd walked in the room.

Maree Davenport.

She was dressed like most of the girls in the place with dark, snug-in-all-the-right-places jeans tucked inside a well-loved pair of brown cowboy boots. To finish the look, she wore a western pearl-snap shirt that was pale pink plaid and also fit just right. The shirttails, tied into a knot at her waist, just barely covered the button of her jeans.

He couldn't take his eyes off her hair, long and thick strawberry blond curls, loose and flowing. Everywhere. He'd never seen it down from her ponytail-bun-thing that she'd had twisted on top of her head every time he'd seen her before. Cascading down her back, it was just begging to be touched.

She didn't seem to wear much makeup, but her lips were glistening, a shiny, peachy pink that beckoned him from the far side of the barn.

He watched on as she and her friend danced to every single line dance that played. They laughed their way through their missteps even though they clearly knew every move. Guys — several of them — tried to dance their way in to get close to the two girls, but each time, they were gently turned away.

The girls went back to the table, caught up in their giggling and pointing. Maree didn't seem self-absorbed, or the least bit worried about being noticed. She looked like she was thoroughly enjoying herself.

He thought she'd catch him watching her when she sidled by on their way to the ladies' room, but she was too focused on trying to hear her friend over the thrum of the music and the crowd. He caught himself grinning at her energy and obliviousness when she buzzed right past him a second time, laughing and interacting with her friend. *Surely she can feel my eyes on her. I sure as hell can't seem to look anywhere else.*

When the karaoke machine came out, Maree and her friend didn't hesitate to put their names on the list. Her friend sang "Girls Just Wanna Have Fun" by Cyndi Lauper. It was upbeat and fun, and she wasn't all that bad. By the end of the song, every girl in the building was half singing, half screaming the lyrics with her, and they were definitely having fun.

Then Maree Davenport took the stage.

No bigger than a preteen, she looked tiny up there, but when she sang the first line of "Sweet Dreams" by Patsy Cline, she brought down the house.

He could see that she was one hundred percent in her element. The entire crowd was spellbound, including Rhys. Every man in that room must have felt as though she was singing only to him, but just as she was singing the final line, Maree looked at Rhys, and their eyes locked.

The moment was fleeting, lasting less than a heartbeat.

The audience erupted, and Maree just laughed. They begged for an encore, and she indulged them, this time singing a much less dramatic, more upbeat tune with Reba McEntire's "Fancy."

Couples went back to dancing after she finished her song,

and Maree walked to her friend who was waiting with a hug. "That was so awesome!" her friend said.

And again, Rhys couldn't help but smile, enjoying seeing her having so much fun. At that, he shook his head; he was just as entranced by that woman as every other poor, lovestruck fellow in Scooter's.

The girls stopped at their table to sit for a minute and finish their beers, and then they wandered to the back to shoot pool. A table was free when they got there, so they racked the balls, and just as Maree was going to break them, he interrupted.

———

$\mathcal{M}$aree couldn't believe her firefighter was there at Scooter's. She'd been hoping he'd come speak to her, and just as she leaned down to hit the cue ball, she sensed his presence. Her heart began its butterfly flutter before he'd even said a word.

"Can I play?"

Landry's eyes expanded to the size of saucers, but Maree just smiled.

"Of course," she answered, standing up straight and turning to face him. "Landry Stark, this is Mr. Larsen; Mr. Larsen, this is my adorable friend, Landry," she said with a smile and a wink to Landry that Rhys could not see.

"Rhys Larsen," he said, reaching out to shake Landry's hand. "How about you girls against me?" he offered, with a small nod to the racked pool balls.

"Sure. You break," Maree said, handing him her cue.

Landry gave her a big-eyed "who, what, when, where, and how???" look as she turned her back to Rhys, but Maree just smiled with an extra sparkle in her eyes.

"Rhys is a unique name. How do you spell it?" Landry asked. Maree could see the intrigue all over Landry's face, curiosity about the strange man who was obviously not a stranger to Maree.

"R-H-Y-S," he answered as one of his buddies, who Maree recognized as one of his fellow firefighters from the grocery store, walked up to join them.

"Do people ever mispronounce it?" Maree asked.

"All the time," Rhys answered. "I get 'Reese' a lot, even a 'Riss' everyone once in a while."

"If I'd seen it written before you said it, I might've guessed 'Rise' like dough to bake bread," Maree commented.

"He claims it's an old family name, but everyone at the fire station agrees with you, pretty lady. No matter the call, this guy always *rises* to the occasion," the second firefighter chimed in while clapping a hand on Rhys's shoulder.

"Ladies, this is Davis, friend, fireman, and full of—"

"Now, now, Rhys, let these two determine my finer qualities for themselves. So, y'all need a fourth?" Davis asked, smoothly inviting himself to play.

They had fun, Rhys and Maree exchanging glances, Davis flirting without restraint, and Landry dishing it right back at him.

The girls held their own, and after four games it was tied two-to-two.

Rhys obviously felt like that was a nice safe place to stop when he set the cue stick aside and reached for Maree's hand.

"Let's dance," he said as more of a statement than a question.

His tone and confidence didn't leave much room for discussion nor deliberation, but it didn't matter. She was terribly afraid that her answer would be "yes" to almost anything he asked.

Following an exuberant Davis and a very bubbly Landry, Rhys walked her to the front and center of the room, where the lack of furniture allowed for the best dancing. Maree liked the warmth and feel of his hand against her lower back as he led the way.

He whirled her under his arm, then pulled her into his body as they waited for the band to start up a new tune. His chest was hard as a rock, but also warm. So warm that she could feel his heat through her crisp cotton shirt. She swore she could hear both of their hearts racing, beating in rhythm with one another.

If the band doesn't hurry up, I'm going to drown in his eyes and his arms and his heat and his heartbeat. Which would have been a terrible shame, as she had already figured out that dancing with him was going to be devastatingly wonderful.

The band must have felt the tension between Maree and Rhys — and possibly her nerves — all the way up on stage, because they finally started their next set. Maree wasn't sure if she'd been saved or sacrificed.

"So, "Fancy," huh? Not a typical choice for karaoke night, I'd imagine," Rhys teased, referring to her earlier choice of a karaoke song, letting her know that he'd been watching. He twirled her under his arm once more as the music started and then into his strong arms which held her firmly but tenderly all at once as they moved in time to "Neon Moon" by Brooks & Dunn.

"No," she chuckled, thankful for the lighthearted banter to defuse the intensity she was feeling. "I just have a thing for the classic queens of country music. Karaoke night is one of my favorites! I especially enjoy torturing everyone here by selecting songs that are old and completely unhip. Thankfully, every-one's pretty used to it by now and willing to indulge me."

They fell quiet as they danced, Maree delighting in the pleasure of being in his arms. She couldn't help but wonder what he was thinking.

———

*S*he's going to kill me with that damn smile, I'm sure of it. The thought hit him hard, out of left field, unapproved and unwanted.

It was followed by an instantaneous moment of panic that screamed "you're a goner" louder than the music blaring from the stage.

A lightning-quick concern popped into his mind that the reason he hadn't been able to look away from her all night was similar to one's inability to look away from a train wreck. A whisper fluttering through his mind said that she might have the power to break through his carefully constructed walls, fences, and all other means of self-preservation.

He'd always been able to squash those internal voices and niggling feelings in the past, and he'd do so again. Feeling confident in this, he figured there was nothing wrong with some harmless flirtations with a beautiful girl.

He'd never let it be more than that anyway.

"You've got some voice for a tiny, little thing," Rhys complimented her, derailing the crazy train his thoughts were on.

"Thank you. I think," she laughed. He figured she was used to being complimented for her voice and also used to being teased for her petite size. It was easy to see that she loved to sing, and obviously, she wasn't afraid to belt out a favorite song. The way she looked up into his eyes, he felt that his compliment had really mattered. No veil or mask at all; she didn't hide a thing. Finally, she glanced away.

He took it as a sign to hold her closer, tightening his grip and pulling her further into the cradle of his arms. Maree fit so perfectly in his embrace that she felt like a luxury. He allowed himself to settle in and enjoy the dance.

———

*L*andry and Davis continued to dance as well, and the next hour went by in a blur of music and twirls, strong arms and warm hands.

And those gorgeous granite eyes. Maree was mesmerized by them. By him. And by the warmth of having Rhys hold her close.

As the night went on, the band transitioned to slower songs, perfect for dancing even closer. Maree hadn't thought there was any space or air left between them, but when they began the AWOLNATION cover of "I'm On Fire," Rhys nestled Maree into his chest even tighter, wrapping both arms around her, hugging her into a soft swaying dance. Maree wasn't sure if he was holding her upright or if she was floating, but she was sure that she was in a dreamlike state. One in which she was perfectly content to stay. Indefinitely.

Sadly, it did end. Knowing the night was getting late and that she was sinking like the Titanic, she gave Landry a look that said it was time to go. Landry rolled her eyes, but she agreed. Their fun was over. At least for tonight.

———

"*W*ell, thank you, Rhys Larsen," Maree said with a stunning smile, stepping out of his arms and walking toward the exit.

It wasn't lost on Rhys that she had just tossed his own words from the grocery store right back at him. He was chuckling and shaking his head once more, and then he called it a night himself.

5

Third Time's the Charm
Folk Belief

 he third time they spoke — not counting that first gaze-colliding event in the Get'n'Go — things finally started moving in the right direction, at least to Maree's way of thinking.

It was a Tuesday afternoon instead of their usual Monday meetings in the fruit and produce department. Maree was shopping to stock Max's house for his stay during his upcoming bye week of the football season. Janie Lyn had been a tremendous help in getting the interior paintwork scheduled and finished over the last few weeks, and while she'd offered to take care of the groceries and "opening" the house for Max, Maree wanted to be the one there to greet him when he rolled into town.

She was lost in her own thoughts, checking off mental lists of what she needed for his house.

"No fruit today?" His voice was like a warm wave washing

over her. She savored it for a fraction of a second before turning to face him with a smile.

"Nope, just the plain old normal stuff," she answered, holding up the bread, bagels, and tortillas that she'd piled into her arms and setting them into her shopping cart. "How about you?" She looked down at his basket, full of household items and staples rather than a specific set of recipe ingredients.

"It's been a hectic two days, so yesterday's crew missed the normal Monday grocery run. The guys are getting what we need for the firehouse; this junk is for me."

"So, who does most of the menu picking and the cooking on your shift?" she asked, genuinely interested.

She was fascinated by his explanation about cooking rotations and his description of each firefighter on his crew and what they liked to cook when it was their turn. She learned that he tended to lean toward some cut of steak on their outdoor grill and a potato on the side when it was his night. Davis was all about Italian foods, while another man Rhys called Roddy let his wife come up to the station to work her magic when it was his turn. He shared that Harleigh, one of the female firefighters on his shift, was an incredible cook but liked to feed them frozen fish sticks and boxed macaroni and cheese just to torture them. His descriptions of each coworker, their food preferences, and their chef personalities turned out to be quite entertaining; she enjoyed listening to him tease about people he obviously respected very much.

He had just confessed that although steaks and potatoes might sound impressive, his cooking skills were considered tolerable but not extravagant when Davis rushed up to them.

"We've got a call," he told Rhys, worked up.

Rhys looked down at his groceries with a defeated sigh.

"Let me get them," Maree offered, quickly digging in her purse. "Here, it's my business card. That's my cell number on the front; call or text when you get off work, and I'll give you the address to come pick up your groceries."

There was no time to discuss, so she stuffed the card in his hand as he turned to hightail it out to the fire truck, climbing up as it was starting to pull out of the parking lot, en route to the emergency.

Maree consolidated their carts, and all of a sudden, the shopping seemed a little more fun. Her face was warm — like it was glowing — and she felt a sense of purpose that had not been there when she'd walked into the store. She refused to admit that there was a little extra spring in her step, and if she was called out for it, she was fully prepared to justify it as excitement about Max coming home for the week.

And she *was* excited!

Maree admired her big brother. Max was big and strong and safe, and she loved the days he spent in Green Hills.

The taxi from Green Hills' airstrip was dropping Max at the house just as she was pulling into his drive from the store. After a huge hug, they carried in the grocery bags together. Then she put away the cold items while he unloaded an extra-large canvas bag, golf clubs, and a backpack from his car.

After Max settled in, he and Maree enjoyed a long walk with his new dog, Hank, through Max's historic Foxtail neighborhood. The subdivision was named for the pale pink and purple grasses that grew wild throughout Green Hills. With her artist's eye, Maree believed it was the most beautiful residential area of town.

Then, while Max went up to the high school to visit with the football coach who had become a good friend over the past two years, Maree unpacked the pantry items and put away the remaining groceries and household items she'd bought him.

When Max returned from the school, he unpacked his duffle bag, and she cooked dinner. They spent most of the evening on the back porch, tossing tennis balls to Hank, eating dinner, and sipping wine while the sun set.

She told him about work and how Main Street Design was coming along, she described her newest fabric collection, and she ran through her updated timeline on the shop renovations. She told him about Landry and Miss Sadie and what was keeping them busy from day to day and week to week. She told him what little more she had discovered about Janie Lyn — the mysterious young woman who seemed to be everywhere and see everything, but rarely said anything — explaining how helpful she'd been in getting his house to its current condition of remodeling completion.

And she told him about Rhys.

Maree was blessed to have a protective big brother, one who cared deeply about his sisters. And one quite capable of reading between the lines. Maree didn't doubt that Max had heard what she *hadn't* said about Rhys as much as he'd paid attention to what she had shared. When there was a firm knock at the door, Max moved to answer it. Maree gave him a look that said "Be nice!"

————

*R*hys was exhausted after a very long day. And he was confused by the guy opening what he believed to be Maree's door. Correction: the very big guy with the *very* big dog opening what he believed to be Maree's door.

"Oh." Rhys stumbled in a little bit of shock and eyed the dog. "I'm...uh..." His explanation died. He ran a hand through his hair. Looking down, he searched for something to say. He wanted to be mad, but he realized that three conversations did not give him any right to — nor any hold over — a beautiful girl.

And he reminded himself, he didn't want a hold over anyone. He was stupid to have thought—

"Looking for my sister, I believe," the huge fellow interrupted his thoughts and finished his sentence for him.

Rhys expelled a relieved sigh. He was grateful that he'd been put out of his misery sooner rather than later. He'd dissect that natural response later.

"Yeah, I'm Rhys Larsen," he offered, putting out his hand to shake.

"Max Davenport." Max shook hands, polite and not quite frowning, but with his overprotective, big brother look still firmly in place. "And this is Hank."

They were standing on the porch with a bright light coming from inside the house, so it had been difficult for Rhys to see his face clearly. Looking more closely, Rhys was shocked that he hadn't recognized the celebrity athlete the second the door had opened.

"Max Davenport," Rhys repeated flatly, the weight of the world on his shoulders suddenly reappearing. "Of course you are." He could only shake his head. That response seemed to be his new norm. This girl was something else, and that *something* was more magnetic, more interesting, and more captivating at every turn.

"Maree, your fireman's here," Max hollered toward the back of the house as he stepped back to let Rhys in.

As Rhys paused to greet the dog with a soothing scratch behind the ears, Maree poked her head around the living room wall with her always cheerful, effervescent smile. Rhys looked up from where he was kneeling in front of Hank, his eyes settling on Maree. Something shifted in his world. An axis righted. The weight lifted.

Rhys was too tired to hide his response to her. Couldn't find the energy required to mask it. He figured Max had seen the transformation. Hell, he could feel it himself. He also had a sense that he'd just passed a test, one he'd not even been aware of taking.

"Come on in," Maree invited. "I left the chicken spaghetti out for you in case you hadn't eaten. Come back here to the kitchen."

He stood up from petting Hank, nodded his head once to Max to excuse himself, and followed Maree.

Just as he turned into the kitchen, Rhys would've sworn he'd heard Max tell Hank, "That smitten boy is toast." Surely not.

When Rhys entered the kitchen, Maree was closing the microwave to reheat his food. It looked like she'd been cleaning up after cooking, just waiting for him to arrive.

"Thanks for finishing up that grocery shopping for me today," he said graciously, but with fatigue in his voice.

"I didn't mind a bit," she assured him. "Long shift?"

"Yeah," he admitted, but found he didn't want to taint his time with Maree by talking about fires that were destroying historical properties in the town she loved. He didn't want to scare her with their theory that there was a serial arsonist behind the incidents. And he didn't want to think through all the implications associated with the urge he felt to protect her from worry.

"Your brother is Max Davenport," he stated incredulously.

"Mm-hmm," she agreed innocently.

He shook his head again.

"Cold beer, sweet tea, whole milk, or water?" she asked, not the least bit concerned that her big brother was one of the best tight ends in professional football.

"Milk and water?" he requested. He loved a huge glass of ice-cold milk, but right now his throat was parched and burning from the fire scene.

"But not together," she teased with a twinkle in her eye, setting a heaping portion of chicken spaghetti in front of him.

"So, you live here with your brother?" He couldn't even say the guy's name; it was all so surreal.

"No," she explained, "I have a design studio downtown with an apartment above it. It drives Max crazy that I won't share this place since he so rarely gets to be here, but this is his, and that — which is admittedly a major work in progress — is mine. Want some freshly grated parmesan?"

"Huh?" Either his brain was scrambled from the call or she was wreaking havoc on his cognitive functions, because he was having trouble keeping up.

"Would you like some fresh grated parmesan on top of your spaghetti?" she repeated, slower, as if speaking to a slow child.

"Uh, yeah, that'd be great," he said, laughing at himself internally.

She leaned over his shoulder to sprinkle the cheese on his plate, her hair falling in front of his face. It smelled like honey, or maybe strawberries and cream. Whatever, it smelled like heaven. He closed his eyes to just breathe.

And he was pretty sure she caught him inhaling the smell of her hair when she stepped back.

Great! I'm going to crash and burn before this "whatever it could be" even takes flight. The thought snuck in. Again. The same thing had happened at the store earlier in the day. He'd been having a good time shopping alongside her. He'd realized that she was very easy to talk to as they'd walked the aisles, grabbing groceries for each of their baskets as they went. He'd been aware that perhaps she was *too* easy to talk to. He'd dismissed that thought immediately in the store, definitely before it had been able to gain any traction. He'd told himself that he couldn't allow that train of thought to garner any importance or significance. Yet he'd just made the same mistake. He reprimanded himself for letting his guard down again. He had to

push that way of thinking out of reach. He couldn't —
wouldn't — go down that road.

Which was fine, since she probably thought he was a hair-
sniffing, watered-down-milk drinking lunatic by now.

At this point, though, he was too tired to care if he
appeared to be half-crazy, too tired to wrangle in wild
thoughts. He was far too worn out to put a stop to crazy
dreams of a future that could never be.

Not seeing any other way forward, he simply dove into his
chicken spaghetti.

---

*M*aree really liked seeing him inhale the dinner
she'd made. She'd read one time that cooking
for others is a sort of love language, and she believed it was
true. She felt revered by his attention, even if he appeared to
be swinging between emotions. He seemed pleased to be there
one minute, and then somewhat withdrawn the next, but he'd
had a rough day, so she was happy to look past the mixed
messages for now.

"Main Street Design, huh?" he asked between bites.

His question both surprised and delighted her.

"You've heard of it?" she asked in wonder.

"Well, I've seen it," he said. "What do you design?"

"Fabric."

"Fabric?" He sounded surprised.

"Well, someone gets to," she teased. She refilled his plate
with another huge portion of pasta and heated it in the
microwave. Then she poured him a second glass of milk and
brought a nice fat slice of homemade apple pie to the table.
She pulled out the chair to his right, sitting down with him
while he ate.

———

*I*t was all very homey. And content. Comfortable.

And it scared him nearly to death. He didn't do domestic. He couldn't play house or pretend to be a family. That was just the way it was.

———

"*I*'ve been doodling and drawing my entire life. In junior high, I learned how to sew and quilt. Somewhere between there and college, I put the two hobbies together and knew what I wanted to do. I studied business at the University of Tulsa, and just before graduation, I discovered Green Hills."

She went on to tell him about the driver sideswiping her car right out of commission. She told him about meeting and staying with Miss Sadie. About their shared love for quilts and quilting. Maree explained that when Miss Sadie had wrapped her in the perfect quilt, she knew she'd found her place. She told him that Green Hills had provided an extended family that grounded her and made life feel stable. She talked while he ate, and she loved that he seemed to soak up every word. Maree was winding down her story when he scraped the last taste of pie filling off the plate.

"Thanks," he said earnestly, looking her right in the eyes. There was that directness, that straightforwardness that affected her so. She wasn't sure if his understated gratitude was meant for the dinner, the dessert, or the distraction. In the end, it really didn't matter. It was sincere, and that spoke volumes.

"You're very welcome." Her voice was soft, acknowledging his appreciation.

"Let me help you finish up here," he said as he set his dishes in the sink.

"I'll wash; you dry," she instructed.

He kept her talking by asking more questions while she washed and rinsed the few remaining dishes. Maree explained the process of taking a doodle and turning it into a fifteen-yard bolt of fabric.

She didn't mind that she sounded like an enthusiastic child, thrilled to talk about her toys which included crayons, colored pencils, paints, and digital design software. She was happy to entertain, happy to share part of her world with Rhys.

Maree walked him through her creative steps, the way she loved to lose all track of time researching vintage quilt patterns from old newspapers printed in tiny towns all across America. She regaled him with stories of how women relied on those newspapers for both new recipes to try and new patterns to piece into quilts.

Maree explained how she took those findings and used them to plan, draw, and color full fabric collections, anywhere from five to fifty unique prints, solids, geometrics, lines, dots, and floral designs that coordinated. The fabrics ranged from soft and muted hues that were considered low-volume colors to big and bright hues that were bold eye-catchers.

His eyebrows lifted with astonishment when she told him that she was working with her sister, who was a photographer, to capture pictures of thirteen recently made reproduction quilts — all using her latest fabric collection. She was prac-ticing and sampling heirloom recipes — hence the old-fash-ioned apple pie with dinner — to pair with the vintage-style quilts. Once the photos of the quilts and the dishes were complete, she would put the finishing touches on her third book, comprised of historical patterns and recipes.

He asked a few questions, so she knew he'd been listening. He seemed interested, yet he was happy to let her do the talk-ing. Besides mentioning that like Max, he too had purchased a home in one of Green Hills' historic neighborhoods, he didn't offer any details about his own life.

She didn't want to push, so she didn't pry. She sensed he was still battling a tough day and wanted to help lighten that burden however she could. She did, however, hope that there would be future opportunities to learn more about him, chances to get to know him much, much better.

With the kitchen put back together, she clicked off the lights, and they walked together into the living room, where Max was watching game film and making notes on a legal pad.

———

*R*hys was still struggling with the fact that Max Davenport was Maree's brother. The man was a living legend, and Rhys was secretly a little awestruck to meet him.

"There she is," Max greeted them, standing up from the couch and getting Hank riled up.

"Here she is," Maree replied, in a way that Rhys knew was a secret language just for the siblings, as she kneeled to love on the dog for a minute.

"Just above edible, huh?" Max said, picking on his little sister, who everyone in the room now knew to be a pretty fabulous cook.

"Yeah, it was rough going, but I choked down two plates of pasta, half a loaf of garlic bread, and ate at least a third of an apple pie," Rhys admitted.

"You gave him my pie?" Max feigned outrage.

"And the vanilla ice cream," Maree confessed as she stood up and walked over to her big brother, sliding under Max's arm for a hug, and teasing right back by patting his washboard abs. "I'm thinking less pie is better for your aging physique."

Max yanked on her hair, again in their own world of

brother-sister communication. A stab of pain punched through Rhys's gut. He experienced a bittersweet taste of longing.

"See you tomorrow," she promised, leaning up on tiptoes and forcing Max to lean down so she could kiss his cheek.

"You seeing her home?" Max asked Rhys, who wasn't the only plain-spoken man in the house. Until that moment Rhys hadn't realized that she was without a car.

"I brought his car from the dealership this morning, so technically, I'm stranded," Maree filled in.

Rhys recovered quickly. "Of course. I'll make sure she's home safe."

It had been a very long time since anyone — man or woman — had intimidated Rhys Larsen, and while he certainly wasn't afraid of Max Davenport, he sensed it was important to make a good impression.

Maree was already out the door, so as Max nodded his acceptance, Rhys grabbed his own grocery bags and followed her out.

Shifting his things into one hand, he opened the passenger door to his truck for her and put a hand to her back as she stepped on the running board to slide into the high seat.

"Good?"

"Good." She smiled back at Rhys. He nodded and stepped back to close her door. He was definitely too beat to fight her smile tonight. His eyes were burning, and his head was swimming. It was all he could do to keep dog-paddling through the muddle of thoughts that refused to leave his mind at peace.

"Where to?" he asked setting his bags in the back and climbing into his seat, turning on the engine, and fastening his seat belt. *Stick to the basics, buddy*, he recited silently to himself. *Surely, you can handle that much.*

"Well, you know where I live, but I'd love to drive by your house if you don't mind taking the long way home."

With a nod of his head, he put the truck in gear and did a U-turn to head the other direction.

―――――

"These historic homes are great," she marveled as they continued across Max's neighborhood and drove through town. Rhys didn't say much, but their quietness was companionable, so neither felt compelled to fill the silence.

"That's it," he said, pulling up in front of a mid-century modern ranch-style home. One story, with impressive windows and a long porch across the front, it was on the last street in a large-lot subdivision on the edge of town. Wilderness and nature were his backyard. She could imagine a sprawling back deck for reading and relaxing.

"It's fabulous," she said.

"Yeah, it's home," he replied, finally with a sound of peace in his words.

"The long lines and flat roof are very striking! And those massive windows are basically one continuous glass wall. I bet the sun shines indoors all throughout the day," she marveled.

"Thanks, and yes, it does," he answered with a hint of pride in his voice. "When I was looking at houses for sale, its simplicity really spoke to me. Since buying it and working to remodel it accurately, I've learned a lot about this style of architecture. I've come to really appreciate how it was designed to incorporate the outdoors."

"The gray paint and the wood accents are incredible. And that double front door — the poppy red has the perfect hint of orange in it. Just like an Oklahoma sunset! You must love coming home to it every day," Maree said keenly. "Thanks for showing me."

―――――

*H*e acknowledged her compliments with a nod and put the truck back in gear, pointing it toward downtown. He was moved by her heartfelt comments and admiration for his house. Buying it had been a huge step for Rhys. She seemed to understand what a big deal it was for him. The realization of how far he'd come made it difficult for Rhys to speak.

She saw so much. Too much. He felt like a plate-glass window that she could see right through. That was incredibly unsettling when he'd dedicated ten years to becoming the exact opposite. He'd worked hard to be there for others, a force of good in a flawed world, but always on the peripheral. Never close enough for someone to really see, to truly understand.

"My apartment entrance is in the back," she pointed out when he pulled up to the town square a few minutes later, "if you don't mind driving around."

———

*N*ot only did he drive her back there, but he also shut the truck off and walked around to her side of the truck faster than she could unbuckle and gather her purse.

"Thanks." She grinned as he opened her door and stepped back for her to hop down.

She didn't say a word when he climbed the stairs with her, and when she dug her house key out of her purse, he opened his palm for her to hand him the keys in an offer to unlock the door for her. Sure, they both knew that she was perfectly capable of doing it for herself, but sometimes it was a treat to hand over the reins.

"Today's flame was the second fire with the exact same MO," he stated, almost professionally, like he was giving a press conference. She sensed the immediate change in his demeanor;

she guessed that he was making an effort to distance her from the ugliness he'd been holding inside all night, so she didn't take any offense to his cold tone, and just listened. "Both times it's been older buildings like these around the downtown square, but so far no one has been anywhere around when the fire started. Thankfully, no one has been injured in any way."

"I'm sorry you've had to deal with that," she said.

He nodded slightly, still looking down at his feet.

"Look, I just want you to keep your eyes open — be careful, okay?" He finally raised his head and looked into her eyes.

"Okay," she agreed readily, stepping into her apartment and switching on a light. He glanced over her head, checking the surroundings just a bit.

"Okay," he repeated. She noted his sigh of acquiescence.

He hesitated another moment. Maree liked that he was finding it difficult to leave, although there wasn't a reason to stay. "Thanks for dinner. And everything. It was great," Rhys said.

She nodded with a smile. "Good night, Rhys." And closed the door.

6

Hello could lead to a million things.
Author unknown

*R*hys picked up his phone a thousand times on
Wednesday. He set it right back down each time
without punching in Maree's number.

He'd endured a fitful night of sleep, and it irritated him
how much he wanted to hear her voice. The problem was that
he didn't *want* to want to hear it.

It didn't matter anyway; he really didn't know what to say.

Instead, he went for a run. He even managed to convince
himself that he had not headed that way on purpose when the
path he followed took him downtown.

He knew she was working in her shop and considered
calling for lunch, but he chickened out on that, too.

Let it go, he told himself over and over throughout the day.

And yet, the harder he fought the urge to reach out to her,
the more she consumed his thoughts.

He tried to do some research on the buildings that had
burned, but his concentration was nil.

Rhys repeatedly chastised himself. Anything — and that included any*one* — that took his eye off the job was a bad influence. He needed to find this arsonist before someone got hurt or killed. That had to come first. Before thoughts about anything else. Or anyone else.

He further convinced himself that distractions were the enemy, things to avoid at all costs. He tossed and turned for a second night.

But still, he did not call.

By Thursday, he was tired, grumpy, and biting the head off anyone unlucky enough to pass near him, be in the same room as him, or heaven forbid, speak to him. No one could do anything right. He didn't want to be bothered. Everyone was grating on his nerves. Hell, *he* was grating on his nerves.

By Friday, he got a message that told him she was done waiting…

- *I just finished eating at Max's house. Taking home leftover meatloaf and mashed potatoes if you're hungry after your shift.*

He read her text again. And then a few more times.

Finally, in a moment of weakness, he typed back:

- *I'm off at 8.*

And that was that.

If she was angry that he had not done the calling, she hid it well. When he arrived at her apartment, she was warm and welcoming. Dinner was incredible. Again.

They sat in her tiny kitchen, at what she called an ice cream table, which he translated to mean itty-bitty table for two. She chatted and laughed and told story after story while he ate. She made it so easy; he envied her skill to do that.

Just like before, he helped her clean up; she washed, and he dried. Aside from asking where to put the dishes, he didn't have much to say. He appreciated that she gave him space to be silent as she hummed a song under her breath while she soaped and swiped the plates. As in the truck when he was driving her home a few nights back, the lack of words was comfortable. He didn't think that she minded the companionable mood, either.

He hoped that if she could see he was experiencing a tug-of-war, she'd assume it was the push and pull of another long shift. He also hoped that she had no idea that, in actuality, she was the rope wreaking havoc on him.

Where do you think you are going to put her inside your life? How can you make her fit? Won't she disrupt the tidy compartments you've bricked into your heart? What if she's worth creating the space? How can you be sure? What if you go to all that trouble and fail? Again.

His logical, scared mind kept demanding answers that his heart could not supply.

They ended up in her living room, sitting not too close on her mini sofa, laughing through a silly comedy they'd both seen a number of times. He had to admit it felt good to laugh.

Again, she made it seem easy.

Whatever *it* was, Maree made it flow…conversing over dinner, meeting her famous big brother, laughing, sharing, breathing, being. Living. Maree made living feel real.

Do you deserve to really live?

After the movie, he stood up to leave, and she followed him to the door. He stepped out onto the stoop; she leaned against the doorframe with one ankle crossed over the other. His weight shifted from foot to foot. Twice. A third time.

She ducked her head, but lifted her eyes, looking directly at him and forcing him to look up from his feet and into her eyes.

"Dinner was good. So good — again — thank you for the offer."

"I'm glad you enjoyed it," she said. Her gaze was true, emphatic. Rhys again felt like a see-through window. He wondered if the saying about eyes being windows to one's soul was accurate. Could she see straight through him, straight to the core of him? Did Maree see his past and his pain. Did she see much more than he was willing for her to know? More than he was willing to concede?

"Max is cooking steaks on the grill tomorrow; you should join us," she challenged.

He wasn't stupid. Maree had thrown down a gauntlet. Would he be a bigger coward for declining and avoiding her, or for accepting the invitation and admitting his weakness for her?

"Five o'clock tomorrow evening. Bring a case of beer," she said, taking the decision out of his hands and standing up from the doorframe. "You've got the address." She smiled, closing the door on his bewilderment.

Rhys managed to sleep a lot better that night; he was in a downright good mood when Davis banged on the door, wanting Rhys to go workout with him. Davis drove to the fitness center, which offered free memberships for public service personnel such as educators, firefighters, paramedics, and police officers. They hit the weights hard, and then Rhys ran the few miles back to his house. Physical exertion further helped lift his spirits.

By the time he made his way to the beer store late in the afternoon, he was in a downright good mood. Without a second thought he grabbed his phone to text Maree.

- *Any preference on the beer?*
- *Yes. Something cold.*
- *10-4*

He stared at the phone, grinning like a goof, actually hoping she would reply again. When he came to the conclusion she wasn't going to, he decided on a Texas beer that went well with red meat, hopped out of the truck, and went into the store. He found what he was looking for in the refrigerated display case and took it up to the counter to pay.

"Looks like a good night ahead," the old man stated, ringing up the sale.

"From a box of cold beer?" Rhys asked without rancor.

"Nah," the old man replied, "from the sloppy grin on your face."

Rhys took his change with a laugh, not denying it, but not quite agreeing with it, either. He was simply getting to know some new friends in town. People his own age, friends not associated with the firehouse.

That was all there was to it. Right? *Right.*

He arrived at Max's house right on time. Voices were coming from the back yard, so he walked directly around the side of the house.

What he found stopped him in his tracks.

Maree was rolling around on the grass, wrestling with Hank, and laughing with a joyful abandonment he hadn't heard in more than ten years. It was beautiful and agonizing in equal measure.

His heart skittered. He was frozen in place. Stuck solidly between fight and flight, he couldn't move forward and he couldn't turn back. Cold chills covered his skin; sweat beads popped up on his temples. Rhys couldn't do this. Seeing Maree in such a carefree manner, enjoying an evening with her brother, frolicking with the dog, reminded him why.

Just when he felt able to lift a foot to dart away, Max came out of the house and onto the back porch. There was no way he missed the strangled look of terror and panic on Rhys's face.

"Rhys," Max bellowed. "Glad you could make it!"

His words, although innocuous enough, seemed to have a hidden meaning, and Rhys was positive that Max knew he was cracking up on the inside. "I'll lighten your load there," Max offered. Then Max walked into the yard to meet Rhys where he was still stuck by the corner of the house. Max's actions were deliberate and reassuring, taking the beer from Rhys, opening the box as he returned to the porch, and methodically setting each bottle in a cooler of ice.

Disentangling herself from the dog, Maree rolled onto her stomach and looked up at the boys on the patio. If she'd noticed the stark terror on Rhys's face, she'd let it pass without comment. For that, Rhys was grateful. Instead, she beamed a smile upon him that radiated a message, a message that declared "I'm really happy to see you." That look, that smile, was an invisible, yet tangible force.

He had a distinct feeling that she had decided — determined — in that exact moment that Rhys would relax and have a good time tonight.

"Hi," she said cheerfully as she hopped to her feet. Rhys didn't say a word, still couldn't seem to move.

For the next sixty seconds, Maree's thorough attempts to dust all the grass off her body went a long way toward helping him recover from his flashback and moment of shock. In the short cut-offs, her legs seemed to go on forever, and she kept sliding her hands up and down them, brushing them off. She leaned over to wipe the clippings off her feet, and her oversized long-sleeved sweatshirt worked its way up to reveal her tight, flat stomach. She swished her hands up her calves, then her quads and the backs of her legs, and finally the arms of her sweatshirt. When he thought he couldn't take anymore, she again folded forward at the hips, this time to shake her hair and twist it up into a ball on top of her head, her silver belly-button ring slightly showing as she fastened the hair tie to hold the bun.

Dear Lord, he was dying.

———

*M*ax, still taking everything in, wasn't sure if she was doing it on purpose or not, but he noticed that whatever had spooked Rhys was apparently forgotten.

"Now that you've undone every hour of my dog's training,

ruined my yard, and tortured my new friend, run inside and grab the baked potatoes for me," Max said with a chuckle in his voice. "Please?" he added with a sugary-sweet, sarcastic smile.

"I did no such thing," Maree argued, "but I will go grab what we need from the kitchen."

Max let Rhys watch her sashay inside before asking, "You all right?"

He noticed how Rhys gathered his wits. It was as though he was shoring up his defenses and re-establishing his walls. The effort was well-practiced, and Max was certain that this was a process that Rhys had gone through many times before, setting his boundaries, securing space and safety. But why?

"Yeah, I appreciate y'all inviting me!"

So, that was how Rhys wanted it. Max could respect him for wanting to keep his thoughts and motivation to himself, but if things continued down the path Max was predicting, they'd have to talk sometime. Rhys had a lot more going on inside than he liked to let on.

———

*R*hys's world was back on an even keel by the time Maree reappeared with baked potatoes wrapped in foil and a strange-looking wire circle threaded with green pods that turned out to be Brussels sprouts. He marveled at the number of new foods she had introduced to him. He usually shied away from the unknown and unfamiliar, especially when it came to food. Meat, potatoes, repeat. That had served him well in the ten years he'd been fending for himself, yet it seemed that every time he turned around, Maree was filling his world with new experiences.

The conversation covered everything under the sun. The topics jumped and the stories flowed freely from Max and

Maree. Rhys was content to sit back and listen. He participated in the exchange, giving tidbits, but never truly opening up.

He told Max and Maree stories about the firefighters he worked with, calls they'd had, and fires they'd fought. He shared that he was twenty-eight years old and had grown up in Texas. He didn't say a word about his family. He knew the lack of personal information was noticeable. The look he saw in Maree's expression revealed that she wanted to know more.

He gave her points for persistence. Never nagging, she tried digging for details, asking very specific questions. He wasn't as immune to her as he liked to imagine. He found himself talking about his education, his time at the fire academy and EMT school. He didn't say where or when school had been, but he did express his love of learning. He shared that he'd earned advanced degrees in fire science.

It wasn't a secret that he'd arrived in Green Hills a few months ago, but Rhys didn't offer any information about *where* he'd come from. He didn't say what brought him to their out-of-the-way, sleepy small town. Green Hills had a magical sense about it, especially because it was *not* on the beaten path. One had to make a conscious decision to be there, to live there… It was paradise on purpose. People rarely stumbled upon such a treasure. Rhys could admit to himself that something specific had brought him to this moment. Maybe 'chased' was a better word; something had chased Rhys to Green Hills. But he wasn't ready to share it out loud.

As the sun went down, the talk turned a little more somber. Maree explained how their parents had died in a car accident just as she was entering kindergarten. Max reached out to grasp her hand, and Rhys selfishly felt a pang of jealousy. He was not so much jealous of Max holding her hand, although he could, in a moment of truth and honestly, admit that he would like to test the softness of her skin.

No, he was envious that Max had the luxury to simply

reach out to console his sibling, of the gift Max and Maree possessed in being together with someone known and loved. Even if they shared sadness and tragedy, at least they had someone with whom to share. *God, how that must feel.*

Max and Maree described their battles against the system to stay together through a series of foster homes. Rhys saw in Max the strength and determination that once forced judges and social workers to bend to his will and now made him a force to be reckoned with on the football field. There was much more to the affable, fun-loving Max Davenport who was so regularly portrayed in social media photos and sports show segments.

When they became quiet for too long, Maree let loose an endearing giggle. Her joy for life literally bubbled out of her, and for Rhys, it was an incredible sight to see.

She dished out dessert — strawberry cake layered with homemade jam and generously covered with a whipped cream cheese frosting — and then went on to lighten things up with hysterical anecdotes about their sister, M'Kenzee, and her wild adventures as a photojournalist.

Rhys connected the dots easily: Max was the eldest, the caretaker, the guardian; Maree was the baby, the creative, and the life of the party. M'Kenzee was the middle child, strong-willed and independent. Again, he reveled in the gift the three siblings had been granted in having each other.

The laughter reenergized them. Without needing a plan, they worked in tandem to take everything inside; Max cleaned his grill and wiped down the table, Maree washed the dishes, and Rhys put leftovers in containers and set them in the fridge.

"I feel like I'm always thanking you for a fantastic meal," Rhys commented as she walked him toward his truck at the end of the night.

"Then there's no reason to stop while you're on a roll. Come to church with us in the morning and indulge in lunch… It's Sunday pot roast, carrots, potatoes, onions, and gravy, with homemade biscuits and more of the strawberry jam that I used on tonight's cake."

"You are the definition of temptation, Maree Davenport," he chided, trying to keep things light and easy. "And you're very persuasive. I'd love to come. Which church, and what time in the morning?"

She gave him all the details as he climbed in the truck, turned on the ignition, and rolled down the driver's-side window.

She stood on the running board to be eye-level with him and, figuring he could ask for forgiveness at church in the morning, he prayed that she'd lean in and end the night with a kiss.

That's when she lowered a hammer to his heart with the softest, kindest words he'd ever been told, "Rhys, I hope that I'm with you again the next time your nightmares hit."

He could not breathe, much less speak. She was too much. She was sweet and understanding, and she was going to kill him. Softly, maybe, but she was going to kill him all the same. He couldn't take his eyes off her face, her gentle smile, the glint in her eyes. He just sat there, not breathing, and not saying a word.

After a long moment, Maree reached a hand into the cab and brushed back his hair, smoothing it from his brow and running her fingertips across his warm skin.

The she turned away and walked back inside the house.

7

The course of true love never did run smooth.
Shakespeare, A Midsummer Night's Dream, Act 1,
Scene 2

Maree had done what she must by calling out his moment of panic. He needed to understand that she was fully aware of the stronghold he kept on his thoughts and emotions. She'd also brushed his hair back, in case it was her only — and last — chance to do so.

She hated the distance he was purposefully putting between them.

He'd come to church as promised. He'd even followed them back to Max's house for lunch as planned. All the while, he was still rather reticent and spoke very little. Almost not at all to Maree.

He and Max talked football. He loved on Hank. He commended her cooking. He helped clean up the dishes.

It was all very proper. It was all too polite.

Max invited him to watch the NFL game that was on after

lunch, but Rhys made an excuse to leave. Maree offered to walk him to the truck. He declined that as well.

"Hang in there, kid," Max reassured Maree as she snuggled up next to him on the couch to watch the game.

The next morning, Maree stopped by Max's to say goodbye before he headed back to Kansas City, so she was later than usual getting to the grocery store. There was no fire truck parked out front. It was his Monday to work, and she'd missed him. She collected her fruit without her usual gusto, ran a few errands in town, and then drove out to Miss Sadie's.

———

*S*adie took one look at Maree's long face and wisely elected to talk about something — anything — not related to fires, flames, smoke, or men.

"I swear my time would be better spent researching the number of students who've perished during medical school," Landry huffed, slamming her massive textbook closed and planting her forehead on top of it. Sadie had reassured her until she was blue in the face, baked every tried-and-true mood-lifting treat, and brewed her very best nerve-calming tea. All to no avail — Landry was still visibly stressed over the exams and clinicals looming over her. Sadie knew in her heart that all would go well, but she was more than ready for Landry to get them over with, so her sweet boarder could relax and get back to normal.

"At least you're taking the time to learn," Janie Lyn replied.

"You can tell us what is going on, Janie Lyn," Sadie said in encouragement. Sadie knew firsthand how challenging a day felt at the local memory care facility where Janie Lyn volunteered. No one should carry that emotional weight alone.

"I'm just frustrated," Janie Lyn admitted. "Why can't people listen to the trained experts instead of insisting they're right? How can they be so determined to have it *their* way instead of what is best for the patient? A patient who they claim is their most beloved family member. I don't understand." Sadie had never seen Janie Lyn look so defeated; she was clearly hurting for her patient.

"Is there anything we can do, honey?" Sadie asked, her voice revealing genuine hope that Janie Lyn would accept her offer.

"I'm sorry," Janie Lyn said chagrined. "I didn't mean to ruin anyone else's day. Someone to listen while I complained was all that I needed. Thanks, y'all," she finished with a sad smile. Sadie's own heart was still bruised from living at the facility with Sam and the ordeal she had been through, watching dementia take his life. Sadie had been open and honest about those months, about the toll it takes on a person. Sadie suspected that to be the reason that Janie Lyn usually kept all her thoughts about her Alzheimer's work to herself, boiling with anger and breaking with sadness at times, but refusing to burden Miss Sadie with her struggles. "Besides, as an unpaid volunteer with no medical training and no authority, there's not much I can do around there anyway."

Miss Sadie hated that all three of her girls were going through low tides.

Life was full of ebbs and flows, highs and lows, peaks and valleys. Sadie knew that to be true, and she knew these were short-term challenges that the girls would wade through and survive. More than survive! They'd learn and grow from every trial, be stronger for grinding their way through every struggle. Yet knowing those truths didn't make it even a fraction easier to watch loved ones maneuver through their challenges, and Miss Sadie didn't like it one bit.

———

*F*or Maree, the week dragged on. Tuesday and Wednesday were spent sewing, sketching, cooking, tasting, editing, and writing. Normally all things she loved to do. That particular week, they were all things she had to force herself to tackle and felt no zest to complete.

Thursday and Friday brought both too much time to think about Rhys, as well as a pleasant distraction, as she made her way over to Tulsa to be the guest speaker at a quilt guild meeting.

The drive there provided the perfect opportunity to take some deep breaths and relax. She found a favorite playlist on her phone and sang along, song by song, while admiring the incredible landscape. No one expected to find such lush, breathtaking terrain in southeast Oklahoma, which to Maree's way of thinking made it that much more beautiful, that much more dazzling. The gentle hills winding through dense green-ery, and the views that seemed to stretch for miles and miles in every direction, created the feeling that she was floating through hidden riches. It was one of her favorite routes, and she always looked forward to a few days spent living on *Tulsa Time*.

Altogether, she was scheduled to be gone for two full days, and the break was a welcome one.

She always enjoyed opportunities to be the guest speaker for guilds, sewing groups, and quilting bees. This time she would be presenting her program at not one, but two meeting times — one on Thursday evening and the second on Friday morning.

Maree treasured the time she spent in that element, because she truly admired and adored her quilting friends and acquaintances, both locally and worldwide. She found that sharing her work with fellow quilters was always a treat. They asked the best questions and were never shy about sharing their own suggestions and critiques.

This trip proved to be no different. When she wrapped up her presentation, several hands shot up from the audience.

"Will you be publishing another book soon? I brought your last one if you don't mind signing it after the meeting," one woman asked.

"I still like last year's fabric line the best," another said.

"Yes, I sure wish you'd rerelease the geometric prints — all the stores are sold out," the guild president agreed.

Maree appreciated their input; it was a great compliment to hear how much they admired her designs. But it was more than flattery; Maree kept files of suggestions from her programs, notes for future projects which helped guide her work.

The program she presented during that visit included a glimpse into her design process, a step-by-step behind-the-scenes look at how she took a doodle, recreated it in digital form, played with colors and composition, worked through "strike meetings" with the manufacturer, and finally sent the approved designs to print.

The design process was fascinating, and the audiences' reactions were encouraging. Without fail, Maree was motivated and ready to work after visiting a guild, vending at a quilt market, or teaching virtually.

She finished her presentation with a trunk show of her finished work — quilts, bags, aprons, pillows, and all kinds of projects that used her fabric lines. The guild members could touch and feel and see up close, creating a lively and energetic exchange. The collection of quilts she'd brought to display on this trip was very special in that it was a series of projects Maree had put together to help Janie Lyn raise funds and spread awareness for Alzheimer's care and support at the memory care facility where she volunteered.

Janie Lyn was all-in with her efforts to end the tragic and fatal disease. On top of that, finding a cure was incredibly important to Miss Sadie after her journey through Sam's dementia and death. Maree knew this selection of crafts and quilts would make a big impact, and she felt called to share them.

"Maree, what can we do to help?" the guild president asked in earnest.

"That's my very favorite question," Maree responded with a smile. "There are so many ways we can use our hobbies, such as quilting, to benefit charitable organizations," she went on to explain, "and as quilters we have a strong and collective voice. Donating finished projects for auctions and raffles raises money that is desperately needed at both local and national levels. Talking about those projects on social media raises awareness, creating a ripple effect as your friends share your photos with their friends. And including how you are quilting for a cause in your posts and captions will start conversations that prompt others to do the same. Gather your quilting friends for community events; if you've never been to one, they are a ton of fun! You can also sew projects like fidget quilts, pillows, and stuffed animals to donate to local nursing homes and memory care facilities," she shared.

The audience members were nodding their heads and taking notes, encouraged and motivated by Maree's passion.

She was equally excited to teach the hands-on workshop. The class she was leading for this trip focused on block and pattern design, color selections, and the software she used to lay out and finalize quilt patterns on the computer. It was a three-hour course centered around a new design technique, and it was chock-full of activities and design exercises.

Workshops were her favorite time to interact with other quilters and learn from them. Wealthy in both sewing and life experiences, the quilting community was a diverse, dynamic group from whom Maree had already gained tremendous insight and wisdom.

Like any good teacher, she believed wholeheartedly in life-long learning, and took home as many notes as her students. Oftentimes, those notes turned into new projects, new patterns, and new book ideas.

The guild she was visiting was the largest in this region. Its members were incredibly talented and very accomplished quilters, so they were a fabulous sounding board to see if this new method of artwork and the patterns it created were worth pursuing. If it went over well, this would be the focus of her website, her next fabric line, and her personal quilt projects for the foreseeable future.

Needless to say, Maree had looked forward to these couple of days away.

In addition to her speaking obligations, she always planned her Tulsa trips to allow her to indulge in some downtime — an afternoon of quilt shop hopping, maybe a run into the shopping mall, and at least an hour to grab a slice of her favorite pizza down on Cherry Street.

It was the perfect distraction.

There was no way Rhys Larsen could sneak into her subconscious to monopolize her thoughts when she was this busy.

And it worked. Mostly.

Aside from the two-and-a-half-hour drive there, a restless night in the hotel, and the two and a half hours spent driving back (when her thoughts drifted disloyally between how much she liked him and when she might see him again), the overnight trip did a wonderful job taking her mind off Rhys.

The feedback from the trip was even better than Maree had hoped, so once she'd unpacked her overnight bag and the suitcases of fabric and materials she'd taken for the trunk show and workshop, she spent Saturday afternoon back at the drawing board, where sketches, fabric design, and digital layouts all came along nicely.

Janie Lyn came over that evening with a fresh and hot pizza topped with all Maree's favorites: Canadian bacon, onions, green bell peppers, mushrooms, and lots and lots of cheese. Maree opened a bottle of her favorite wine to go with it. The dinner was delicious, and the company was even better.

"Tell me about Tulsa," Janie Lyn prompted Maree.

Maree came alive sharing all the specifics, the questions, and the comments. Both girls got a little teary when Maree described how focused and inspired the quilters had been to begin quilting to end Alzheimer's disease.

"I never paid much attention to quilts before I started helping you in the studio," Janie Lyn said. "Now I notice them everywhere I go. I've even been bidding on a few vintage quilts that I found online. They are so beautiful!"

"Beware," Maree warned. "Collecting quilts is just as addicting as making them. I have a hard time turning away from any that I find at an antique store or a thrift shop. I've even found incredible quilts and unfinished toppers at garage sales. So much work went into them — it breaks my heart to see them being sold for next to nothing."

"I might need to avoid antique stores, thrift shops, and garage sales," Janie Lyn admitted with serious concern.

Maree burst out laughing. Within seconds, Janie Lyn joined in.

The unplanned party didn't end until Janie Lyn had logged onto the virtual auction site to show Maree the quilts she was trying to buy, and then teased Maree for being a terrible influence when she convinced Janie Lyn to up her bids. On all four quilts!

The girls were both laughing and giggling again when Maree walked Janie Lyn out well after midnight. Maree was grateful for their budding friendship.

Rhys was not at church on Sunday.

After services and lunch, Maree spent the afternoon and evening sewing a Christmas quilt pattern that featured a holiday fabric line she would soon unveil. The finished quilt would be featured on the cover of a national magazine in December to highlight the collection of cool wintery blues, bold cardinal reds, and deep forest greens. She was teaching Janie Lyn how to use the longarm machine to do custom quilting, the work that sandwiches the three layers — the pieced quilt topper, the center batting, and the backing fabric — and stitches them together to finish the project, so she set the completed "flimsy" to the side to save for her new friend to finish as she wished.

On Monday, Maree shopped for fruit as usual, visited Miss Sadie, and put the final touches on a calico and chintz spring line that would roll out next February to introduce her new artwork technique. The prints were reminiscent of woodblock designs that had been produced in India between 1600 and 1800 and portrayed tiny flowers in beautiful colors on light backgrounds. Maree was sure her new version of exquisite antiques would be well-received.

She even finished the mock-ups for the magnificent pine shelves that a local woodworker was contracted to build for the shop. She envisioned them lining two walls of the building from floor to ceiling, with custom library-style, rolling ladders attached. They were going to be perfect for accessing fabric bolts, arranging her vast collection of books, and hanging finished quilts that served as decorations as well as a way to display her fabric lines.

She accomplished a lot of work. But she never heard from Rhys.

While eating her lunch on Thursday, Maree decided that she'd had enough. She had given him enough space. Distance was — at least to her — not the answer.

She had a habit of going after what she wanted, and she was done letting him retreat. There was more to *whatever* they were, and she was ready to reach out to him. She intended to do just that when his shift ended at 8 a.m. the next morning.

After she locked up the shop that afternoon, she ran back by the grocery store to pick up enough breakfast ingredients to create a feast that would kick-start their day.

She decided they would make a full day of it, so she also grabbed hamburger meat and buns to throw on the grill, and a bag of potatoes for making homemade French fries for their dinner.

She added two handfuls of peaches to make a cobbler for dessert that he'd positively drool over. She wasn't above finding the way to a man's heart through his stomach.

She bought a couple of flats of fall flowers to plant in the beds along his front porch. She could start the project while he slept for a while, and then after he'd had time to rest, she hoped he would work by her side to finish the job.

He could have all the time he needed to open up to her about the demons haunting him, but he could not continue to shut her out. They had something worth exploring, Maree was sure of that. Too sure, in fact, to let him toss it — or her — aside.

She heated up leftovers from her fridge to nibble on while she baked the cobbler and made a batch of homemade vanilla ice cream. She would let it set in the freezer overnight, and it would be perfect to pile on top of the golden-brown cobbler crust tomorrow night. With her plan in hand, she cleaned the kitchen while humming Dolly Parton classics; if anyone knew how to take charge and fix a situation, it had to be Dolly.

She showered and gooped her hair with leave-in conditioner and gel, fixing it in a "pineapple ponytail" to set her curls while she slept. She brushed her teeth, flowed through her nightly skincare regimen, and went to bed feeling the most encouraged she'd been all week.

She woke up to find Green Hills in a whirl.

In the very early hours of Friday morning, there had been a large explosion just outside of town. The whole community was abuzz; an abandoned warehouse was on fire, releasing who-knew-what-toxins into the air. Worst of all, it was common knowledge around town that Mr. Armstrong, an elderly veteran who kept to himself because he suffered from PTSD, often slept in the woods during the warm months or in that old building when it was cold. They couldn't find him anywhere.

Rhys had been on shift when that call came in, and she knew he wouldn't quit until the fire was out and Mr. Armstrong — or, God forbid, his body — was discovered. Although his shift had technically ended, it could still be hours and hours before he would leave the firehouse.

Maree had a very healthy imagination, so it was a short leap for her mind to fill with worries and what-ifs. She was far too concerned to accomplish much of anything; she didn't even attempt the flower beds. Her day simply consisted of mindlessly walking in circles around the shop, using a fancy and practically foolproof machine to cut fabric into quilt kits, and listening intently to the local radio station for updates. It was all she trusted herself to accomplish with her attention on what was going on and none of her focus on what she was doing.

By 8 p.m., reports confirmed that the fire was contained. The warehouse and the surrounding outbuildings were a total loss. Mr. Armstrong was still missing.

Hoping that he'd be found very soon, and that Rhys would be headed home, Maree pan-fried the hamburger patties and potatoes. She wrapped them up and put them both in a paper sack, then grabbed a quilt from the stack under the coffee table and went to wait for him.

Whenever his shift ended — *however* his shift ended — he was going to need her. And just as she'd told him, she would be there for him. Whether he liked it or not.

8

*Sometimes, the best way to help someone
is just to be near them.*
Veronica Roth

*A*n intense warehouse fire and a manhunt for a possible victim of that fire had consumed a full shift plus an extra eighteen hours. Driving home from the station, Rhys focused on keeping his eyelids open and his truck between the yellow lines. It felt like he hadn't been home in forever.

In fact, it had been almost two days since he'd left to work the twenty-four-hour shift which had turned into forty-two. It was 2 a.m., and he was bone-tired. On top of the fatigue, Rhys was starving, but he was too exhausted to fix or find anything to eat.

There was absolutely nothing good about days like today.

He'd showered multiple times at the station, trying to wash off layers of grime and soot. Yet his body still felt coated in smoke; his eyes were burning and begging to close. He was not paying much attention as he dragged himself up the porch steps and jiggled the key into the front door lock, so he almost didn't see the bundle on the old wooden bench in the far dark corner of his porch.

Sitting sideways and leaning against the back of the seat, a beautiful angel was tucked tight in a blanket and fast asleep.

His first thought: *I don't deserve this gift.*

Man, had he missed her. His self-imposed exile was proving to be useless. Even when he didn't see her in person, she haunted his dreams; when he didn't call her, he heard her voice in his head. The more he swore he didn't need her, the more possessively she took up residency in his mind. And in his heart — his greatest fear coming to fruition.

His second thought: *Maybe there is something good about this day after all.*

Rhys finished unlocking the door and pushed the door open enough to toss his gear on the floor just inside the entryway. Going back to where Maree slept, he kneeled down to be face-to-face with her, and his heart skipped a beat. The weight of the last day and a half lightened just a tad, and a semblance of peace settled in.

She was stunning. And she was carrying a bag of something that smelled homemade and delicious, even if it was cold.

Yep, an angel.

As smoothly as he could muster, he stood back up, lifting Maree into his arms and holding her close to his chest as he snagged the food bag and walked through the doorway. Balancing on one foot, he lightly kicked the door shut behind him, then reached out to lock the handle.

He walked to his oversized recliner, sitting down with her still in his arms and settling her even closer to his body. His stomach growled with hunger. Using one hand, he looked inside the bag to find the burger and fries. He enjoyed a few of the fries, but he still couldn't muster the energy to do more than that, so he set the bag on the floor beside the recliner. Just as he was resting his head back against the seat cushion and closing his eyes, hers opened.

"Hi," she whispered, looking up into his face.

"Hmm," was the best he could respond, and he definitely could not wrangle the energy to open his eyelids. He was also half-afraid to let her wake up for fear that she would take off now that he was finally home.

"Are you okay?" she asked.

"Working my way there," he replied, picking her up in his arms just enough to nestle her even closer.

"Please stay," he said, so low that she might not have even heard him.

Either way, he wasn't letting go.

Sometime during the early hours of the morning, Rhys lifted the foot of the recliner, and Maree stretched out on her side, halfway leaning on him and halfway wedged between his body and the arm of the chair. Her head rested on his chest, and her hand rested on his heart. Her leg was slightly bent and draped over one of his. A corner of her quilt was still encircling her, while the rest of it draped over their feet and fell to the floor.

This was how he awoke around six o'clock, his normal time to go for a run before breakfast. Not this morning. He would have happily stayed stone-still and remained just like that forever if he thought it possible. Since he figured that was unlikely, he used his free arm to reach over to the couch, where an afghan was draped over the arm. Moving as slightly as possible, he pulled it over them to keep her warm and covered her hand with his own.

He dozed, he dreamed, he awoke again, and this time he could tell from the rhythm of her breathing that she, too, was awake. He took one deep inhale, savoring the moment just one extra second.

"Your hair smells like life." His voice was gravelly, as much from sleep and fatigue as from the smoke at the fire he had worked. He worried that she would think him crazy again for loving the scent of her hair, but it was true. There was something vibrant and alive about her, and he couldn't seem to get close enough. He couldn't do this long-term, but he couldn't muster the willpower to walk away. Not today, at least.

With a gorgeous grin, she turned her face up to his, lifted her chin until her lips were close enough to kiss his cheek, and then snuggled in and hugged him tighter.

Taking this as a sign that their night in the chair was over, Rhys dropped the foot of the recliner and helped her to her feet. Maree stood first, and Rhys was about to heave himself up, when his arms — of their own volition — turned her to stand square in front of him. With his hands firmly on her hips, he leaned the top of his head into her stomach, closed his eyes, and stole just a few more heartbeats of her comfort. She stepped closer, turning his head to the side, so she could clasp him to her, sheltering him as one harbors a wounded soul. She seemed content to stay just as she was, for as long as he might need.

But the world had other ideas, and the doorbell rang, disrupting their embrace.

She leaned down, kissed the top of his head, and headed down the hallway toward the bathroom as he walked to answer the door.

The sun and the human on the front stoop were both a little too much, too glaringly bright, and Rhys really wished he could turn the clock back just enough to go back to holding Maree close in his arms.

"You're still in your clothes from yesterday," Davis pointed out needlessly.

Rhys merely grunted a sort of answer, hoping that if he didn't speak, his friend and fellow fireman might take the hint and turn around to leave.

No such luck.

"Are you going to let me in?"

"Do I have to?"

"Why wouldn't yo—" Davis stopped mid-question as Maree entered the hallway from the bath. Looking back at Rhys, Davis simply raised an eyebrow to ask his question.

"Please, do come in," Rhys invited, his voice dripping with sarcasm, and rolled his eyes while opening the door and stepping back. He lifted his arm with a grand, albeit grumpy, gesture for Davis to enter.

"The grocery girl we saw at Scooter's?" Davis whispered, this time raising *both* eyebrows at Rhys as he walked by him. Then Davis plastered on his most enchanting smile and headed straight for Maree.

Rhys closed his eyes, attempting to will away the pain starting to form in the center of his forehead. He took a deep breath, holding it while he counted to ten for patience, and then closed the door as Davis turned on the charm. Why gaggles of girls fell all over the guy, Rhys could never understand.

"Good morning," Davis beamed.

"Hi," Maree replied with that brilliant smile. "It's nice to see you again. Thanks for dancing with Landry the other night; she was ridiculously stressed over medical school. Being out on the town for a few hours did her a world of good."

If Rhys was worried that she would feel embarrassed about being "caught," he had wasted his concern.

She was open and honest and not the least bit bothered by being discovered at Rhys's house so early in the morning.

Her confidence was disarming Davis and delighting Rhys, who was ducking down the hallway himself; obviously, she could hold her own.

Rhys emerged from his room a short fifteen minutes later,

freshly showered and sporting new clothes, but Maree was already gone.

"Where is she?" he asked Davis as he poured a cup of orange juice and grabbed a carton of eggs from the fridge.

"*Who* is she?" countered Davis.

"An angel, I've discovered." Rhys heated a skillet to fry the eggs, having fun avoiding Davis's inquisition head on.

"Do you know anything else about this angel?" Rhys could tell that Davis was chomping at the bit for some info. Rhys enjoyed making a game of dragging it out, just to mess with his friend.

"How many do you want?" Rhys asked, pointing the spatula toward the egg carton.

"Three," he huffed in response. "Please," he added grudgingly.

"Your wish is my command," Rhys teased. "And throw a couple of bagels in that toaster, will ya?"

"The warehouse makes three suspicious fires. We have a bug," Davis said as he popped in the bagels, poured himself a glass of juice, and grabbed the butter and a jar of jam from the fridge.

"That's what I'm thinking, too. Thank God that no one has been hurt. The buildings he — or she — is burning have been old, empty, and already in need of destruction. Anything that could've blown was moved at least twenty yards from the point of origin. Is he a firebug or a vigilante?"

"Doesn't matter. A fire's a fire." Davis's voice was laced with disgust, and Rhys agreed completely.

With that, both men dug into their breakfast plates. This was a regular occurrence, breakfast at Rhys's place. They often met up when they were both out running the path at the city park a few blocks over. They would finish their run together and end up here at Rhys's house, hungry.

They had only known one another the few months since

Rhys arrived in Green Hills, but some people became instant friends when they met, needing neither extra time nor conversation to understand one another perfectly. Rhys appreciated the companionship, and he respected Davis for his skills in the field. Each man was equally glad and humbled that the other had his back.

"Damn, this jelly!" Davis commented slathering another healthy heap on top of his bagel.

"It's strawberry jam. Maree made it."

"Maree made it?"

Rhys couldn't keep himself from smiling. Again. This seemed to be happening quite a bit. He didn't think he minded that fact as much now, at least not as much as he had at first. Maybe.

"Yeah," Rhys conceded. "She's a great cook."

"How would you know?"

"Well, the chicken spaghetti she made last Tuesday was incredible. Her meatloaf and mashed potatoes hit the spot Friday night. Saturday, she grilled perfect steaks with baked potatoes and Brussels sprouts — which I didn't even know I liked. Sunday's roast and veggies after church were sinful, and I won't even bother you with the details of her desserts."

"You've been holding out on me, buddy," Davis complained.

"Yeah, I guess I have," Rhys admitted, pushing the eggs around his plate; his tone was less playful and a bit introspective. "I have enjoyed getting to know her, but nothing can come of it, so there wasn't any point in making a big production of spending time with her. Besides, almost every one of those meals took place at her brother's house and were by no means dates."

Rhys went on to tell Davis the whole story...how she had offered to finish his shopping, how he'd met her brother — who just happened to be Max Davenport. He told of how he'd managed a dinner invitation almost every night for a week. He even confessed how she was creeping into his thoughts more and more when he least expected it.

The part he did not share was just how much this attraction — this woman — scared the life out of him. Nor did he reveal how fastidiously he'd spent the last few days purposefully ignoring her, thinking that if he pushed her to the back burner, the fascination would fizzle out. He absolutely did not confess that his attempts had only caused him to think about her more.

"And she was just *here* when you got home after the warehouse last night?" Davis asked.

"She'd brought burgers by for dinner. I guess she fell asleep on the porch waiting for me to get home."

"What did she say when you woke her up?"

"She didn't. I didn't. I just picked her up, set her in the chair with me, and we slept there until about five minutes before you showed up ringing the doorbell."

"Nothing else happened?" Davis's voice held a hint of doubt.

"Nope."

"Would you tell me if it had?"

"Probably not, but nothing did happen last night, or this morning — whenever."

"What do you plan to do about her?"

And with that, Davis had asked the million-dollar question.

9

Kiss me and you will see how important I am.
Sylvia Plath

*R*hys had not seen Maree since after the warehouse fire, but he hadn't sought her out, either. He wasn't sure what was happening between them, and although she was never far from his mind, he wasn't sure if he wanted her there.

He still thought he had a choice in the matter.

So, when crew #33 stopped by the Get'n'Go for groceries to cook over their shift, of course, she was there.

"Hey, Maree," Davis boomed, walking her way. She was sifting through the plums, engrossed in her fruit selection, and jumped a little at Davis's enthusiastic hello.

Rhys grimaced, and the other three firemen walking in with them looked back and forth between the pretty girl they often saw in the store and the two guys — one all grins and giggles while the other was brooding. As a unit and perfectly in sync, they changed their direction to follow Davis curiously.

"Ah, hell," Rhys muttered, following reluctantly.

"...do you have a ticket?" Davis was asking Maree as Rhys approached.

"No, I've never been," she answered, "but I do love seeing the photos from each year's gala."

"Dav—" Rhys began in a low, growling, reprimanding tone but was interrupted as Davis continued.

"You've got to come! The Fireman's Ball is a blast. It's unforgettable, unlike anything you've ever seen. Please say you'll come wi—"

"She's with me."

With that blunt, brook-no-argument announcement by Rhys, the entire group — as well as a few random shoppers whose interest had been piqued — all froze to watch the drama going down next to the banana display.

Rhys stepped up to Maree with his usual confident air, yet his nerves hummed like a guitar string strummed too tight. On impulse, he reached out to move a curl away from her eyes, but realizing his hand's intention, he stopped himself midair.

She watched him and waited patiently as he cleared his throat, shifted his weight from one foot to the other, and finally strung a few words together.

"Our annual fundraising event is this coming Friday night. Being so new to Green Hills, I've never been, but I hear it's a pretty big deal. Will you go with me? Please," he added, sounding like a man stepping in front of a firing squad.

He could only imagine what must've been a hangdog expression on his face. Luckily, she didn't make him suffer long. Maree threw him a bone and answered instead, "I'd be honored, Rhys; thank you for inviting me."

Damn, her smile. It gave him a sense of relief and made his heart race all at once. With a look of silent instruction from Rhys, the rest of the guys and the random bystanders got the hint and went on about their shopping.

"What's on the list for Miss Sadie today?" he asked. He

didn't care how pathetic and obvious the attempt to switch gears had sounded. He was grasping for more even footing, and would take whatever he could use.

"I've got berries — strawberries, raspberries, blueberries, and blackberries — for cobblers and pies, plums and grapes for snacking, and I'm just going to gather a dozen of these bananas for their breakfasts this week," she recited while counting out the final pieces of fruit.

"That's all you need?"

"Yep," she answered, walking to the register. He stood silently while she paid.

"I'll walk you to your car," he offered — no, commanded — grabbing the paper bags and waiting for her to lead the way out the door and to her car.

"Do you need to get your own groceries?" she asked, pausing and glancing up at Rhys.

"Nah, they've got it covered," he said, hands on the grocery cart and eyes on the automatic doors ahead. He couldn't get out of that store fast enough.

———

*S*he opened the back hatch of her small-sized SUV, slid an armload of fabric bolts in plastic bags over to one side, and he set the bags in the back.

She walked to the driver's door. He put his left hand on it just as she went to reach for the handle. She reflexively turned toward him, giving him the opportunity to put his right hand on the car too, effectively trapping her between his arms. She looked up into his eyes, those incredible gray pools.

He took a step closer. And another. Until she was backed up against the car, Rhys's heat radiating down the front of her body as she tried to control her very erratic heartbeat.

She'd been patient all week, waiting for him to make the

next move. That wasn't her strong suit: waiting for things to work themselves out, and particularly *on their own*. She preferred to guide life, taking no chances on fate hijacking her happiness again. She believed that with enough effort and grace, good would always defeat evil, love would always prevail. Loosening the reins of control, letting life take its own course, was a challenge for her. For Rhys, Maree was willing to try.

Fireman's Ball tickets were hard to come by, so she had no intention of giving him an out on that. She also knew very well that his invitation had been coerced and under duress, so she needed the proverbial "ball" to stay in his court. She knew how she felt about their budding relationship, but she guessed that he wasn't so clear.

Or maybe he was.

"I've missed you."

His voice was so low that she worried that perhaps she'd dreamed the words out of his mouth. But she didn't have time to figure it out.

He lowered his lips to hers, with his hands firmly planted on either side of her, his body pressed so very close to hers.

His touch was like coming home, like discovering the place you belonged. The kiss was warm and tingling and everything that a first kiss should be.

She couldn't stop her inclination to rise up on her tippy-toes, an instinct to get closer. He continued to taste her lips, but never deepened the kiss. He nibbled the corner of her mouth, and then settled back on her lips. She was certain that she would slide to a puddle on the pavement if he released the cage of his arms, the only thing that held her upright.

"Larsen, let's go!" Davis yelled from across the parking lot.

He kissed her a fraction of a second more, then winked and smiled an indulgent little grin.

And just like that, he was gone.

10

*If you could kick the person in the pants responsible
for most of your trouble, you wouldn't sit for a month.*
Theodore Roosevelt

"*O*h, dear," Miss Sadie expelled on a deep breath upon
seeing Maree standing at her back patio screen door.

"I'm in big trouble, Miss Sadie," Maree confessed, setting
the fruit bags on the kitchen cabinet, and promptly turning
into Sadie's comforting embrace as she buried her face in the
soft shoulder being offered.

"Now, now; it's never as bad as it seems," Sadie sympa-
thized. Maree must have herself in something awful if her
flushed cheeks, glossy eyes, and bewildered look were any indication. "A cup of tea and a scone with some clotted cream and
my plum jam will make everything bearable."

"Jam is what got me in trouble in the first place," Maree
grumbled.

"Impossible," Sadie countered, offended by the mere
suggestion.

"Oh, Sadie, I could love him."

"Oh!" Sadie was caught off guard. "Ohhhhhhh," she restated with understanding.

Now, this was a horse of a different color. Her precious girl had an enormous capacity to love; all she needed was to find the right person to recognize this gift, to tend it and treasure it. Since the very first time Maree had hinted about her handsome hero from the grocery store, Sadie had felt that this man could be that person.

"He kissed me." Maree was gazing off into space, dreamily, her expression very un-Maree-like.

Even better than Sadie had imagined! She needed to tiptoe carefully through these tulips.

"And when he holds me, I feel safe and secure, but never smothered or constrained." Her voice had a tone of wonder and awe.

"Sounds terribl—"

"Oh, no, Sadie, it's truly wonderful."

Sadie was going to say *terribly irresistible*, but she didn't think it was prudent to say so now. Instead, she simply frosted her scone with cream and jam and settled in to live vicariously.

"He's so strong. And I don't just mean physically — although, boy, is he built! His character is strong. How else could he run toward danger when every God-given instinct would scream self-preservation to the rest of us? And although he's ripped with muscles, he is so kind and gentle that I am continuously amazed by his touch. And those eyes! They're gray — almost silver, really — like steel, but not cold. Maybe more like flint, but not hard. He kissed me; did I tell you that? I felt my insides go to mush, my entire body tingled, and butterflies took up residence in my stomach. Oh, Sadie, I never wanted it to end."

"Oh, dear, indeed," Sadie acquiesced, feeling utter delight and joy, licking the jam from her fingertip and picking crumbs off the tablecloth.

"He's asked me to the Fireman's Ball."

"The Fireman's Ball!" Sadie exclaimed, putting down the rest of her snack.

The Fireman's Ball was *the* formal affair of the year in Green Hills. Maree had never attended, as invitations were quite expensive and incredibly exclusive, but Sadie remembered her days of attending. As one of the largest, wealthiest, and most influential cattle companies in the state, Marshall Cattle Company was always toward the top of the invitation list, and Sam had always been very proud to enter the gala with Sadie on his arm.

The event included a cocktail hour for mixing and mingling, followed by a five-course dinner presented by an iconic chef flown in from a famous restaurant, and the night culminated in dancing until the wee hours of the morning. Celebrities, sports figures, and politicians came from near and far to enjoy the event. Yes, tickets were not easy to come by, and her sweet Maree was invited to attend.

"Under duress," Maree confided. "And ridiculous peer pressure from his friend, Davis — that might be his first name, or it might be his last, as it's all that I've heard. But Rhys could have let it go; he didn't have to say I was his. Not his. I'm getting it all mixed up. He said, *'She's with me.'* He didn't say I was his. No, not his."

Maree was rambling and going on and on at warp speed. It was plain to see that she was lovestruck, awestruck, and possibly even thunderstruck. Sadie loved it.

"Oh, Sadie, what shall I wear?" she asked when she finally came up for air.

"I have just the thing," Sadie answered.

11

People will stare. Make it worth their while.
Harry Winston

$\mathcal{S}$ ince Monday's showdown in the fruit department, the extent of Maree's contact with Rhys was a voicemail on her cell phone explaining that he needed to meet her at the gala because he was covering part of a shift for a friend; therefore, he would come straight from the firehouse and most likely be a few minutes late. Not the most reassuring message after the way his arm had been twisted to extend the invitation in the first place.

Still, she refused to be swayed from her enthusiasm for the night, so she took her toiletries and makeup over to Miss Sadie's to get ready for the ball. She luxuriated in a hot bubble bath, slathered on glittery body butter, and spritzed her skin with her favorite perfume. She applied a light touch of makeup, including a peachy lip gloss, and once her hair was piled upon her head in an intentionally messy updo that looked both classic and sexy, Miss Sadie helped her slide on the dress that Sadie had worn to this same event over fifty years ago.

The vintage ball gown was incredible, and after a few slight alterations, it fit her perfectly.

Sadie had put her foot down when Maree said she intended to drive herself to the ball, but they did both agree to Landry dropping her off at the venue after they'd taken a few photos outside the mansion.

Maree imagined herself very much like Cinderella, being fussed over by her loving fairy godmother and precious friends. She felt like a princess in her dress, and she definitely saw Rhys as her charming, handsome, and worthy prince.

Maree stepped out of Landry's car and walked toward the immense double doors of The Conrad, the oldest, most exclusive hotel in town. She fought the urge to pinch herself, just to make sure she was still awake and not enjoying this fairy tale in her dreams.

Looking up the eight floors to the elegantly pointed, arched rooflines, Maree was enthralled by the building's design elements. She was an artist, after all, and she couldn't stop herself from taking a moment to admire the building. Recognizing the English Tudor architectural style from the form and art history classes she'd taken during college, she was amazed by the huge windows, the elaborate buttresses, and the cathedral-like spires built upon the building's corners. Sadie had told her tales of cattlemen, oilmen, and famous politicians visiting the hotel — tales that were wilder than fiction. The Conrad was magnificent.

So much history, and here she was…Maree Davenport, Cinderella at the ball. She reached a gloved hand out to feel the aged wood of the intricately carved doors. They had to be at least twenty feet tall. Incredible!

Assured that this was indeed real, Maree took a deep breath and entered the ball. A greeter took her wrap and handbag as she stepped into the atrium where the cocktail hour was set up. Walking down the grand staircase and across

the twinkling room to find the bar, she tried to be inconspic-
uous since she was dateless.

Hopefully, not for long.

She figured she would walk slowly to use up some time,
making her way to find a glass of something to hold, simply so
she would not be empty-handed and completely out of place.
She smiled kindly as she went, but no one said more than a
pleasant greeting; most just nodded their head in a nonverbal
hello. There were so many people.

As luck would have it, the young man tending the bar was
someone she recognized from the Italian restaurant on the
square around the courthouse downtown. Luca's was very
upscale — glitzy and swanky in an old Hollywood fashion. It
was located on the street adjacent to her shop and apartment,
and it was one of her favorites. Although she didn't know the
boy's name, at least his was a familiar face. She could hang out
close to the bar — but out of the way, of course — until Rhys
arrived.

"A glass of wine, Miss Davenport?" the young man asked
as she approached.

"Oh, yes, please," she said, looking at his engraved, metal
name tag. "White, and something on the dry side, if possible,
Joshua."

"Just Josh." He grinned, grabbing a bottle from the enormous silver chilling tub behind him.

"Is the whole staff from Luca's here tonight?" she asked,
desperate for something to say so he wouldn't shoo her away.

"You remember me?" he countered, sounding somewhat
shocked.

"Of course, although to be honest, I don't recall ever
hearing your name before. I promise that I'll remember from
now on. Even though it's not part of my typical food budget, I
can't resist the pasta and bread at Luca's. I have to stop by to

splurge at least once a month," she confessed with a huge smile.

"I know exactly what you mean; the best part of working there is the meal tasting before each shift," he agreed. "Have fun tonight, Miss Davenport. You look amazing."

"Thank you, Josh! It was a treat to see you here," she said, laughing at his own confession and smiling graciously as she took the wineglass that he handed her over the high bar.

———

*I*t took Rhys less than a second to set eyes on her when he walked into the building and stood at the top of the stairs. At the far end of the room, the bartender was handing her a glass of wine; the lucky, besotted fool made her laugh and was being rewarded with that smile, the one that chased away devils and lit up the dark.

Right then, she turned toward the staircase, their eyes met, and the smile was all his. It was a sucker punch to his solar plexus.

When she'd been facing the bar, the commanding, deep-red gown was beaded and appeared to have a full skirt. But when she turned toward him, Rhys realized it was actually fitted — like a second skin — and *very* sleek from the strapless neckline to her tiny belted waist and flowing all the way down to the floor-length hem. She was wearing long white gloves, and a stacked choker of pearls was protecting the exact spot his lips were aching to kiss, just under her jaw.

Just as he took the last step down and she reached his end of the room, Davis appeared at their side, smiling like a fool himself. Before Davis could utter a word, Rhys reached for Maree, essentially pushing Davis aside with a gesture little more than a touch, but getting his point across, nonetheless.

"Exquisite." Literally dumbstruck, it was all Rhys could muster to say.

His compliment made her light up, bringing an innocent blush to her cheeks that belied the sophistication of her dress in a big way.

———

"Thank you," she replied, a little lost for words herself.

Taking her hand in his arm, he led her back to the same smitten bartender to order his drink — and stake his claim. It was silly and archaic, and yet the young man behind the bar didn't miss the message. Poor Joshua, an innocent bystander in her fairy tale. Maree figured men had a language all their own that each could comprehend, and while Josh was simply a sweet kid whom she was glad to have seen tonight, she was not one bit embarrassed to admit to herself that Rhys's possessiveness brought a thrill to her already-erratic heart.

Picking up his drink with one hand and placing the other at her lower back, Rhys guided Maree toward a garden door that was open to the terrace. Stopping just in the doorway — neither in nor out — and without a word, Rhys moved the hand at her back to lift her chin with his thumb and a finger as he lowered his head to meet her in a kiss that was also meant to send a message. With those two small points of contact, she felt their connection deep into her being.

Yes, she thought, she was in serious trouble where this incredible man was concerned. His kiss was perfect: prudent yet seductive, judicious yet promising.

"Thank you for being here tonight," he told her, looking into her eyes from mere inches away. "With me," he added with another hint of that finality that was starting to make her nerves hum — in a very good way.

It took her a second to snap out of the trance in which he

had her, at which point she realized that they were the main attraction.

"Everyone's staring," she pointed out.

"Yes, they are," he agreed with a saunter and a wink as he led her back inside to mix and mingle until dinner.

12

I could have danced all night.
Audrey Hepburn as Eliza Doolittle
in My Fair Lady

hys introduced Maree to every fireman she had ever
seen in the grocery store plus the fire investigators
and dispatchers from firehouse #2 as well as the fire chief,
Miles Everett, and his wife, Sasha. She introduced him to a
couple of NFL players she knew through Max, and a few other
friends, mostly other business owners and quilters she had
come to know during her two years in Green Hills.

After that, dozens and dozens more partygoers stopped to
meet and greet; a seemingly endless stream of people that
neither of them knew made sure to make their acquaintance as
they passed by. As two relatively new residents to the community, both young and dynamic, Rhys and Maree seemed to be
an item of big interest.

The names and faces were starting to swirl in Maree's
mind, and yet, everyone was very friendly, saying how much
they'd enjoyed watching her design studio take shape. Although

she'd been in Green Hills for two years, they were re-welcoming her into the fold of this majestic town. Without realizing it, they were re-establishing that this was exactly where she was meant to be.

When she was sure she could not come up with another topic of small talk or memorize another name, the chime rang for dinner. The dining room was positively magical. Swags of gauzy ivory and white fabrics were draped across the vaulted ceiling, creating soft light enhanced by lanterns that appeared to be floating across the room.

There were massive balloon arches with layers and layers of white, ivory, and metallic gold balloons of all sizes strategically anchored against the side walls. The tables were dressed in white tablecloths with swaths of sheer ivory voile fabric; gold chargers and flatware framed delicate stacks of bone china place settings. More balloons were artistically arranged to create floating centerpieces that featured immense bouquets of white flowers — roses, calla lilies, white dahlias, tons of tulips, and many more flowers whose names Maree couldn't even guess. Altogether, the ambiance and atmosphere were breathtaking, and served to further magnify the feeling that this night was a mystical dream that she would never forget.

The dinner was impeccable.

"Garlic grilled prawns and buttered scallops on a balsamic reduction," Rhys read from the menu once the appetizers were set in front of them. "Sounds fancy," he said, smiling at Maree and following her lead on which fork to use.

The next course was a butternut squash and apple soup with cinnamon agrodolce. "Rich, but not too sweet, even with the cooked apples," an older woman at their table said with approval.

"Reminds me of an amazing apple pie I had recently," Rhys told the group, with a gleam in his eyes that was just for Maree.

Next, they were served a marinated beet salad with seasoned almond slivers and whipped goat cheese. "Give the goat cheese a try," Maree whispered to Rhys when she saw him selecting around it. "You'll love it," she promised.

The entrée was Maree's favorite part: ginger salmon with honey-mustard glaze and cabernet filet mignon. She couldn't believe how impossibly delicious the filet mignon was — she'd had steak before, many times, but never like this. It almost melted on her tongue. "Wow," she commented to Rhys after her final bite.

"This dress was not made for this meal," she groaned quietly to Rhys as the dessert plates were served. Eight-layer chocolate cake with hazelnuts, chocolate mousse, and chocolate ganache, topped with a dollop of vanilla-enriched cream and garnished with sugared berries on the side. "But who am I to say no to dessert?"

"Definitely not a quitter," Rhys teased as they both took a deep breath and dove into the dessert. "And I'd say your dress still looks just right," he said for her ears only. Maree blushed and savored both the chocolate and the compliment.

"That was without a doubt the best meal I've ever had, beginning to end," Maree declared when the waitstaff — decked out in black tails and white gloves — removed her last plate.

———

*R*hys agreed it had tasted good. Really good. And knowing Maree to be quite a food aficionado and a pretty fantastic cook herself, he was not surprised to see her slide a copy of the menu into her purse.

He simply raised an eyebrow to let her know that she'd been caught when she looked up from committing her crime to see him watching. She charmed him again by softly insisting that he "shhh" with a delicate finger against her way-too-kiss-able lips, even while a guilty giggle escaped and a slightly wicked gleam shone in her bluer-than-sky eyes.

He wasn't alone in falling under her spell; the entire table seemed eager for her next story, hanging on her every word. Even the waitstaff beamed from her comments and gratitude when they cleared the table. She made everyone feel special, important — without having to try. She was open and gener-ous, as comfortable listening raptly as she was carrying a conversation. It always came back to ease. Maree made life look easy, beautiful. That effect drew people towards her; they all shared a sense that if they got close enough, that peace and contentment might rub off, might be absorbed by mere proximity.

As after dinner drinks were served, Maree swapped recipes — and her contact information — with the couple to their left, with a promise to email the written instructions first thing tomorrow morning. As they sipped coffee and hot tea, the two matronly women to their right recruited Maree to join their Tuesday night book club at the Library. Her enthusiasm over that invitation prompted another one from the woman who'd liked the soup so much, this time a standing appointment to play Mah Jongg, also at the library, but on Thursday after-noons. When Maree declined, admitting that she'd never played, the woman refused to take "no" for an answer. She dismissed Maree's concern with a promise to teach her, herself, which was apparently a big deal by the reactions from the other women at the table.

Rhys marveled and shook his head with a grin as cups were refilled. It was incredible. Maree gathered humans the way a grass rake gathers leaves. She skimmed across the conversa-tions, open and airy, letting people be themselves and liking them for it, and ultimately snagging new friends along the way.

Maree was incredible.

When Rhys had shared her as long as he was willing, he determined dinner was done and hastily wrapped up the conversation.

———

"*S*hall we?" he asked of her.

Maree had no idea to what she was agreeing, but declining him was out of the question, so she simply nodded: yes.

Rhys folded his napkin as he scooted his chair away from the table, making their excuses to leave the table. He stood behind Maree to help with her chair. When she stood, she felt his hands at her waist and his breath on her neck. A delectable warm shiver ran across her skin.

And then they danced.

Whereas snuggling in his arms while sleeping in his recliner had felt safe and secure, dancing in his arms was invigorating and thrilling. She literally laughed out loud with glee when he picked her up on a waltzing twirl. She felt incredibly empowered when he dipped her low on a samba. Her heart stopped completely when he brought their bodies together for a tango. Maree'd known he was a fabulous dancer from their night at Scooter's, but the tango? Maree had learned it in a dance class that she'd taken as an elective in college, but she couldn't believe he knew the steps. She was thoroughly delighted by the discovery.

Fairly early in the dancing, Davis tried to cut in, and Maree did not even chide Rhys when he completely ignored his best friend and spun them away. They wanted only to be together, and everyone in the room knew it.

"Want a break?" Rhys asked after an exhilarating set.

"Yes. No. Sure," she decided, and he led her to the bar for something to sip while they walked from the elegant ballroom, through the atrium, and back to the doorway leading out to the gardens.

"Where did you learn to dance like that?" She had to know.

"My mom," he said with a soft smile. "She was an accomplished dancer, even had opportunities to dance professionally before meeting my dad and getting married. Instead of a daughter she could dress in pink tutus, she had three boys who loved dirt and worms and fishing and sports. But being an outdoorsy kind of a kid didn't get me off the hook. Long before I was old enough to attend junior high dances, she forced me to practice every kind of dance known to man. She'd tell me to sweep the barn floor, then she'd pull out her old record player, and we would have dance classes right then and there. She taught and I practiced until Dad couldn't stand it any longer. He took over as her partner, which gave me the green light to escape. They thought I didn't notice the picnic basket and bottle of wine that he'd brought with him. Or that they'd walk back up to the house tucked into each other's arms hours after I had gone to bed."

Maree waited to see if Rhys would continue, but the reminiscing was over, and he fell distant and silent. It was the first time he'd ever shared even a slice of his personal life, his family, or his history with her.

"You are a mesmerizing storyteller, Rhys. And it sounds like your mom is a wonderful dance instructor," she nudged.

———

*W*as, he thought to himself, responding with only a slight nod as they continued to walk around the decorated grounds.

"I like this spot," Maree confessed, tugging him to a stop

and pulling him out of his reverie. It was the exact place they'd been standing when he had kissed her just hours ago.

"Do you, now?" he teased as he turned toward her, enjoying her playful pout and placing his hands again upon her hips to pull her close.

She looked up into his eyes with a nod, and he could clearly see her interest.

———

*S*he also had hope. She wondered if he could see into her soul, read the emotion warming her chest and tingling her skin.

The lighthearted, almost mischievous, glint in his arresting gray eyes turned into something much more serious, almost smoldering, as he continued to look down at her.

Maree could not breathe. When she thought she would faint from lack of oxygen, he finally lowered his lips against hers. With his hands holding her in place, her own hands were free to slide up his chest, along his jawline, and into his hair, so that she could pull him closer, finally deepening the kiss.

And he responded.

Her waist was so slight that his arms wrapped completely around her when he pulled her against him. Keeping one arm firmly across her waist, the other hand found its way to the center of her back, just between her shoulder blades and above the strapless dress.

———

*H*er skin was warm. Perhaps it was heated from their dancing, or maybe it was their kiss. Rhys liked to believe it was simply from their proximity — his whole body was on fire for her.

With that realization, a small semblance of sense returned. He had the presence of mind to lift his lips from hers and break their kiss. He didn't make it far, resting his forehead on hers as they both attempted to catch their breath.

Good Lord. I'm like a pinball shooting from feeling to feeling, all these emotions coming at me from every direction. It's too much.

On a deep breath and a cleansing sigh, he loosened his hold and took a step back from her, a step that he needed to make as figurative as it was literal. Perhaps even more.

———

"More dancing or shall we continue our stroll, m'lady?" he asked with a bow.

The moment was over, which was probably for the best. She felt as though she was in way over her head. And yet, she wanted to jump in even deeper.

He may have been cooling things off for himself, but she figured she could use the opportunity to get a hold of herself, too.

"A bit more of our meandering, I think, sir," she deigned with a slight curtsy, which was all the magnificent dress would allow.

He laughed a little at her matching folly and set her hand in the crook of his arm as they headed off onto the well-lit garden path.

"Did you know that 'meandering' is how I best love to quilt a quilt?" She launched into an explanation of the final steps to finishing a quilt and shared a little history of quilting motifs. It reset the air around them; it was what they both needed to breathe.

They talked of this and that, just random things as they walked. He asked great questions about everything that mattered most to her. He asked about her fabric designs, and she explained her passion for textiles and colors and textures. He asked about her plans and goals, and she told him about Main Street Design. He asked about her hopes and dreams, and she told him about Sadie and Sam, about their incredible love story; she told him about Sadie's undying devotion, even when Sam no longer knew her name. She decided not to talk about her parents or their deaths, wanting to keep things lighter on such a beautiful night. She asked about why he became a fireman, and he responded, "I'll have to tell you that story sometime," so she knew he, too, had things they could save for later.

She hoped that later would come.

When they made their last turn in the garden and were heading back to the terrace, Rhys removed his tuxedo jacket and draped it on her shoulders without saying a word. He put his arm around her shoulders, and they walked the remainder of the way back to the bright and shining hotel atrium without saying a word.

The shift from chatter to silence was again symbolic. Maree was certain of it; she just didn't know why. When they had kissed, his passion had been so true that Rhys was nearly shaking with rigid control. She knew that she'd not imagined it. Then he was calm and distant. As warm and welcoming as the heat from his jacket felt, she could not suppress a slight shiver caused by his cool and collected demeanor.

"Ready?" he asked once they were back to the atrium.

"Yes." She nodded with another smile, although this one, while no less brilliant, was a bit more introspective and knowledgeable.

The valet brought his truck, and he helped her up into the cab, cautious of the vintage dress.

"You are gorgeous," he told her, looking across the seat once he was in the truck. She noted a sad, wistful hint to his voice.

"Thank you," she replied, looking down at the fabulous dress.

And, determined to end their night on a happy note — a beautiful note — she forged ahead to tell him the tale Miss Sadie had told to her. About the times Sadie and Sam had gone to the Fireman's Ball, the larger-than-life characters Sadie had described, and then she rambled on like a kid in a candy shop, sharing more details about the color, the cut, the style, the beads, and the history of the dress than he could ever want to know or even remember.

When her gusto to be upbeat finally ran out, he nodded slightly in agreement.

"Yes, the dress is pretty, too," was all he said in return.

He pulled up to her shop, drove around back to the driveway and the entry to her apartment above the store. It didn't escape her notice that he left the truck running. He held her elbow as she made it up the stairs in her high heels, and he stood quietly while she found her key in her little handbag. Just like before, he unlocked the door.

"Thank you, Rhys," she said, in a voice much breathier than she had intended, but breathing was becoming a chore. Again.

"I don't know what to do about you," he confessed, looking down at her as if she was the most inexplicable puzzle. "One moment I want to set you on a pedestal under a glass case to protect you forever, and the next second I want to absolutely, positively ravish you. All the while knowing I can't have you."

She didn't understand that last bit — she'd made it crystal clear that she wanted to explore a world in which they were close — but she could tell he was struggling, fighting an inner battle that only he could navigate.

"Well," she conceded with an apologetic turn of her head, "I'm certainly not a trophy or a trinket that warrants a glass case, but I've also never been the ravishing, one-off kind, either, Rhys." She tried to exhale the breath she'd been holding, but it came out as a deflated, defeated sigh. With a sound of regret and a sad half smile, she added, "I'm the forever type."

They both stood there for a brief moment, things hanging in the balance.

"Good night," she paused, "and thank you! Tonight was a dream," Maree said. She dug deep inside her heart to look right into his eyes and bestow her truest smile upon him one last time. Miss Sadie always said to "fake it till you make it," and she would end this night with a smile if it killed her.

Rhys watched her. She knew that he saw her valiant effort, his perceptive gaze scanning her eyes, her lips, her face, as though memorizing each part individually as well as the whole. But he didn't say a word.

"Truly, it was the night of my life," she said as she used one still-gloved hand to reach up and push the hair from his temple one more time, as she'd done through the window of his truck outside Max's house, as she'd wanted to do again and again since their first conversation in the grocery store.

Then she lifted onto her tiptoes and guided his cheek down, so she could kiss it, before going inside and softly closing the door.

13

*The hardest thing I'll ever do
is walk away still loving you.
Author unkown*

R hys stood in the glow of her porch light, in a bit of a trance after she closed the door. She'd done everything right and said everything right. He knew she'd let him off the hook with a graceful and gracious parting, but he'd seen the glisten of tears in her eyes as she wished him good night. Absent-mindedly rubbing his chest where it burned, he tried to take a deep breath, but his lungs felt constricted.

She'd said it herself — she was the one-love, till-death-do-you-part, forever kind.

And he was not.

Forever was a risk he could no longer — would no longer — take. She'd asked why he became a fireman as they walked in the garden, and he'd deflected smoothly. Just as he always did when anyone asked. It was a story — a vivid nightmare — that he still did not share.

In contrast to Maree's tumultuous childhood, Rhys's had

been idyllic. He'd grown up living on a beautiful plot of land just outside a small town in Texas, about an hour from Fort Worth — a few hundred acres full of deer, turkey, and quail and a freshwater tank perfect for fishing and swimming. He was the oldest of three boys; Radley and Redmond were his twin baby brothers — a "surprise" bonus born to their family when Rhys was twelve years old. His mom was an interior designer who worked from home and stayed overscheduled and difficult to book due to high demand. His dad was a finance officer at the farm and ag bank during the week, and an outdoorsman every Saturday and Sunday. Their home was full of love and laughter. His family was close, spending tons of time together and having fun at every stop along the way. Life was about as perfect as a seventeen-year-old could imagine.

Rhys was a very good student and a great athlete.

Academics came easy for him; his mom often teased that he would meet his match in college and be in a pickle since he'd never cracked a book or learned how to study. His dad always waved away her predictions with his own joke that Rhys had inherited his intelligence from the Larsen side of the family; therefore, he was simply born brilliant.

From an early age, it was also apparent that Rhys excelled at sports. Little League baseball led to traveling all-star teams. Natural speed led to summer track meets. Little Dribblers led to early placement on the varsity basketball team as a freshman in high school.

But football was his favorite.

Rhys was a workhorse running back on the state-championship football team. He started his Saturdays in the fall by driving into town early to grab breakfast burritos with his friends, then watching film in the field house to grade the prior night's football game, followed by weightlifting and stretching to recover from the stress and strain put on their bodies the night before.

He would shower in the locker room before heading home to grab lunch, and then take the twins fishing or help his dad with a project, usually tackling the honey-do lists that his mom loved to create for them. By about four o'clock, they'd all five end up lounging around the living room, his dad in his recliner, his mom flipping through house magazines or knitting sweaters and scarves while she sat on the couch beside the lamp, and all three boys sprawled out on the floor in front of the TV, half dozing and half watching whatever college football games were on that weekend.

After a nap — almost always interrupted by monkeys jumping on his back to wrestle — he'd shower and dress to meet up with friends, maybe take a girl to the movies.

Most nights, they'd simply sit on the tailgates of their trucks in the football stadium parking lot at the high school, dreaming about what their futures would be like, boasting about what was coming: their next opponent and how they'd find a way to beat 'em; their senior year, which still felt eons away; and where they'd eventually go to college to razzle and dazzle on the football field while the college girls swooned at their feet and they lived like the kings of the campus. It was all so carefree, so childlike, and so incredibly innocent.

Until the week of Thanksgiving.

It was a special week in Rhys's junior year. Since they were still practicing football, it meant the team had made it a few rounds deep into the state playoffs. The coaches made a big production about workouts on Thanksgiving morning, and the whole town came out to watch the boys prepare.

The team ran through drills and one-on-one sessions before finishing up with special teams and a field goal competition. They started early, but no one minded a bit because all the moms brought baked pastries, muffins, and casseroles to enjoy for breakfast. Everyone — players, coaches, families, and fans — devoured the communal feast as soon as practice was over.

While the ladies fussed over the food, the dads and all the old-timers manned the coffee station, treating the players' younger siblings to hot chocolate complete with marshmallows and whipped cream on top. "Remember the game when..." seemed to be the way every second or third sentence began, and those fellas never forgot a play.

As practice was winding down that particular Thanksgiving morning, Rhys noticed the twins' absence. They should have been running wild with their friends, as all the little kids were trying to catch the punts and field goals from the varsity kickers. Just as Coach was finishing his remarks to dismiss the boys, sirens could be heard in tandem. Police cars, fire engines, and ambulances all raced past the school and headed out of town. Headed out toward Rhys's house.

Something wasn't right, Rhys could feel it.

"Coach, I think I gotta go," he interrupted. He didn't see the nod of agreement that his coach gave as he sprinted to the locker room to grab his truck keys. He didn't even change out of his cleats. And to this day, he didn't remember the eight-minute drive out to their place.

Whereas he had no recollection of those few minutes, he couldn't force his mind to forget the scene that appeared when he barreled up the drive. The image of the house up in flames, his mom screaming and flailing to get inside. His dad had been physically restraining her to hold her back while the firemen, police, and EMTs helplessly sprayed the fire that was ravishing his world, stealing his brothers, and forever altering his life.

In the commotion, no one noticed him drive up, so he was able to run right past them and into the side door to the kitchen. No one had to explain that the twins were inside. Hollering their names and trying desperately to see through the smoke, Rhys had taken no more than a step over the kitchen threshold when the entire structure collapsed. Three stories, including the attic the boys loved to play in, were engulfed in a raging inferno. The heat, the smoke, and the flames would be no match for two five-year-old bodies.

The air was too hot for skin to tolerate, too thick for lungs to inhale. The entire world was black and raging with fury. Although he was screaming and crying out as loudly as possible, the roar of the fire drowned out all noise. It was the deafening sound of death.

Rhys knew they were gone.

He wanted to go up in flames with them.

He stood frozen in place, eventually falling to his knees, crying in pain and disbelief, waiting — hoping — to be engulfed, too.

But instead, a fireman grabbed him, hoisting him across his shoulders, regardless of the fact that Rhys didn't want to go. He carried Rhys to the lawn, where he fell to his knees, dropping them both to the ground and keeping a grip on Rhys in case he tried to run for the house again.

"I'm sorry, son," the fireman said in a flat, final tone.

Something about the truth in his voice hit Rhys like a sledgehammer. He closed his eyes in acquiescence, rolled to his side, and started throwing up. His body jerked and rejected the smoke he had inhaled while his heart shattered with the knowledge that his world would never be right again. A sense of loss stronger than can be described washed over him. Once his body purged the smoke in his lungs, nausea over the circumstances kept him dry heaving as tears streamed down his face. Somewhere across the yard, he could hear his mom wailing, repeatedly crying out "no" while his dad held her, but he had no words to soothe her.

This was the horror Rhys relived daily. It was the nightmare that woke him every single night. It was the story he could not tell. He'd cried just that one time since the fireman had picked him up off the kitchen floor and carried him out of their burning house, saving his life. Since the episode lying in their yard, he'd not relinquished control over his pain. Ever.

Instead, he'd put a thick barrier around his heart. His burns had been significant enough to require a few skin grafts, but the scars served as reminders that what one held dearest, what one loved and treasured could be yanked away in an instant.

As soon as he was released from the hospital, Rhys walked away from football and the other sports that had brought him so much joy. He withdrew from the friends with whom he'd been so close. He finished high school early to get away from the town he'd once adored, but where he could no longer stand to be. Upon graduation, he attended the fire academy and earned an online bachelor's degree at the same time.

Then he became a fireman, so that he would never be too late again.

He had not saved Radley and Redmond, but he honored them in every call he took, at every fire he fought, and through every person he saved. He couldn't bring them back, but he would never forget them.

Nor could he love again. He'd tried. With his parents — who'd never recovered from losing the boys, either. And with girlfriends — who were really just acquaintances he'd taken on dates over the years. But the mechanism, the valve, that allowed one to open up and risk loss, was missing from his heart, burned up and turned to dust.

So, there it was. As much as he wanted to give Maree all that she needed and all that she deserved, he just wasn't the guy who could do it for her. He'd like to be that man. But wishing simply wouldn't make it so.

She was one hell of a lady — sexy and wholesome, honest and mystical, kind and spunky — and she would spend the rest of her life showering her huge heart and her amazing love on some very lucky person.

It simply could not, *would not*, be him.

Realizing and comprehending that sooner rather than later was a godsend, really. He would give her some space, keep his distance, and she would realize the exact same thing. She'd been just fine — living a wonderful life, in fact — before he'd arrived in Green Hills a few months ago, and she could be just fine with a wonderful life without him.

He hoped he could go back to being fine, too.

14

Perseverance is placing one foot
in front of the other, even if it drags.
T.B. LaBerge

After closing the door and clicking the lock, Maree forced herself to walk to the end table by her sofa, went through the motions of turning on some lights, changed out of the lovely dress, and put away her handbag. She tried not to, but she listened, knowing that Rhys stood on the porch for a very long time, holding her breath that he would knock on the door and make a stand for what was blossoming between them. He never did, and eventually his truck door slammed, and his truck revved as Rhys drove away.

The days went by, time went on. Hours turned into weeks.

Maree refused to change her life or alter her schedule, so she saw him on Mondays when he was on shift. She'd always say hello if their paths crossed in the grocery store, but Rhys did a pretty adept job of avoiding the produce section and the checkout lines when she was in them.

It was almost surreal the way they had been so perfectly in

sync one moment and then were ships passing in the night the next. She still did not fully understand what had happened to cause the distance, but she knew it was something that Rhys had to tackle, or at least trust her enough to share with her if the chemistry and friendship between them stood a chance at developing and succeeding.

She had not done anything wrong, and trying to imagine or guess his problem would only drive her mad.

No, she absolutely would *not* allow herself to go down that path. Instead, she became even more resolved that she would persevere through her heartache and come out stronger on the other side.

She gave herself fantastic pep talks and halfway believed them, but she was also honest with her reflection in the mirror and knew she had limitations to what she could endure.

She both wanted to see him and dreaded seeing him, all at the same time.

For the longest time, she adamantly refused to go out with Landry and their friends. She told herself it was just to be safe; willing to admit that seeing him out, especially if he happened to be out with another girl, would be more than she could handle.

But her friends and family were persistent and wore her down. Although Green Hills was a small town with few options when it came to nightlife, she managed to get through a couple of trips to Scooter's without seeing him and was actually beginning to relax when she was there. She'd been able to put together a cute outfit, fix her hair and makeup, and plaster on a smile to appease Landry and Miss Sadie. They thought she was finally getting over him, and she was willing to put on her game face and suffer through if it made them happy.

But, alas, Green Hills really did have a very limited social scene, so it was only a matter of time before they both ended up at Scooter's on the same night.

*A*lso hounded by well-meaning friends until he gave in and joined them at the bar, Rhys walked through the door and his eyes fell immediately upon her. She was sitting at a tall cocktail table by herself, eyes drifting down in deep thought, watching the straw make circles in her drink. Irritated with himself, Rhys determined with a grumble that he must have an internal radar where Maree was concerned.

Her friend, Landry, and another woman he hadn't met but knew from photos as Maree's sister, M'Kenzee, were engaged in a friendly battle at a pool table nearby, but Maree was alone. Her drooping body language and the distant look in her gaze were blatant signs that Maree was feeling *very* alone.

As much as those facts slapped him in the face, Rhys still slunk close to the bar and settled in a dark corner in hopes that neither she nor Landry would see him there. It didn't make him feel any better seeing the proof that she was going through the same misery that he'd been feeling. In fact, seeing her natural zest for life so muted forced him to confront a massive dose of guilt — he was perfectly aware that their current and less-than-ideal situation was completely his fault.

He told himself that he should have stuck to his guns when Davis and the guys begged him to go out with them. He could have been enjoying a ball game on TV from the comfort of his own couch, ordering a large pepperoni pizza for one, popping the top on a cold beer or two, instead of hiding in the back of Scooter's, drinking in the sight of Maree while praying that she didn't have that same radar for him.

He lucked out and stayed incognito as the girls finished their game of pool and returned to their table and Maree. She made a stalwart attempt to cheer up, plastering on what Rhys recognized as a forced, false smile. A waiter tried flirting with all three of them when he delivered a heaping pile of bacon cheese fries along with two glasses of wine for Landry and M'Kenzee and a glass of ice water for Maree. She returned the server's smile, but the gesture never reached her eyes. Her valiant effort to engage in their girls' night out wasn't lost on Rhys; he knew she was too kind to let on how miserable he figured they were both feeling.

He tried to give the same effort and attention to Davis and the guys. They all deserved a fun night out after a week of long shifts and yet another fire in the same pattern, which had led them to further believe that they might have a serial arsonist on the loose in Green Hills.

He was once again — for no less than the billionth time since the Fireman's Ball — arguing with himself. *Why is being apart from the greatest girl on earth the best course of action? Because in the end, I will be alone anyway, so it's not worth the pain. Why is walking away from her harder than it's ever been with other women? Because she's the perfect complement to my life and everything I could have dreamed up in a woman. Why do I lose everyone I've ever loved? Because—*

His internal debate was interrupted by whoops and claps and hollers erupting. The karaoke machine was being set up on stage. He couldn't halt the flood of memories; he immediately thought of their first encounter at Scooter's.

Her enchanting, entrancing singing, how alive she'd been on that stage — bewitching, really. How she'd seemed to cast a spell over him and how right it had felt to hold her in his arms as they danced and talked and teased and laughed. How it had felt even better to clutch her infinitely closer when the music slowed to a sultry beat.

Please don't sing, he caught himself repeating. *Please don't sing, please don't sing, please don't sing* Just like the little engine that could, he adopted the chant to get himself past this challenge. *Please do NOT sing!*

Luck was not his friend that night. After much begging and pleading from her friends and the rest of the bar patrons, resignation fell across Maree's face followed by cheering and laughter all around her.

Everyone was used to her shining in the spotlight, working the room like a professional entertainer, and no one could imagine that she did not have any desire to delight them as usual.

The moment she conceded and stood to walk toward the stage, Rhys headed straight for the door. Hearing her voice would be his undoing. It would stop his heart, prompt cold sweats, and utterly break him. He knew he was a coward, but running felt like his only option. So, running was exactly what he intended to do.

He didn't tell the guys he was leaving, didn't say a word to anyone. He threw a twenty-dollar bill on the table, which would more than cover his part of the tab. And he made a beeline for the exit.

Just as he reached out to push open the door, he heard her opening note, and it stopped him in his tracks.

"Swwwwweeeeeeeeet dreammmmms...of you."

She sang in an unnerving but beautiful tone, not boisterous and fun like the first time she'd sung this same song, but haunting, deep, and sorrowful. Before, she had sung with reverent respect for the original artist, Patsy Cline. This time she sang with wretched firsthand knowledge of desolate despair. Her words and her voice gave him cold chills, and he simply could not get his feet to move in order to force his body out the door.

Dropping his head in defeat and slamming his hand against the wall in frustration, he turned around to watch her sing.

Maree worked the crowd unknowingly, without making eye contact with a single soul in the audience. She managed to look sexy and innocent all at once. She should look boring and frumpy in the long flowing skirt and vintage-style block heels, with her hair piled on top of her head. Her innocuous librarian look was in stark contrast to her skintight, wrap sweater, which hugged her figure in a way that made his hands tingle to smooth over the fabric, encompass her ribs, settle a hand on her back. The tendrils and curls falling out of the messy bun were like silk; they begged to be touched. Her tiny stature with her big, rich, melodic voice captured the attention of every person in the room.

Boring and frumpy, she was not. Without a doubt, she was as sexy as hell, which just happened to be the exact pit where Rhys found himself.

Even the catcalls coming from men of all ages in the audience were voiced with respect and awe. Just like last time, she had every man in that barn eating out of the palm of her hand.

"You can dream of me every night, honey," one fellow called to her.

"Never stop singing, darlin'," from another.

"Damn, I wish someone would sing to me like that," Rhys heard some poor sap wish aloud.

Rhys wondered if steam was visibly emanating off him. He wanted to wrap his hands around each of their necks. And yet, he certainly couldn't blame them. Selfishly, he wanted her dreaming of him every night. He wanted to listen to her sing indefinitely. He wanted to hear her babble, chatter, ramble, joke, tease, and giggle. And, yes, he wanted her to sing to him. And only him.

But more than that, he knew that he'd given up those gifts; he'd surrendered any right to be jealous. He, too, was just another besotted fool on the dance floor. One that was living through the agony of a nice strong punch to the gut.

"Instead of having sweet dreams…"

Just as she came to the final two words, her eyes locked on to the deep, dark gray depths of Rhys's.

"…aaaa-booouut youuu."

There was no doubt to any living soul in that room to

whom she was singing. He realized that she'd known he was there the entire night. She'd been every bit as aware of him as he'd been of her. In that, they were still perfectly — and painfully — in sync.

"Lucky bastard," one man said in a tone of loss, as if he'd ever stood a chance.

Rhys couldn't move. Like always, she rendered him powerless against his own feelings for her. His feet were rooted in place, and no matter what his brain ordered, his body refused to obey.

She handed the microphone back to the DJ, casting a spell over the entire room with her humble smile, mesmerizing and magical after bringing down the house. Again.

There was no other way to put it: she was astounding and overwhelming.

She was amazing and incredible.

Several men stepped up, vying for her attention, asking her to dance, asking her to share a drink, asking her to marry them. She gave each man a small smile, shrugging them off in a friendly but quiet dismissal.

They all pretended to be crestfallen and broken-hearted, but they had no idea. Rhys and Maree both could have explained with great honesty and precise detail how tangible a broken heart felt. How it stole one's breath and crushed one's chest. How the act of inhaling air past a broken heart seemed to require deliberate instruction and purposeful intention. After so many days and weeks, they could describe that debilitating pain with perfect accuracy.

But Rhys knew she would refrain from doing so. He watched Maree lift her chin, plaster on a look of gratitude for their praise, and make it through this moment. He saw her steely determination and knew that she would continue to survive. He would force himself to do the same. If only he could get out of this damned bar.

She wound her way back to her friends. He made his way through the crowd to step into her path. She looked up into his face, pain and heartache clearly evident in her eyes.

"Rhys," she said in a sad, resigned voice, with an almost imperceptible shake of her head, and with the weakest, most worn-out smile he'd ever seen on her gorgeous face. Her body language screamed that she did not have it in her to deal with him, nor the myriad of emotions that swept through her body simply because she was standing in front of him. He sensed it was more than she could muster through. Physical pain pierced through him when the best she could manage was a half-hearted nod.

With that, she stepped past him, grabbed her purse, and headed for the door.

Her eyes were an open window into her thoughts, and Rhys hated that he was the one responsible for putting that forlorn misery in their depths. It pained him to know that the sadness in her voice was completely his fault.

"*Shit,*" he muttered under his breath, and turned to follow her out the door.

He tried to catch up with her, but too many people had comments and judgments to make. Everyone in Scooter's knew he was the world's biggest fool. They had no intention of letting him go without telling him so. She was their darling, sweet all-American girl, and he was the monster that had hurt her. They took no mercy on him, and he didn't blame them. He agreed with every one of them; he didn't deserve her; he couldn't protect her. Didn't they know that was precisely why he'd let her go in the first place? And yet, the unseen, magnetic force pulling him toward her was like no other.

By the time he made his way to the parking lot, Maree was pulling her car out of the parking lot, onto the highway, and heading for home.

For the third time that night, Rhys stood there, glued in

place. He was fighting an inner battle. He waged war upon himself, and either way he was going to lose.

He wanted to chase her. He wanted to follow her home, make things right, and hold her in his arms. He wanted to kiss that strawberry gloss right off her lips and take the first deep breath he'd known in weeks.

But what could he say? Nothing had changed. It was true he wanted to be with her. He thought about her all day and dreamed about her every night. He yearned for her in a way he'd never known was possible.

But it was also true that wanting wasn't enough. He couldn't keep her safe, and he sure as hell couldn't risk losing her.

Unaware of how long he stood there fighting his own mind, Rhys was finally alerted out of his stupor when a truck wanting to pull out of the parking lot honked and hollered for him to get out of the middle of the road.

With his own sad and resigned sigh, he headed for his truck and drove home. The night could not have gone any worse.

15

Never say never.
Pickwick Papers by Charles Dickens

t was a few weeks later when they saw one another at the grocery store. Rhys was walking in as Maree was walking out. They were moving toward a head-on collision with one another.

She was looking down to tuck her receipt and change into her wallet while pushing her basket out the doors. His voice caught her off-guard, which surprised her as she heard it in every dream, every night.

"Hi." He paused, and the whole of crew #33 paused with him.

"Oh," she started, automatically looking up into the deep gray of his eyes.

"Hey, guys," she added, realizing they were not alone. She acknowledged the group with a polite smile. Too polite, actually.

The silence became very awkward, very quickly.

"Can I help you out?" he stammered and shuffled over the five little words.

"No," she replied immediately, a knee-jerk reaction. They all saw her panic for what it was: self-preservation. "Thanks, but I've got it."

She let him off the hook with a little less vehemence in her voice. Then she gave a nod and a smile of goodbye to the guys and pushed past them to get to the safe haven of her car.

She was very proficient at trudging through these days. This time she just had to make it to the car. She kept repeating her new mantra to herself, "One foot in front of the other. Just keep moving forward," over and over and over in her mind.

No one watching would have guessed that her hands shook and her nerves quaked as she unloaded the bags of fruit, returned the basket to the stall, settled into her driver's seat, fastened the seat belt, started the car, and pulled out of the lot. All terribly normal tasks that one typically does without intention or thought, but tasks that now took every ounce of her concentration after that brief encounter with Rhys.

What was this invisible hold that he had on her? He didn't want her, so how and why could she still — so desperately — want him? How long until her heart fused its shattered pieces back together? This was ridiculous. He was *one* man. (Granted, he was the one man she cared for deeply and the one man she yearned for with all her being.)

But still, in a world of quite literally billions of men, he was just one man. One who obviously didn't feel the same way she did. She chided herself, feeling foolish and weak. Then she began reprimanding herself in earnest — for the umpteenth time. Why couldn't she move on?

Why was the one man who had rejected her so thoroughly the only one she seemed to want? To need? To love?

She was pondering these futile questions, feeling low but knowing that if she could just make it out to Marshall

Mansion, Miss Sadie would say just the right things, spoil her with hugs, fatten her up with something sweet, and soothe her nerves with her favorite cup of tea.

Putting one foot in front of the other — both figuratively and literally — she forced herself to keep moving. Keep going. Keep living.

She stopped by the dry cleaners to pay for a few items that Miss Sadie had said were ready to be picked up. While she was there, she mustered up a genuine smile and a good ten minutes of small talk with the sweet couple who owned the business.

One foot in front of the other. Just keep moving forward.

Next, she pulled into the full-service station and filled up with gas. Again, she managed a legitimate smile and conversation for the kind gentlemen who pumped the gas, checked her tires, and cleaned the windshield.

One foot in front of the other. Just keep moving forward.

She'd made the best of a tough morning. She felt a little silly for it, but she was really quite proud of herself for managing so well. And now she was on her way out of town, headed for Miss Sadie's, and feeling rather accomplished.

Her thoughts were ricocheting like pinballs in her brain as she waited for the last stoplight at the edge of Green Hills to turn green. She replayed the split second she had spent with Rhys in the store. It had forced her back a step or two, but she was okay. She'd visited with Mr. and Mrs. Wynn at the cleaner's. His voice had made her heart skip a beat, and then stop altogether. She still loved him too much. She'd done normal-person things like getting gas and making coherent conversation. He was too thin; his eyes looked sad. Was he sick, was he eating?

Sitting at the stoplight, her mind was absolutely all over the place.

Finally, the light turned green. She looked both ways,

reined in her errant thoughts, focused on the road, and pulled out into the intersection.

One foot in front of the other. Just keep moving forward.

It was quickly becoming more than a mantra; it was now her own personal motto.

The intersection she was driving through was between Main Street, which turned into the farm-to-market road leading out to Marshall Mansion, and the ramps to enter and exit the interstate turnpike that ran across Oklahoma.

Hidden under the dense blanket of trees, Green Hills was a quiet stop along the highway, mostly just locals driving back and forth to the city, and a decent number of tourists exploring the chain of quaint small towns on quiet weekend excursions.

Today, however, someone was in an all-out hurry to get into Green Hills. Barreling down the turnpike exit ramp, the driver sped through the red light just as Maree reached the center of the intersection — essentially, a sitting duck. She saw the vehicle and braced for impact just as the SUV T-boned her car.

The force of the collision pushed her car sideways. She couldn't guess how far — the screeching was a great disso- nance ringing in her ears, but she thought that something had stopped the car sliding across the blacktop. The vehicles were two chunks of metal that crunched, smashed, and pretzeled together on her driver's side. It all happened so very fast. One second was quiet and calm; the next utter chaos.

She'd been pushed toward the center of her front seat area, the door rammed against her left shoulder. But when she tried to move, her legs were stuck under the steering column. She was pinned in place. She was aware that blood was streaming down her face; the metallic scent of it hung in the air around her. Yet, oddly, she did not feel pain. Only the warm wetness of the blood.

With her right hand, she felt around the console underneath her right hip and located her cell phone. It was still exactly where she had set it in the cup holder, plugged in to charge, as if the massive collision had devoured the entirety of her world but not even moved the molecules around that one cup holder.

Word traveled faster than the speed of sound in Green Hills, so someone would know about the wreck already, but she dialed 911 anyway and did her best to report the crash as coherently as possible. She knew she was still lucid, but the edges of her peripheral vision were getting dimmer and fuzzier by the minute.

---

*R*hys and the guys were in the process of checking out and paying for their groceries when the call came over their radios.

"All units: 10-36 code three at the intersection of Interstate 75 and Main. Possible 10-24 and 10-36 code four," the dispatcher announced in a perfectly calm, clear, and precise voice. All that jargon indicated an injury traffic accident at I-75 and Main Street that included a possible car fire and tool-assisted vehicle extrication.

Rhys felt a cold, absolute certainty that he'd known only one other time in his life. The sensation lasted a fraction of a split second, but that was all it took to be transported back to the moment he saw the first responders whiz past football practice. *Coach, I think I gotta go.* It was ten — almost eleven — years ago now, but he could still feel every hair lifting on his neck, still feel his heart skipping erratically and his blood running cold. He'd simply known then, too.

That intersection was on Maree's route out to Sadie Jones' house. He tried to rationalize that too much time had passed since their conversation in front of the grocery store. He'd watched as she left the parking lot even before he'd grabbed a basket. He and the guys had divided and conquered to save time, but they'd still been in there for at least fifteen minutes. Probably more. Had to be closer to twenty-five. She was already at Marshall Mansion. She was most likely there already. Safe and sound.

But he knew. He just knew.

16

*Avoiding danger is no safer in the long run
than outright exposure.
The fearful are caught as often as the bold.*
Helen Keller

"Truck 33 en route," Rhys spoke into his radio. "Come on, that's Maree," he instructed, running for the truck waiting outside.

Davis and their crew were surprised into action, but they didn't question. They were the closest engine to respond anyway, so they left their groceries where they sat on the conveyor belt and bolted out the door.

The color was completely drained from Rhys's complexion. His eyes looked dead. He was too calm — beyond detached — which is what worried his guys the most.

"You don't know that." Davis tried to reason with him as they flipped on the lights and sirens and pulled away from the store. "Rhys, you can't know that."

*R*hys didn't bother with a reply.

He was out of the fire engine and running toward her car just minutes later. Davis had his back and would get the status information from the uniformed police officers on site. His only thought was to get to Maree.

Instinct and training were deeply ingrained. Numb to the fear that was clawing at his chest, Rhys followed protocol to keep her safe. His fellow firefighters liked to tease him about his name, saying that he was like a phoenix, always rising out of the ashes to save the day, but it wasn't far from the truth: he was methodical, systematic, and precise every time he went on a call. This time was no different.

Assessing the likelihood that her car could catch fire, he ran back to the fire engine, grabbed an extinguisher, and began spraying the motor, gas tank, and undercarriage of her car.

"Maree, I'm here. Open your eyes," he called to her through the heap of twisted metal as he sprayed.

No response.

"Davis, we need the jaws," he called out, with his usual calm-in-the-storm, take-charge behavior. Rhys was grateful for his friend and coworker in that moment. Davis would have seen the car, recognized it as Maree's, just as Rhys had when they drove up. Davis wouldn't challenge Rhys; he'd understand that Rhys was working off of ingrained skill. They all understood it was every first responder's worst nightmare: to drive up to a loved one on-scene.

Rhys squeezed between the light pole that the door was bent around and the metal framing that had once been the side window to crawl through the passenger side of Maree's car. He yanked off shattered bits of metal and debris, tossing the rubble aside, as he went.

"Maree, come on, baby, open your eyes," he commanded. Panic was not an option, but damn, he wanted her to respond.

He kept talking to her, determined to reach her through the fog of her shock. At the same time, he called out directives to Davis, who had taken lead on the extrication.

"Rhys?" she breathed, barely audible.

"Maree, I'm here; can you open your eyes?" he asked, speaking slow and loud and clear, exhaling a slight sigh of relief. He hated that his voice contained a trace of his inclination to beg her; he knew he had to keep his tone calm and be a source of reassurance for her.

Her eyelashes fluttered, as if her eyelids were too heavy to lift. He wiped blood away from her eyes with a swath of cloth that Davis had handed him. So much blood. A head wound could easily gush, but it was too much blood. Folding the rag over again and again, turning it in search of a clean, dry spot, he continued to apply pressure and wipe away more blood.

When, finally, she cracked her right eye open to him, he tried to not look too terribly fierce. "Hi," he greeted her, forcing an infinitesimal smile to hide how terrified he felt.

"Twice in one day," she faintly whispered, trying valiantly, but losing the battle to keep her eye open.

———

*S*he'd both dreamed and dreaded seeing him. But never like this.

Her mind was reeling. Rhys was speaking to her. He was calling her "baby" and soothing her. He was barking information to someone else. She was confused, but as usual, she clung to the sound and thought and image of him all the same.

Through the misty haze of half consciousness, Maree heard his voice continuously, calm and yet underlined with urgency and command, but she couldn't make out all the actual words he was speaking. While he spoke, deafening commotion commenced all around her. She assumed shock was setting in as her body was jostled and pulled onto a back-board and out of the car. She sensed the movements, but everything was foggy and distant.

And then came the pain.

Perhaps it was the straightening and unfolding of her limbs, now flat on the gurney. Maybe it was the fresh air that was seeping into every cut and slash on her flesh. Whatever the reason, her nerves were now in stark awareness, and the pain was unreal.

Tears were streaming down her cheeks, mixing with blood, and she was trying desperately to speak aloud before they shuffled her into the ambulance.

"Rhys," she called, but no one could hear her thready voice.

"Rhys," she forced louder.

Still, no one seemed to notice.

Panic settled in. She needed to see him, just once more. In case it was her last chance.

Her breathing had sped up. Her attempts to call out had become frantic.

"Larsen!" someone yelled. "We're ready for transport."

"Hold up, guys," Rhys called, jogging over to Maree.

"Hey." He smiled down at her. His presence was reassuring as they rolled her toward the ambulance. Maree saw panic and urgency underneath his veil of control; it was in his eyes and the strain of his face. She wanted to sooth him as he was doing for her. She wanted to assure him that everything was okay. She hated to see him looking so scared. But she simply couldn't keep her eyes open.

She was thankful that she could still hear him. And feel him.

"You're in great hands now, and you're going to be just fine, Maree. Max is meeting you at the hospital, and I'll get there just as soon as I can, okay? I'll be there, I promise," he vowed, brushing her blood-matted curls back from the gash on her forehead with a caress soft enough to break her heart. He was so solid and strong that his presence made her feel more stable.

If her eyes would have opened, he'd have surely seen in them the incredible love she felt for him. Even in this horrible state, she couldn't help but wonder why he couldn't see how much he cared for her in return. She didn't know what might be wrong with her physically, she didn't know how severe her injuries were, and she didn't know any prognosis on her well-being. In that moment, she was too frazzled to know much of anything. But she did know that they belonged together. She decided right then that if she survived this, she would no longer take "no" for an answer.

With his other hand, he found and held her hand. She was just lucid enough to realize that his heat against her frigid cold was an indication that shock was setting back in. He helped load her on the wagon, kissed her icy fingers, reached out to touch her cheek one more time, and jumped from the ambulance so they could transport her.

She wanted to say thank you. She wanted to hold on to his hand and never let go. But more than anything, she wanted to succumb to the sleep that was overwhelming her. She couldn't accomplish the first two, so she gave in to the third.

17

They invented hugs to let people know you love them
without saying anything.
Bil Keane

he next thing she knew, Maree was lifted from the gurney to a table with a huge X-ray machine looming over it. Her body was jostled. Again.

An IV was inserted into her right arm. She closed her eyes, trying to focus, to sense or mentally feel for injuries, but she couldn't be sure. She didn't trust her own mind, couldn't decipher which pain was coming from what area of her body.

Within seconds, the warming sensation of fluids flowed throughout her body and the pain receded.

The X-rays didn't take too long, but the technician left her on the table while the films were read, just in case they needed additional pictures, he'd explained. She faded in and out of consciousness, and while she was waiting, a sense of calm came over her. Maree was just lucid enough to attribute the improvement to the meds that were now pumping through her veins. Her jaw relaxed — how long had she had been clenching it tight. Her forehead was awfully heavy, and her neck seemed to give up supporting her head as it sank deeper into the pillow.

A memory popped into her thoughts, an out-of-body view of herself in a yoga class, lying back during those final ten or fifteen minutes of the practice, when the instructor leads everyone to *Savasana* for a final rest and talks the group through calming the fluctuations of their minds until they are balancing peacefully between sleep and awareness. *I really like that feeling; truly, it's my favorite part of going to a yoga class*, she thought to herself. Or maybe she said it out loud. Like before, she couldn't be sure.

She thought she might have giggled, finding it funny that such random images were popping into her mind. She was trying to focus on each memory — or were they dreams? Regardless, they were iridescent bubbles that floated away too fast. She wanted to chase them down the track that her train of runaway thoughts seemed to be riding.

The world felt confusing and sporadic. Maree knew the cocktail of drugs going through her IV was responsible for this serene sensation, and she was thankful for a respite from the pain and fear that had gripped her since the first jolt of impact in the wreck.

All too soon and without any explanation, the medical staff returned, moved her back onto the gurney, and rolled her to a private room, which seemed surprising until she overheard a nurse say that Sadie Marshall Jones had called to arrange the "best care available." That made Maree smile — a full smile that might have been visible on the outside but was definitely gleaming on the inside, because Miss Sadie only resorted to throwing around her maiden name when she wanted things done in a certain way and in a hurry.

She faded out again and awoke to notice the sun setting through her window in the most exotic colors of orange, peach, red, and burgundy. *Nothing like an Oklahoma sunset*, she mused, proud of herself for stringing together intelligent facts.

Just then, Max's voice rang out in the hallway, commanding both information and attention, accompanied by the thud of jogging steps. *I guess Max and Sadie are two peas in a pod*, she joked, finding herself quite clever. *These meds are really doing their job.* Max's voice sounded very far away, like in a canyon or cave, but there was no doubt that her brother had arrived.

She grinned a loopy, sloppy, drug-induced smile. She was loved, and that was a very good feeling no matter her current predicament and the challenges that were undoubtedly ahead.

———

"*A*h, there she is," Max gushed with relief when he walked into the room to find her somewhat alert and trying her best to smile at him.

"Here she is," Maree mumbled, slurring her words, yet working hard to keep up their special tradition, the same way they had greeted one another since she was a little girl forcing him to play dress-up and school and dolls.

Max had hoped to never see a loved one in another car accident as long as he lived; Maree had now experienced two in two years, three in the course of her young life. His stomach had plummeted when the call came in that she was being transported to the hospital. He'd jumped into his truck and driven as fast as he felt was safe to go. The entire way, he feared what he'd find when he arrived. He was overwhelmingly relieved to see her conscious and communicating, even if her end of the conversation was in and out and all over the place.

"What have the doctors told you?" he asked, gently stroking the least bloody side of her forehead.

"Nothing yet," she replied in a whisper, pausing between

the words. "I was hoping...you...could...fill me in," she confessed in fading words as her eyes closed and she succumbed to sleep again. With that, Max was back out the door commanding more attention to garner more information.

———

*S*he had no concept of elapsed time and might have slept for five minutes or five hours. Or perhaps five days. She could not have guessed. She vaguely remembered a gorgeous sunset, but now the light through the window was strong and bright.

Regardless of what time — or what day — it was, the room was empty when Maree fully awoke. She managed to gently wiggle herself halfway upright in the bed and began mentally checking and testing her body parts. She'd tried this once before, she remembered, but had not gotten very far. This time, she was somewhat coherent and had some luck. *Surely they would have restrained anything that shouldn't be moving,* she told herself to justify the mini-experiment to determine the extent of her injuries.

Right arm was fine, a little bruised and achy. Right leg was terribly sore and achy. Neck was incredibly stiff and hurting with deep consistency, but not with sharp or scary pangs. She quickly discovered that her left side was not good. In fact, she deemed it in very bad shape. She could not seem to lift her left arm more than a few inches from her side without triggering excruciating pain. With her right hand, she felt around on her face and found a lot of bruises, scrapes, and cuts, as well as a large piece of gauze that was covering what she guessed to be a very deep gash that was stitched but still oozing fresh blood along her left temple and hairline. The car windshield must have shattered against her head, which would also explain the intense, throbbing pain she felt. Talk about a headache!

As she was finishing her inventory, a take-charge and bois-terous nurse came into the room. "Tsk, tsk," she chided. "Now what are you all about, getting that blood flowing again?" The nurse immediately grabbed new gauze and began applying pressure while wiping Maree's cheek and neck.

"Sorry," Maree grimaced. Even the gauze seemed to inflict spasms of sensitivity, and someone touching it was turning her green around the gills. "I was just trying to see how much damage I've done."

"Well, I don't have those answers, but I do know we can wash this cut again, get it rebandaged, and get you into some-thing less blood-soaked," the nurse promised, preparing a basin of warm water and arranging a tray of larger sheets of gauze and first aid supplies like bandages and tape.

"I've also been told that you didn't cause this damage, but some fool driver from out of town running through a red light on the frontage road," she said in defense of Maree, while shaking her head in disgusted frustration. "You're lying here a torn-up heap of a mess, and that idiot walked away with barely a scrape. Now you lie back and let me worry over this; just close your eyes, dear."

Maree felt instant adoration for this sweet woman. She did exactly as she was told with what she hoped was a friendly smile. For someone so beat-up, she wondered at how smiley she felt.

Maybe it was the drugs? Maybe it was Max running around like a bull in a china shop, or her nurse and new best friend worrying over her like a momma bear? Maybe it was the care and concern she had clearly heard in Rhys's voice?

Maybe it was all of the above.

The next time Maree opened her eyes, it was to find another huge bandage above her left eyebrow and a hospital gown. Max was leaning his hips against the countertop by the sink and typing something in his phone, but he looked up immediately when she rustled in bed. A wave of distress washed over his features, and she was determined to put him at ease.

"Take it slow," he reminded her as she inched her way higher up on her pillows.

"Well?" She had to clear her throat to speak. "What's the verdict?" Maree asked, resigned to whatever report he gave and fully aware that it could have been much worse.

Max set his phone to the side, folded his arms across his chest, and went on to explain Maree's injuries. She had a broken collarbone on the left side. It had already been set and required the sling that was around her left arm and neck. Her left knee would require surgery to repair a shattered kneecap and torn ligaments, so they had her leg in an immobilizer. The surgery would not take place until she met with an orthopedic specialist, once the swelling subsided. Broken glass and metal shards had become embedded in her face, neck, and arms that were exposed during the crash. She had a concussion, but the trauma team was pleased that she'd had strong vitals throughout the past thirty hours that she'd been under observation in the hospital.

The doctors had advised her to stay another night so they could keep an eye on her, but since they couldn't find any medical data to demand that she do so, they agreed to provide very specific care instructions and release her whenever she felt up to the ride home. She would be horrendously bruised and sore, but with medication to manage the pain and nausea, the doctors said she was free to feel bruised and sore and from the comforts of home, rather than amid the bright lights and disruptive beeps of the hospital.

She was elated by that news. No matter how bad things were, she was a firm believer that they would seem a little less *bad* at home.

"Can I get some real clothes to wear out of here?" she

asked Max, feeling ridiculously weak, but determined to appear strong enough to leave.

"In the chair over there. Sadie went by your apartment and brought everything she said you would need for a few days," he explained as he stood from his perch.

"How long have I been sleeping?" she asked. How had she missed the treatment of her collarbone and the stitching of her cuts, as well as Sadie's entire visit.

"A good while, but setting an arm in place for a broken collarbone to heal correctly is rough. Being out cold made that and sewing you back together tolerable," Max replied.

"But how long ago was the accident?" she asked again.

"Yesterday, midmorning. It's almost four o'clock Tuesday," Max informed her.

"A day and a half. I had no idea." Bewilderment took over as she looked down at the sling.

"Good. I wouldn't want anyone to have a memory of what you've been through. Keep resting, and I'll go get a nurse to help you," he offered.

"Make sure it's the cheerful one who helped me clean up," she requested as he turned to leave her to change.

"That would be Ruthie, your number-one fan. She's been like a mother hen pecking around you every half hour. I'll go find her and be right back," he said with a wink. Max grabbed the bag of clothes and belongings from the chair in the corner of the room and placed it on the bed next to Maree's right leg, opposite the worst of her injuries. Then he put the curtain in place and left the room.

When Ruthie arrived, Maree was using her good arm to sort through the items Sadie had packed. It was amazing that Sadie knew exactly what she would have grabbed for herself if that had been an option. *Of course, if that was an option, I wouldn't be in this predicament!*

"Are you sure you want to go home so soon, honey?" Ruthie inquired as she entered the room.

"Absolutely positive," Maree answered as she decided on a pair of soft fleece shorts with an oversized one-thousand-times-washed Walk to End Alzheimer's t-shirt. "Will you give me a hand?"

What should have taken one person two minutes took two people ten, but they got her dressed as much as possible by leaving her left arm in the sling but loose under the big t-shirt. Then Ruthie went to locate Max and give him the all-clear.

———

*M*ax had sent Rhys several updates via text messages, but Rhys had been impatient and worried all the same. It had been a very long day — two, actually — helping with the reports, cleanup, and debriefing of Maree's collision. Then they'd had call after call throughout his shift, ending with another fire set by their local arson bug, who was getting more aggressive and daring with when and where he or she was setting his fires. The fact that they had absolutely zero leads on this guy was beyond frustrating. Hunting for something — anything — all throughout the night, this morning, and into the afternoon meant that Rhys hadn't been home yet. Nor had he slept in well over thirty-six hours.

Rhys stormed through the glass doors and immediately saw Max standing against a wall to the side of the waiting room, talking on his cell phone. Rhys walked toward him, prepared to talk over whatever conversation Max was having regardless of how rude it was to interrupt, but Max motioned and mouthed the room number, "114," with a toss of his head toward the hallway behind him. Without breaking stride, Rhys was off to find Maree.

He walked into the room to find her sitting on the very

edge of a chair, trying to accommodate the massive brace on her left leg while struggling to put a sock and tennis shoe on her right foot, all with only one hand. The exertion had her face flushed. She was trying so hard to do a simple task she'd done a million times. He could see both determination and frustration in her swollen, bruised face.

"I shooed Ruthie away, adamant that I could put on one sock and one shoe by myself. But it's turning out to be more challenging than I expected," she confessed. Then she looked up, probably assuming that Max was back. A warm blush spread through her cheeks, and a smile blossomed on her face.

He dropped to his knees in front of her, moving her hands away and taking over the task with overly delicate movements, as if he was doing open-heart surgery. As if he was sliding a glass slipper on the foot of a princess.

"I won't break," she told him softly, leaning toward him and tilting her head to the side. He sensed Maree willing him to look up at her.

But he didn't. His only response was a gruff grunt.

He still couldn't look at her, but he did set her foot on the ground a little further to the outside so that he could kneel closer to her chair. He continued staring at the floor, trying to pick a path. Resigned that he had no choice but to move forward, he finally made a move, putting his hands on the chair just outside her hips.

Rhys closed his eyes, as if he was in physical pain. He *was* in physical pain. For Maree. For all she'd been through.

She reached her right hand out to stroke his hair, and that was his undoing. His arms slid behind her, hugging her so lightly that Maree urged him closer, shifting so that the crown of his head was resting against her right shoulder, and her cheek was resting on the top of his head. She'd positioned him as close as they could get while avoiding her sling and injuries.

Tremors were escaping Rhys's body. When he moved to

back away, she only held on a little tighter. Since they'd met, he'd been as drawn to her as she was to him. Only she had been brave enough to embrace that fact. Their chemistry was magnetic; he couldn't deny that he cared for her. Even so, he was surprised by the amount of pent-up fear and uncertainty working their way out of his system. His angel, she gave him all the time he needed.

———

*M*ax entered the room unheard and unseen. He took stock of the situation and decided that he'd been right all along. They were a perfect, complementary set: Rhys looked just as bad as Maree did, maybe even worse. Max set the flowers he'd just bought in the gift shop on the counter by the sink and silently backed out.

———

*I*t was a long time before Rhys felt composed enough to talk.

"I've never known fear like that," he said. It was the truth. It was an acknowledgment that she couldn't begin to understand, but the magnitude of it was not lost on Rhys. As horrendous and helpless as he'd felt when that fire destroyed his life ten years ago, seeing Maree in her mangled car had been even worse. He didn't know how that could be. He didn't understand how anything could be worse than what he'd felt back then. Nor every day since. But arriving on the scene of Maree's accident had been a deeper level of hell than he had known existed. He felt like he was being shredded from the inside out.

Maree lifted his chin to see his face. He could read her emotions; it was plain to see the unapologetic, unabashed love that she had for him. It was written all over her scraped, bruised, exhausted face.

She also looked sympathetic, like she hated seeing him in agony, like she would have done anything to spare him this moment. Yet here they were. The pain he'd vehemently run from had found him anyway.

"I'm so sorry, Rhys."

18

In any given moment, we have two options:
to step forward into growth or
to step back into safety.
Abraham Maslow

"All right, sweetie, you're free to go," Ruthie announced as she bounded into the room. Maree giggled that the nurse was not fazed in the least by the appearance of a fireman, on the floor, wrapping his arms around her patient.

"Take me home?" she asked Rhys, holding her breath, hoping he would say yes.

"I think Max is here," he replied.

Did that mean he didn't want to give her a ride? Take her home? Be with her at all? Or was he simply stating that they needed to find Max before he took her out of there?

Her mind was mush. Her brain was overtaxed. Her emotions were frazzled. She was overthinking this, and she knew it.

"Since your brother is the guarantor on your insurance, he signed all the paperwork so you didn't have to hassle with it,"

Ruthie filled in. "He also left this for you, and he said to enjoy the flowers." Ruthie set an envelope under the bouquet that Maree had just noticed for the first time.

Well, that was decided. Whether Rhys liked it or not, Maree figured.

Ruthie settled Maree in a wheelchair and rolled her to the entrance where Rhys had pulled his truck up to the curb. He put her bags in the back and pushed the button to move her seat as far back as possible to make room for the leg brace, which wouldn't bend. He grabbed a blanket from the back seat and set it on the middle console to cushion her left arm and sling.

"Let's see if you can maneuver yourself on that right foot," Ruthie offered, but Rhys swooped in, lifting her out of the wheelchair and setting her on the truck seat without hesitation.

"I guess that works, too," Ruthie muttered.

"It's like you rescue people for a living," Maree half teased through clenched teeth. She was bracing herself against the pain and making a valiant effort to show a brave face. She hoped that Rhys appreciated the teasing for what it was — an attempt to lighten the mood — but at that moment he seemed to be hyper-focused. She could tell that nothing would distract him from getting her in the truck with as little discomfort as possible.

———

"*B*ye, sweet Ruthie; I appreciate you so much," Maree said, gripping the hand of her new friend. She amazed Rhys. He marveled at how she could bond with a person so genuinely, so honestly, a person whom she had known for a mere matter of hours. It was incredible.

"Call with anything you need, you hear? Either of you!" Ruthie made them promise, reluctant to let them leave.

"You okay?" he asked before he put the truck in gear. Getting right back into a vehicle after a wreck was often hard for people. Given the seriousness of her accident, he imagined that being on the road might make her anxious.

"Almost," she replied. He jerked his head up to look her up and down, worrying about her injuries.

"Seat belt," she pointed out, making an effort to twist her torso to grab the clasp. He reached across her body to get the fastener. When he was close, she settled back against the seat and reached her right hand out to cup his cheek and jaw, pulling his face to hers. He closed his eyes, frozen in place, but she would not be deterred.

––––––

*W*hen Rhys had left Maree in Ruthie's care to go get the truck, Maree had admired the beautiful flowers that Max had sent to her room. The bouquet was a gorgeous mix of poppies, roses, and carnations in vibrant pinks, deep oranges, and golden yellows. The bright colors were a wonderful energizer, and they smelled lovely and sweet.

Then Maree had opened the envelope. Max's card consisted of two sentences: *He loves you. So do I.*

Maree was taking her big brother's message to heart. As Ruthie had wheeled her out of the hospital, Maree had made up her mind: she would not make it easy for Rhys to push her away this time around.

"Thank you for toda— Yesterday, I mean. All of it," she whispered. Taking advantage of his close proximity and her hand on his cheek, she stroked her thumb across his bottom lip. She had often declared — in the privacy of her own mind — that no man should be gifted such kissable lips. Then she replaced her thumb with her own lips. Perhaps the pain meds were increasing her boldness. Maybe she had missed him too much these past weeks. Whatever the influence, it did not matter. Giving it her all, she caressed him with a kiss meant to melt.

Maree worried that she tasted and smelled like blood and trauma, but she kept nibbling and teasing his lips.

---

*U*ntil he couldn't take it anymore. He finally responded by participating in the kiss. He dropped the seat belt, ran his hand up her non-injured arm and framed her face to hold it very tenderly but just where he wanted it as he took over control of their kiss. He deepened the kiss, fighting a desperation he had never felt before. Coming up for air, he kissed the corner of her mouth, the ridge of her jaw, and the softest skin just under her ear. And then he came back to her mouth, very aware and protective of her bruises and swelling, yet plundering and ravishing as he went, a man starved for the sweetness of life.

She must've been pretty starved for him as well because she met the kiss head-on, taking and giving in equal measure. Whereas he was terrified to cause her any further pain, she seemed happy to stay there for an eternity.

But Ruthie wasn't going for it.

It took a few knocks on the window, but the nurse finally got their attention, "Y'all take that on home, and don't forget to get some rest, child!"

Maree laughed a little at being reprimanded for too much PDA, her chagrined giggle startling Rhys from his deep mood. Looking fully into her eyes for the first time all day — for the first time in weeks, if he was being honest — he felt all the air escape his lungs on a sigh. A sign of resignation? Of acceptance? Of declaration?

Ah, shit. This must be what a tug-of-war battle feels like eighty feet high on a tightrope with no net to catch you when you fall. His chest burned with that same shredding ache he'd felt earlier.

"Seat belt," she whispered again, a challenging reminder that made him chuckle, really more of an acquiescing guffaw. He reached again for the fastener, clicked it into place, and put the truck in gear to leave the hospital.

"My stairs won't be all that convenient, so I should probably crash at Max's house for a while," she explained as she relaxed against the headrest. "I'm sure that's why Sadie packed so many clothes for me. He won't care, and I have the keys and alarm codes if he's not there when we arrive."

Rhys glanced over to find her eyes shut. What a couple of days; she had to be way beyond weary and spent. God, what he'd have given to spare her this pain. As well as the pain to come. Those bumps and bruises were going to get worse before they got better. Her leg and shoulder were going to begin to throb and ache. He imagined that within forty-eight hours, it'd be near impossible for her to find a comfortable way to sit, stand, or lay down. And that's before the knee surgery. It wouldn't be a simple arthroscopic procedure. No, Maree was in for reconstruction if not a knee replacement, either of which would be accompanied by a brutal recovery and months of physical therapy. She'd been through a lot, and she had a long way to go before she'd reach the other side of this ordeal.

Without asking permission, he drove to his own house. He parked in the driveway and came around to open her door. She had fallen asleep, so he was careful when he unfastened her seatbelt and eased his arm under her legs, being especially aware of supporting the leg brace. In slow motion, he slid her across the seat. When he lifted her into his arms, she raised her right arm up around his neck to help hold on. He carried her up the walk and used the hand behind her back to unlock the door, resting her weight against his chest. Once he had it opened, he reached inside to flip a light switch.

"You don't have to do this," she whispered. "You can take me to Max's."

"I want you here," was all he replied. She didn't argue.

He set her on the couch, placing her leg brace along the back of it and situating pillows between her hip and arm to keep her sling in the best position. Rhys brought her a glass of water, and he set extra pillows on the floor within her reach.

"What else can I do to make you more comfortable," he asked.

"Not a thing — I'm good, really, Rhys. Thank you."

He sat on the edge of the coffee table, studying her expression to decide if he believed her. Then he grabbed the TV remote, handed it to her, and announced, "I would love a very quick shower, and then I'll fix us something to eat, okay?"

"Of course," she said. "Take your time. I may just rest my eyes for a sec while you're in there." Her voice was fading even as she said the words, and he knew she was asleep before she finished her sentence.

He took the opportunity to soak in the sight of her. He indulged himself for just a minute. To study and stare and say *thank you* that she was alive and strong, and right here. The significance wasn't lost on him. It had been a very, *very* long time since he'd felt thankful to a God that had abandoned him and his family years ago. Sure, he'd been to church over the years, celebrated religious holidays. But since that day, Rhys's faith had been severely lacking in presence and strength. But today felt a little different.

Before heading for the shower, he sent a quick text to Max, letting him know they were out of the hospital and settling in at Rhys's house. Then he went out to the truck to get her bags. When he returned, she was clutching the afghan they had used in the recliner the night of the warehouse fire.

Man, that feels like a lifetime ago.

He set her bags inside the door and adjusted the blanket on

her. He could not resist feeling her skin with a touch of her cheek and a light kiss on the top of her head.

"Thank you," she murmured as he walked away.

———

*W*hen she couldn't quite get comfortable a few minutes later, she managed to get up onto her one functioning foot. Taking the afghan with her and using the one crutch she'd been sent home with, as well as the wall down the hallway for support, she limped her way to his master suite. Luckily, the doctor had allowed her to bear weight on the injured, braced leg, but it was still an arduous endeavor. She was sweating with exertion by the time she got there.

There was a dim lamp shining on a bedside table alongside a phone plug, so she guessed that was his side of the huge bed. Clutching anything she could reach to stay upright, she hobbled her way around to the other side. She maneuvered to take off her one shoe by using the metal bed frame to ease her heel out of it. Maree let her shorts fall to the floor so they wouldn't ride up when she slid onto the bed. She tried to ease out of the t-shirt, from which she could still detect the smell of the hospital, but she couldn't manage it.

Finally, finagling the sling out from under the soft shirt and feeling less encumbered, she lay down on top of the quilt, propping her left arm on pillows and pulling up the afghan as best she could. Even with the dulling effects of the pain meds, everything hurt.

Maree took a shaky yet deep breath, trying to ease the tension that held a vise grip on her entire body. She focused on her breathing, on the splash of the shower water running in the bathroom. It was soft and soothing. She was out within seconds.

———

*R*hys stopped short when he came out of his bathroom to find his angel sound asleep on his bed. Making her way to the back of the house must have been excruciating, but she finally looked restful and at peace. He figured he had two options: move her to the guest bedroom or move himself to the guest bedroom. He was happy to do whatever would make her most comfortable.

At the moment, though, he was starving and needed food, so he made the executive decision that figuring out where to sleep would have to wait.

Rummaging through the fridge revealed some leftover spaghetti, which he heated in the microwave. He doused the pasta with parmesan cheese and paired it with a huge glass of very cold milk. He turned the TV on to watch whatever sports were on while he ate, but he couldn't keep his mind from wandering.

She'd been so polite at the grocery store. Had that really been yesterday morning? It seemed like he'd lived a year — or three — since then. He remembered thinking that she was being too nice to him. Like he was any other casual acquaintance from town. Like she had placed a veil between them. And he'd hated it.

Then, when the call came in for a 10-36 with a code three, he had sensed that she was in trouble. He'd known that feeling before, felt that exact chill when the sirens blared past the practice field all those years ago. He'd never imagined he could withstand that feeling a second time.

That was why he had pushed her away, to avoid that depth of fear. But he'd felt it anyway. So, if he was going to feel that way about her even when they weren't together, why was he torturing both of them by keeping them apart?

Because he couldn't handle loving and losing her.

Damn, his thoughts were running in circles, quickly driving him mad.

He pushed the plate away. Nausea overtook him, and he worried that the spaghetti was about to come right back up. His appetite was gone.

Before his fears could escalate, there was a knock at his front door. Thankful for the interruption from his own thoughts, he looked out the window to see who was on the porch.

"Hey, Davis," he answered, opening the door for his friend. "Come on in; I was just finishing up a plate of spaghetti, if you want some."

"I'm good, but thanks. How is she?" he asked, sitting down at the kitchen table, across from Rhys's plate of food.

"Broken clavicle, several issues going on in her left leg that require a tough surgery or two and an even worse recovery afterward, nineteen stitches scattered across several deep gashes in her head that I don't think she's aware of quite yet. Bumps and bruises — *lots* of bumps and bruises," he listed while clearing his now forgotten spaghetti and setting the dishes in the sink. "Lucky," he added at the end and then joined Davis at the table.

"That's a rough road over the next few months, but you're right, Rhys: she's either insanely lucky or she's got a guardian angel watching over her."

"Maybe two of them," Rhys thought out loud.

"How's that?" Davis asked, not understanding the comment.

"Nah, nothing, man. My mind is scattered."

"I can imagine. We were all worried about her, but I know you care about her. More, I mean." Davis seemed to be trying *not* to say whatever it was he needed to say.

Rhys waited for a pause in Davis's hemming and hawing, then raised his eyebrows in a silent question.

Davis still fumbled a bit before finding his voice…

———

"*I* went to the salvage yard to check the car one more time for any personal belongings." He paused a long time. He struggled to string the words together in the most accurate way, focused on sounding professional, detached, and impersonal. He tried to simply state the facts.

"Rhys, she shouldn't have survived," he confessed when he could find no other way to say it.

"Yeah, I know she's lucky to have basically minor injuries in the grand scheme of things," Rhys agreed. Davis bristled at his casualness.

"No, you aren't listening. There is zero space left in the driver's position. ZERO. Very little visible light in the passenger side, and the door that impacted against her is shaved into slices of metal that are sharper than shrapnel. I can't explain it; I can't even fathom it."

———

*D*avis was visibly shaken by what he had seen. Rhys thought about that, bewildered. And queasy. Again.

"Thanks for telling me. I'll go check it out tomorrow, but I don't think she needs to see it. She doesn't need to know that part right now."

Davis nodded his agreement. "Did her brother come to get her?"

"He was at the hospital, stayed until I got there. He was able to talk with the doctors and take care of all the paper-work, so she wasn't burdened with it. Then he slipped out without a word," Rhys hedged.

"So, is she home alone? She's in pretty bad shape and definitely going to need some help. Probably for a while. I'm sure—"

"She's here," Rhys interrupted before Davis could make his conscience feel any more stressed.

"She's here," Davis repeated rather than questioned. "As in, here in your house?"

"Yes, she's here. Asleep in my room. As we speak." Irritation edged his tone, but Rhys wasn't the least bit sure at whom it was aimed. Was he mad at Davis for asking the obvious, at Maree for making him care about her, or at himself for allowing all of this to happen in the first place? Or was he simply fed up with a world that punished everything — everyone — he dared to care about?

————

*D*avis could hear the anger in Rhys's voice — it only added fuel to the fire of his own concern for Maree.

"What are you doing, Rhys?" Davis demanded. He lowered his voice, which should have taken some of the bite out of the accusation but somehow made it worse. "Look, man, she's in love with you; surely you can see that?" His tone was incredulous, and by the expression on Rhys's face, Davis guessed that his words were like salt in an open wound to Rhys. "She has been through hell and back. She doesn't deserve to be toyed with." Davis was now good and ticked off on Maree's behalf.

"I wouldn't do that," Rhys tried defending himself, but his protest sounded weak.

"Then what *have* you been doing?" Davis demanded again. "You've done nothing but reject her for weeks. And now, when she's about to fight one hell of an uphill battle, you decide it's a good idea to bring her home with you? Damn, Rhys!"

———

*N*o matter how angry Davis got, Rhys was too physically, mentally, and emotionally spent to take the bait. He didn't have the energy to fight back.

With his elbows on the table, Rhys lowered his head into his hands, rubbing his face, pressing on his temples, which felt as though they were about to explode out the sides of his head. "I was just sitting here trying to figure that out when you showed up."

"Well, Florence Nightingale, please, explain away."

The questioning expression on Davis's face didn't budge. Instead, he slid his chair back and crossed one ankle over the other, sitting back and settling in. Rhys could tell that Davis was more than eager to give his undivided attention. At the same time, Davis's body language continued to convey that he would not be satisfied with whatever lame justification Rhys was going to spew in defense of the asinine decision-making skills he seemed to be displaying. No, Davis clearly didn't have any intention of letting Rhys off the hook.

But Davis was patient. He held his words until Rhys gathered the courage to unload his thoughts. Rhys appreciated that Davis was willing to wait all night if that was what it took. And it might.

Davis really was a good friend. And Rhys knew that extended to Maree, knew that Davis wouldn't hesitate to take her to her brother's house or to Sadie's if Rhys's explanation didn't satisfy Davis's moral code.

Rhys had never mentioned even one word about his family to anyone in Green Hills, so Davis could never have guessed what that explanation would be until Rhys finally began to share.

19

> *These mountains you are carrying,*
> *you were only meant to climb.*
> *Najwa Zebian*

*A*fter several minutes of them sitting in silence, Rhys lifted his head out of his hands and took a deep, steadying breath.

"I think about her all day, and I dream about her all night." Rhys started, and then stopped, stunned. Putting two and two together, he realized in that moment that his nightmares of the twins had ended when Maree came into his life. The night terrors had vanished. He had not noticed their absence because Maree had taken up residence in his mind.

"When I'm not around her, I crave her. Literally *crave* her. It's crazy, I know, but my hands twitch to touch her, to hold her hand, or sit close to her. When I am around her, I'm constantly dogpaddling to keep from drowning in her. She knocks me off-kilter, like I'm fumbling around, unsure of what to say. Like I'm back in seventh grade or something."

"You're in love with her," Davis provided with clarity.

"I can't be."

Rhys could tell by the look on his friend's face that his statement didn't make a lick of sense in any possible way, so he was grateful that Davis chose to wait him out. Again.

It took a little longer this time, but after ten years of carrying around guilt and loss and sorrow and raw, gut-wrenching pain, Rhys opened up to someone.

Finally, he shared his burden.

He told Davis everything. He shared about his family. He told him about his idyllic childhood. About becoming a big brother — times two — just before going to junior high. About small-town life in Texas, about playing sports, and about loving his life and his family.

He told Davis about how the fire investigators determined that the twins must have unknowingly knocked over a candle when they were running through the house. He described how they had been trapped once the fire took hold, and that the boys died in those flames.

He detailed how his mom, who was once strong and smart and savvy, died of a broken heart three years later. He confessed that when his dad died of a rare strain of pneumonia a couple of months after his mom, he was flat-out jealous that they were free from the pain he could never escape.

———

$\mathcal{D}$avis was dumbfounded that though he'd spent so much time getting to know Rhys since they'd met, he'd had no idea what his friend was carrying around. He knew his response here was critical.

"I can't fathom the loss you've been through," Davis told him, choosing his words with care, making sure they sank in through the sadness permeating the physical space in which

Rhys sat. "I am so sorry that you had to deal with so much, and yet, those experiences brought you to this place. Maybe it's selfish, but I am glad you're here. At our firehouse. On my crew. Now. In Green Hills. There is no one else I trust more when we are fighting fires."

"I app——" Rhys began, but Davis cut him off.

"I'm not quite done, Rhys. And I sure as hell don't want your appreciation. I'll give you my two cents' worth, and then I'll get out of here," he pledged, and barreled ahead.

"The reason guys float from date to date and girl to girl is because we are holding out for what you've been gifted. We are waiting for the One: one amazing, one smart, one funny, one gorgeous, one caring woman, who loves us more than we could ever earn or deserve or justify. We are desperately seeking *that* one person. We are looking for her every place we go and in every girl we meet. She's *here*. In *your* house. Asleep in your bed. Can you comprehend that, Rhys? It's not like you're going to take advantage of her or ravish her in her sleep; I know that. She's just been through hell, and she's going to go through it on a daily basis over the next few weeks. Maybe even months. But right now, she needs you. She wants to be close to *YOU*. Do you see that? Do you understand that you're a total and complete idiot if you don't kick me out of here, lock the door behind me, turn out the lights, and go rest your head next to the treasure you've found? You've had a terrible journey to this point. But here is where you are. For God's sake, Rhys, go grab hold of the life you've been blessed to live and do it in honor of the ones you lost."

With that, he got up from the table, squeezed Rhys's shoulder, and left, tossing a final "good luck" at Rhys on his way out the front door.

———

That was a third option that Rhys had not considered: just climb in next to her.

Could he lie that close to her and not gather her into his arms? Did she want exactly that? Was that why she went to his bed instead of the guest room in the first place? Did she crave his nearness as he did hers? Was she looking for his strength and comfort, as he gravitated toward hers? If he allowed himself that glimpse of heaven — allowed himself that luxury even once — would he ever be able to sleep again without having her close?

And at the end of the day, could he accept the risk of something happening to her just so that he could love her? For that matter, could he stop loving her if that last answer was a resounding *no*?

He was falling down rabbit holes again, so without over-thinking it — at least any more than he already had — he pushed back his chair, stood up, and shook his head to dispel the thoughts filling his mind like dark smoke choking out daylight.

Then he did exactly as Davis had recommended.

He checked the locks and turned off the lights, except for the entryway lamp, just in case she tried to find her way in the dark during the night. He took her bags with him into his room, setting up her suitcase on a chair and putting her toiletries in his bathroom. He moved her one shoe away from the side of the bed so she wouldn't trip on it.

He was indulging in the sight of her sleeping when she stirred. It took her a moment to focus and locate where he was standing. When her gaze found his and she tried to smile up at him, her eyes were, once again, an open book.

He read a myriad of emotions. Fatigue and weariness, grat-itude and indebtedness, fear and uncertainty, pain and discom-fort, affection and adoration. And deep, abiding love.

He couldn't look away.

His heart beat out of rhythm, his stomach fluttered, and again his brain turned to mush.

"How do you feel?" he managed to ask, helping her when she tried pushing herself up to sit on the edge of the bed.

"Starting to throb all over. I think I'll take another pain pill and borrow the bathroom for a sec."

She shifted to get up. He couldn't stand to see her struggle, so he scooped her into his arms and deposited her in the bathroom. "I'll set this here in case you need it," he said, placing her crutch against the vanity and closing the door behind him as he walked back into the bedroom. While she was in there, he went down the hall to the kitchen to get a glass of ice water, a cup of applesauce, and a few crackers for Maree to take with the pain pills so they wouldn't make her queasy.

When he returned to the master suite, she was just coming out of the bathroom, balanced on the metal crutch and eyeing the expanse of flooring she needed to cross. Standing still and shoring up a deep breath, she was framed in the doorway. Maree had just flipped off the light switch, so the nightlight in the bathroom created a glowing halo around her slender form. Her curls were wildly mussed and falling all around her shoulders and back. The threadbare tee did little to hide what was underneath. He was momentarily dumbstruck.

"Rhys?" she said softly, breaking his trance. "Could you get the medicine bottles that are in my purse? I think I left it in your truck."

"I've got them here." Why was his voice so gravelly? And what kind of horrible person was overcome with desire when the object of that desire had been through a horrendous ordeal and was in considerable physical pain? The very worst kind, he assured himself with disgust.

"I brought you some crackers and a glass of water. I even found some applesauce in the fridge." *As if she couldn't see that for herself*, he thought caustically. Seventh grade! Talking to her sent him straight back to the awkwardness of junior high.

"That's perfect — thank you." She gave a feeble attempt at a smile as he stood close and reached around her to set everything on the bathroom countertop. When she hobbled a bit to turn back to get the pills and crackers, he placed a hand on her side to help her balance. The heat of her skin radiated through the make-do sleepshirt. She was the perfect combination of soft and supple. Her cheek was close to his chest, and her head was the perfect height for touching his lips to the top of her head for a soothing kiss.

He was in so much trouble. He wanted to be noble and honorable and valiant and chivalrous. But he wanted to feel her warmth and hold her close even more.

"I think I'm good now; surely that'll kick in pretty quick," she said, swallowing the pills. "I'd like to take the snacks over to the bedside table, if that's okay." She turned to make her way to the bed, bringing them face to face.

He meant to step aside, to help her across the room. He would have sworn his intentions were good. But he couldn't seem to move out of her way.

She'd had that effect on him since the first day he'd seen her in the grocery store. She was a magnetic force where Rhys was concerned. Just as he'd told Davis, he was drawn to Maree like a moth to a flame.

His right hand lifted to mirror the left one, still resting on her waist. He set his lips on the top of her head. Maree laid her right hand over his heart, so he knew that his touch was welcome. Her eyes met his as she gazed up at him.

That was all the encouragement he needed.

Using just a finger to lift her chin, he looked down at her, slowly lowering to meet her. So slowly that it seemed to take an eternity to seal their kiss.

The sensation was well worth the anticipation.

He started with the lightest touch, barely brushing his warm lips to hers. When she tried to move closer, he shifted toward her right side, being so very careful to avoid her left arm, which was bent by her ribs but not in its sling. He leaned against the doorjamb, nestling her right hip between his legs, the firmness of his thighs and the texture of his jeans in stark contrast to the smoothness of her leg. He sensed when a shiver traced down her body.

Maree leaned into his chest and reached her right hand down to hold her injured left arm. He traced her jaw back and forth, hesitant to lose the connection with the velvet feel of her skin. Then Rhys lowered his right hand to replace hers, taking the weight of her left arm into his hand while his left hand slid up her ribs and along her back until it was buried in her long, heavy hair and supporting her head. He'd found a way for them to fit just right, where he was taking on her weight while protecting all her areas of aches and pains. Rhys wished they could have stayed just that way forever, sharing one another's strength, and confirming there was still beauty in life, perfection in this world.

But alas, he ended the kiss.

"Let's get you tucked back in," he suggested, a little breathless. He lifted her into his arms again, something that seemed to be occurring quite often, and a habit he could get used to without any trouble.

He set her on the edge of the bed first, tossing the afghan out of the way and pulling back the quilt and covers. As if she weighed no more than a bag of fruit, he picked her up and resettled her, yanking the layers free from where the sheet and blankets were firmly tucked under the mattress. He wanted to create plenty of room for her leg brace, so the covers would not add any weight or pressure that might intensify the pain.

"Are you sure you want to sleep with your left leg on the outside?" he asked, worried. He was concerned about everything across the board, but specifically worried whether the heavy leg immobilizer would move too close to the edge as she slept.

"I'm happy to switch sides," he offered. "If you want."

———

*H*is words were music to her ears. Hearing that he was, indeed, going to stay with her felt like a balloon of joy bursting in her heart, and a huge brilliant smile erupted on her face. She had been afraid to hope and way too scared to ask. She wanted to let him know how happy he'd just made her.

But all she could do was nod. An enthusiastic nod, to be sure! But she couldn't make her vocal cords work when she felt giddy with emotion, so a nod was all he got.

"Yes, you're sure, or yes, you'd like to switch?" he asked, lifting an eyebrow. He teased her gently, the corners of his mouth lifting.

"Yes, this is perfect," she confirmed in a breathy voice, sliding down to put her head on the pillow. "Thank you," she exhaled, settling into place.

"Stop saying that," he countered in a kind and gentle tone.

"Yes, sir," she agreed playfully as she closed her eyes.

———

*H*e was finding her smile contagious and starting to feel a little delirious himself. How incredible that she was jubilant, that she was smiling, that somehow she felt peaceful and content after such a harrowing day.

20

Healing is the application of love.
Iyanla Vanzant

*R*hys took his slow, sweet time getting ready for bed, thinking that stalling would make it easier. In all truth, he couldn't explain what "it" was that felt so difficult. He just knew without a doubt that he didn't want to make any mistakes. He also knew with acute accuracy that he'd caused them both a ton of hurt these past couple of months; he absolutely could not stand the thought of adding to her trials right now.

When he'd stretched out his normal routine as long as he could, he walked to the bed, trying to be as silent as possible. He was nervous and jittery, and he assumed that having Maree so close would prevent him from getting even a wink of sleep. But once he finally gathered the gumption to crawl in, he had a sense of relaxation that he hadn't felt for years; a decade, actually.

He pulled the covers up over her once more. As she reached for his hand under the covers, all the weight of the day seemed to evaporate. His limbs felt like dead weight. He was asleep in mere seconds. He slept soundly for the first night since they'd shared his recliner that perfect early morning several weeks before.

When he awoke the next morning, he was sleeping on his stomach, facing Maree, hands still entwined but now holding hers with his right hand. He'd obviously shifted in the night, but he couldn't remember a thing. He had been enjoying the "sleep of the dead," and coming out of it took a second to adjust back to the real world.

Finally, he rolled onto his side to face her, blinking a few times to open his eyes the rest of the way. She was already sitting up in the bed, and she managed to smile down at him. But her smile was strained, and her face was too pale. She was clearly in pain.

"You should have woken me up to get your medicine; what time is it?" The fog of deep sleep instantly evaporated, and he moved much faster. He dashed off to the kitchen. In the blink of an eye, he returned with a fresh glass of water, two buttered pieces of toast with her homemade strawberry jam, and the maximum dose of pain pills and anti-nausea tablets.

"Thank you," she said in a hoarse, flat voice as she swallowed the pills. The roughness of her usually silky tone caused Rhys to frown even more.

He recognized that she was trying to be a good patient after he'd fixed the food for her. She worked on the toast, but the best she had managed was two or three birdlike bites.

"Rest for a second and see if you can eat any more," Rhys encouraged. "I'm going to brew a pot of coffee, and I'll be back in less than five minutes. Don't go anywhere."

When he returned, one mug of coffee and one mug of hot tea in hand, he again found her asleep in his bed. The sight stopped him in his tracks. Just like the night before, he simply stood there and stared for a second.

He'd thought it would be awkward or uncomfortable waking up with her — with anyone — stretched out next to him. He'd thought wrong. Somehow, his subconscious knew she was there all throughout the night, and that awareness brought a sense of peace and serenity that he'd not known since tragedy had struck his family and his life had fallen apart.

He let his gaze take in every cut, every scrape, and every bruise inflicted upon her. God, she was gorgeous. All he saw were the beautiful features under the painful reminders of her trauma.

Good Lord, I'm losing it. His mind was whirling around like an Oklahoma tornado, but he couldn't seem to calm it.

He couldn't take his eyes off of her, and he couldn't stop thinking how right she looked, right where she was. In his life. In his house. In his bed.

He wanted this. He wanted her. He wanted to give her the forever she demanded and deserved. But his past experiences told him that loving him would destroy her, and that was the one thing he could not handle. He was still waging a war with himself, battering his heart in the process, and ensuring that nobody emerged a winner.

His mind continued to whirl.

He was shaken out of his trance when Maree stirred in her sleep, trying to shift into a more comfortable position, but grunting with frustration at her inability to move or adjust. He could tell she wanted to roll over, but she couldn't with the large leg brace and her arm and shoulder secured to prevent too much movement of her broken collarbone.

Working off instinct, a strong desire to hold her, and a desperate need to help her, he slowly eased his weight onto the mattress, sliding as gently and gracefully as possible onto her side of the bed. He wedged himself almost under her so that she was partially on her uninjured right side while he was supporting her injured left side.

He had a quick mental image of them playing a brutal game of Twister, arms and legs intertwined in a miserable attempt to hold it all together without causing anyone to collapse. It was not a reassuring vision.

But he would happily fold up like a contortionist if it eased Maree's pain.

He was so careful not to jostle her that he had to remind himself to breathe, all the while continuing to berate himself silently in his own mind... *How can I fix this, how could I let her get hurt, why can't I ever protect the people who matter the most, who am I to think I deserve someone this good, God, she's beautiful, what a monster I am to want her this much when she's hurting this bad, what's wrong with me, I have to help her, how can I fix this?*

Rhys managed to tear himself off that roller coaster by focusing on the fact that regardless of whatever monologue battled in his own head, Maree mattered most. He would do whatever he could to keep her comfortable. In this case, it was matter over mind, and the erratic thoughts finally ceased.

Maree never awoke, but she did relax against him. She exhaled, releasing her tension and allowing Rhys to absorb her weight. She nestled into the pillow and fell deeper asleep now that she wasn't flat on her back or trying to balance on her good side.

Rhys was rolled on his right side, his arm under the pillow that was supporting her head. He reached his left arm over her to grab extra pillows off his side of the bed and managed to create a prop for her left arm. Without putting too much weight on any part of her body, he found a way to leave his arm wrapped around her to hold everything in place.

Assessing the situation, he figured they had moved beyond the vicious round of Twister to resembling a pile of broken pretzels. He was good and stuck. She was cocooned within the shelter of his body. And it was heaven.

Rhys never fell asleep, content to simply hold her in place

and listen to her soft breathing. What would it feel like to nap this way on a Sunday afternoon? Maybe a football game on television after church and feeling overstuffed from one of her Sunday dinners? No injuries to avoid, no bruises turning her delicate skin purple. Was that even possible? Was that what normal people did? People who weren't too scared to share themselves, to share their life with someone wonderful? People not afraid to laugh and to giggle? To settle in and to snuggle? To love?

Rhys could hardly imagine it. And yet, he yearned for it. He wanted this so much that it evoked a physical ache deep in his chest.

A long while later, the cadence of her breathing changed. He could tell that she was starting to wake up, and Rhys wasn't surprised when she said his name in a groggy voice. He thought even that was sexy. How could that be?

"Hmm?" he answered.

"I think my drugs are working — I feel like I'm floating."

"I won't let you float away," he promised, hugging her just a bit tighter to prove his words.

"I thought I might yesterday, sitting in the car after the wreck."

He was fully alert now but had no words for that, so she continued.

"A warm peace came over me, and although I expected to be scared and panicked, I felt an odd sense of serenity. It's not easy to explain, but I didn't feel distant or alone. I didn't even feel any pain. Isn't that strange?"

A wave of cold chills washed over his body. A lump of nausea formed in his throat. He felt hollow inside for just a second. It took him a minute to gather the words to answer.

"I think that maybe you had a couple of angels watching over you," he admitted, recalling the way Davis had described what was left of her car.

"My parents, you mean?"

"Maybe them." He knew they had not survived a car accident her family was in when she was a child. He felt certain that those memories would have flooded back as she waited for help after yesterday's collision.

"Maybe someone else," he said. Could he retell his story twice in the span of a day?

"Maybe two small someones who wanted you to be okay for me," he added with reverence.

———

*S*he wondered if her head was too foggy to comprehend his words. She was having a hard time following what he said. Then he took a ragged breath, and she had the urge to snuggle in tighter.

Even though he was clearly there to take care of her, Maree knew instinctively that Rhys was struggling, and that this — whatever he had to say — was very important. She needed him to know that nothing he could say nor confess would ever change the way she felt about him. She needed him to feel how unconditionally she loved him. Now and always.

———

*S*lowly, taking breaks and long pauses to gather his thoughts and his energy, and drawing in a settling breath when needed, Rhys told Maree his story, just as he'd shared with Davis.

He could never have guessed how cathartic that unburdening would feel. The animosity was missing from his tone, and the anger had fallen from his words. The unmistakable change felt odd in his mind. He couldn't remember a time when the pain, hot and fiery and debilitating, had not been his constant companion.

Rhys laid it all out for her. He shared memories of good times with his mom and dad, of being an only child and king of the castle before the boys were born. He talked about how they all referred to the twins as their favorite double surprise, about how their world had organically shifted to revolve around the boys and their exuberant approach to life from the moment they'd arrived. He told her stories about playing football, working Saturdays and summers with his dad, and being proud and protective of his mom. He took his time, selecting his words with care. He spoke openly and eloquently. He painted a beautiful picture of his life.

"It sounds better than a dream, Rhys," Maree commented.

"It was. It was better than the best dream you can imagine dreaming. Of course, I didn't realize that at the time — I mean, I loved my life and knew we had it pretty great. But I didn't realize how special it was or that it could end in a heartbeat, be ripped away so fast."

"A fire?" she asked.

"How—" he started to ask, but he didn't know how to word his surprise at her astuteness. He'd worked so hard at concealing his past. He thought he'd been pretty adept at constructing walls to keep well-meaning friends and curious dates at arm's length. How had she seen right through each of his carefully constructed barriers? Had she guessed his demons this whole time?

"I just figured something big had to be the reason you chose to fight fires with such unyielding passion and determination," she offered. "The intensity with which you work is incredible. In a moment when so much is going on, when so many critical factors must be considered, you still have this singular focus that keeps you calm and in control. You're amazing."

"Not amazing," he contradicted, growling a bit more emphatically than he'd intended, "just desperate." His tone softened, a trace of defeat in his voice. "Desperate to make up for failing my family. For not getting the boys out of the house that day."

Years and years of repeating that erroneous opinion had turned it into a cold, hard fact in his mind. That was his truth. He could not see it any other way.

"How could that be your fault, Rhys?" she asked. Her question sounded considerate, but without any judgment. He appreciated that she wasn't trying to change his mind. They were treading on thin ice here; a dangerous and precarious thread was holding this together in his head and in his heart.

"Throughout football practice that day, I'd noticed the twins weren't there. They should have been. I knew that they should have been. Nothing would have kept the boys away. And Mom would never have been late to help set up the Thanksgiving potluck breakfast with the other team moms unless something was wrong. Very wrong. I noticed. I knew they should have arrived already. I could feel it. But I didn't do anything about it. We went through the entire practice. *The entire practice!* Shorter than a usual workout, but easily an hour and a half, almost two hours. All the while, I should have been at home. As Coach was ending his comments in the huddle, fire trucks, police cars, and ambulances all raced by, and I knew I was too late. I knew they were headed for our house, for my family. When I got to the house, the structure had to have been at least ninety-five percent engulfed in flames. With the boys trapped inside. It collapsed just after I got there. I didn't save them."

———

er instinct was to soothe and comfort him. She wanted to beg him to see it as she did — as she knew the rest of the world must see it — but Rhys was finally talking. This was too critical to smooth over. She was desperate to keep him talking, opening up and going through it with her. He had to get all the way to the end, regardless of how much it hurt her to imagine what he'd gone through. And what he continued to put himself through every day since the horrific accident.

"Your burns? That's where they came from? Going into a burning building at the age of — what — maybe seventeen? To me, that doesn't sound like doing nothing."

The first time she'd actually spoken to him at the grocery store, she had noticed his hands, wrists, and arms were disfigured with healed but visible scars.

Maree was still lying in the hollow of Rhys's body, her back to his chest and stomach. His words, spoken in his deep, rich timbre next to her ear, were a palpable stream of emotion. And yet she wanted more.

She needed to create another strand of physical connection, so she picked up one of his hands. She traced along his fingers, explored his palm, and rubbed the back of his hand with her thumb. The pads of her fingers stroked along his wrist and up his arm as far as she could reach with a touch as light as a feather. She decided that the brutal imperfections made him look more like a real human and less like the magnificent superhero that she normally saw in him. She knew in that moment that the experience that had caused his scars was something painful, yet something vital to what made him the man she loved. Her Rhys.

He let her study his scars; she did not see them as proof of failure. She wished he would accept her understanding and empathy, would use them as a path toward letting go of his guilt. But after a few moments Rhys replied, "Certainly not enough." Self-loathing had crept back into his voice.

She heard it, recognized it, and wanted to keep that from taking over. She would not let him push her outside his walls again.

He tucked his hand back under her ribs, where she couldn't continue to touch and feel the evidence of his trauma, but he hadn't extricated himself from holding her. She took that as a good sign.

"So, you finished high school the next year? And then straight to fire school?"

"Pretty much. Even after I walked away from sports and doubled up on classes to graduate early, I had a few offers to play ball at small schools. But I was ready to fight fires. I needed to fight something. I agreed to start online college classes to appease my folks, but I entered the fire academy the week after my high school graduation.

"Our fabulous home, one that had been so full of love and laughter, was a pile of ashes. Mom and Dad rented a place down the street from the high school. We had nothing personal — no photos, no furniture, no knick-knacks — from before. It was all gone. The rental house was barren and sad; none of us had the motivation to do anything other than survive at the basest level. I needed out of that house and out of that town.

"Mom tried, I think, but her will to function was gone. Her fervor for life and people and design was gone. She had no interest in creating, no drive to put one foot in front of the other to advance past the pain. Dad couldn't help her and couldn't move forward himself. She lived in a frail state of depression. Soon she suffered from every ailment you can think of.

"Dad walked away from his job, and spent every minute back at the old place, on the land he still owned but couldn't stand to rebuild. He claimed he was farming and ranching, and

I guess he did just enough to pay the bills in town since Mom wasn't working anymore, either. But all I ever saw him do was sit and stare at the dirt. I know he used to take a pole and fishing tackle to the tank, but I never once saw him cast a line after the fire.

"Three years after the twins died, I was a year into my job as a Fort Worth firefighter and halfway through a bachelor's degree in fire sciences when the call came that Mom had died peacefully in the hospital. As I mentioned, she'd become frail, as if her body just couldn't operate anymore. She simply drifted away. I know that she died of a broken heart.

"At her funeral, I could tell that Dad wasn't far behind; I wasn't surprised to get another call a few months later that he'd succumbed to a pulmonary virus, some rare strain of pneumonia that I'm sure he contracted sleeping on the cold, wet, hard ground out by the burnt ruins of our old life. In a horrible way, I'm glad they're both gone. Now they don't have to suffer through life without Radley and Redmond."

"Rhys, Radley, and Redmond," Maree recited. "I love that your parents were like mine, equally stuck on one letter for all three of their kids. I can just picture the twins. Miniatures of you, attached to you like shadows, and totally in awe of their big brother," she said with a small respectful smile as she scooted over toward his side of the bed just enough to lie on her back and look up into his beautiful face. Needing him to feel her warmth, something full of life, she reached up to stroke his cheek, so he wouldn't be alone in his memories.

"Actually, I do have a few photos packed away," he said, surprising her. "After the fire, friends and family members tried to help by donating furniture and clothes, cooking for Mom and Dad, and filling that cold rental with any little mementos they could find that were shared memories of vacations or experiences with my family. I was in the Parkland Hospital burn unit during that time. Although Mom and Dad were too numb to process the gifts, they did have the presence of mind to put all the photos that people brought — copies they had of school portraits, newspaper clippings, and snapshots that included the boys — into a box that I found tucked away in their closet after Mom died."

"I can't wait to see them," Maree responded with genuine interest. "Although," she nudged him with a smile, "I'm very confident that the picture in my head is spot on."

He'd never talked about the boys this much. Not to anyone. Not ever. And he couldn't remember the last time he'd allowed himself to smile over them. Without consciously deciding to do so, he leaned down and kissed her. Just a light kiss, but one that made her smile grow. And when he pulled back, ending the kiss, he paused just to look at her. She beamed up at him, and he simply soaked up her beauty. She was so good for him. Too good for him. God, he wished he could be good for her, too.

The day remained lazy and cozy. Rhys helped Maree run a bath. She wrapped herself in a big bath towel, so he could remove the leg brace and set her in the tub to soak away some of the soreness.

"How ya' doing in there," Rhys asked from outside the door.

"The soapy water stings every cut and scratch, but it's worth it," she replied.

"Want a few more minutes, or are you ready for some help?"

"Maybe a little longer. I would hate to waste this nice warm water."

He stayed there, listening for sounds that she needed him. He was sure that she was doing the best she could washing with one hand, but it couldn't have been easy. Not three minutes had passed when the swooshing ceased. He knocked before slowly opening the door. It only took one glance to see that she was physically spent.

Again, incredibly lucky that she was allowed to put light weight on the injured leg — at least as much as she could tolerate — and relying heavily on her good arm and leg, Maree had managed to stand back up in the tub. She'd rewrapped the towel around her as the water drained, but the actual drying off must've been too much. When Rhys entered the warm, steamy bathroom and saw water droplets glistening like pearls on her dewy skin, his breath caught. The jolt of attraction nearly stopped his heart.

A vision of the gala, the young bartender, and the look of adoration on the boy's face flashed through Rhys's mind. He decided right then that they would *not* be hiring a home health assistant as the hospital had suggested; he'd happily be her caregiver for as long as he was needed. In that moment, he nearly convinced himself that he could be here for her forever. Nearly.

They managed to get her dried off and dressed without compromising her modesty. He graded it as a supreme success that he came out on the other side of the endeavor more or less still sane. He situated her on the couch with instructions to find a movie or ballgame or whatever she liked on the TV. He disappeared into the kitchen, returning in about fifteen minutes with fresh grilled cheese sandwiches and bowls of steaming tomato soup.

"The lunch of recuperating champions," he boasted, setting up a TV tray in front of her and one in front of the recliner for himself.

"It looks great, Rhys. Thank you," she said again.

———

*H*e'd told her to stop thanking him so much, but how could she? He'd proven to be tender, thoughtful, and considerate. He was anticipating her needs and struggles, and he seemed to be a helpful step ahead of her at every turn. She knew that Max, M'Kenzee, Sadie, and Landry would have all dropped what they were doing and volunteered to help her through this. Probably even Janie Lyn in her giving-yet-mysterious way, but she loved that Rhys was the one with her.

"What to drink?" he asked, walking back toward the kitchen.

"A cup of hot tea?" she ventured, not sure if he drank tea. Or coffee, for that matter. She loved him, and believed they shared a meaningful connection, but she still had quite a lot to learn about Rhys.

"I can do that," he called from the other room, and returned a few minutes later with a massive glass of cold milk for himself and an oversized mug of heated sweet tea for her. Not a fancy tea set or flavored bags that needed to steep, but a glass of sweet iced tea that had been poured into a mug and heated in the microwave. It was perfect, and she readily admitted — only in her mind, of course — that she was smitten.

"What are we watching?" he asked while commercials played on the television.

"The 'Stros game," she replied while blowing on a spoonful of soup. Thank goodness her right arm was working; otherwise, she'd be wearing the bulk of this lunch.

———

"*T*he Houston Astros?" he whined to tease her. He was surprised to catch himself being silly; despite that part of his character being MIA for the last ten years, doing so was easy with Maree and felt incredibly good. "Maybe the Rangers are playing instead?"

"Nope," she replied with a conviction that brooked no

argument. He grinned at her fake bossiness — in truth she was the least clingy, pushy, or bossy woman he had ever known — and sat down to eat his lunch.

In the first inning, she was digging into her soup and sandwich with gusto, making Rhys proud that he'd cooked something she liked, even if it was only canned soup and a toasted sandwich... In the middle of the third, she gave up on trying to eat anymore and pulled herself to the other side of the couch, clearly running out of steam... By the seventh inning stretch, she was out.

Rhys covered her up with what he now thought of as *her* afghan, adjusted the pillows so they were supporting her arm sling and the leg brace, smoothed her strawberry blond curls back from her brow, and touched his lips to her forehead before taking all their dishes to the kitchen and putting the TV trays back in the coat closet. He was watching the final two outs of the game when his cell phone rang.

He saw it was Max and clicked the mute button on the television remote.

"Hey, Max," he answered.

"Rhys. How's she doing?" Rhys respected how Max cut to the chase. He knew it was tough to let someone else take the lead with her care and recuperation. Rhys was humbled by the trust Max had placed in him.

"Sleeping soundly. *Again*. I know they said the CT scan was clear, but she can't stay awake more than a couple of hours at a time." Rhys was determined not to worry her, and he didn't want to give value to something that was nothing. But he was a bit worried all the same. "I'll mention it when the doctors come by tonight."

Perks of a small town: Rhys and Max had made a few strategic calls, and all parties involved were willing to be flexible in scheduling appointments, which allowed for house calls and a little VIP treatment for Maree.

"That's happening at 7:30?" Max confirmed.

"Yes, Miss Sadie left word on Maree's phone that she'll be by this afternoon to see her and is apparently bringing dinner. Then the orthopedic surgeon is supposed to be here around 7:30. And the general physician said she wants to come by for a quick exam when she leaves the hospital, which should be pretty close to the same time."

"You better make plenty of room in your fridge if Sadie is bringing food," Max advised with a chuckle. "Be prepared for a veritable feast! You think I ought to make my way back to Green Hills for the doctors' visits tonight?" Max asked his final question in a more serious tone.

"After the gourmet soup and sandwiches I made for lunch, I am sure we will both welcome Miss Sadie's offerings," Rhys admitted. "And tonight, well, that's your call. She loved your flowers and card — whatever you wrote in there did the trick. I don't think she feels abandoned or anything; she kept telling me she could use your house to avoid her second-story apartment. I ignored that, but it's obvious that she knows you're here for her if and when she needs you."

"Okay, then," Max conceded. "Ask about the fatigue and excessive sleeping, maybe we need to run more tests. See what the surgeon recommends about scheduling the knee repairs, and I'll check in later tonight."

"Sounds good."

"Rhys?" Max continued, "You sure you're up for this? It's going to take more than a couple of days to cross this bridge. I don't doubt you care for her, and I know with every degree of certainty that with *you* is where she most wants to be. But I want you to know that you are not trapped. You don't owe her — or me, or anyone — anything at all."

"I appreciate you saying so." He was trying to decipher if he should be grateful or offended, so that was all he had to say back.

"But she's staying put?" Max asked.

———

*M*ax was grinning on the other end of the phone. He'd heard the quick shift from easygoing to slightly-hacked-off in Rhys's voice. He appreciated the man's willingness to serve, but he had to put it out there all the same.

Maree and Rhys had endured a tumultuous few months before this. Twice now, Rhys had cut bait and bailed when he'd felt their relationship progressing. Max and Maree both knew through life's hard lessons that a happy ending was worth working for, worth waiting for, even when the path to get there was rocky terrain. Maree had been willing to let Rhys find his way back to her in his own way. And while a scare like Maree's accident changed one's perspective and reset priorities in a more correct order, it didn't erase those weeks of difficulty. Max truly liked the guy, but Maree was his baby sister; that trumped everything else.

———

"*S*he's staying put," Rhys answered. Although the two men were close in age, Max was clearly secure in the role of older brother. Rhys could live with that, but he fully intended on taking control on this one. His tone left no room for argument or negotiation.

"Okay, buddy," Max said, and Rhys accepted Max's attempt to smooth Rhys's ruffled feathers for what it was: a mild apology. "Call or text if anything changes, if y'all need anything at all," Max said once more.

"Will do." And with that Rhys, disconnected the line.

21

Pain is inevitable. Suffering is optional.
Haruki Murakami

*A*fter ending the call with Max, Rhys stayed put, alternately reining in his thoughts and questioning what he was doing. He was still sitting in place, frozen in that chair, staring at nothing, when he heard voices on his front porch.

Opening his door to check it out, he found Davis carrying an armload of casserole dishes and vegetable bowls. Sadie Jones, who was also loaded down — with a cake carrier, a cookie tin, a breadbasket, and what looked like a bag of ice cream from the grocery store — was hot on Davis's trail. The trunk and one back-seat door were still open, indicating that there was even more to unload from the car.

"Miss Sadie," he greeted, taking the packages from her arms, "you should be more careful about picking up strangers; this one here can be a real pain in the—"

"Careful, Larsen," Davis shot back good-naturedly, "or some of this food will magically and mysteriously disappear."

"Now you boys hush," Sadie chided when they walked in and she saw Maree sleeping on the couch. "Maree is resting." Rhys and Davis stepped around Sadie when she stopped mid-stride. Rhys understood; he'd needed to stop on several occasions to take in and savor the sight of Maree safe and sound — the worse for wear, but alive and healing. Rhys glanced back to a see tears gleaming in Miss Sadie's eyes, but she blinked them away, took a deep breath, and continued into the house.

"In fact," she directed, "set those things in the kitchen and grab your shoes, Rhys. Daniel was in the middle of his run when he stopped to help me unload. Now you can join him for the rest of it."

"Daniel? Who's Daniel?" Rhys teased. Rhys had known that Daniel was Davis's first name, but he'd never actually heard anyone use it before. A uniqueness of growing up in a small town is that folks knew everything about you, and they weren't afraid to tell it.

"Very funny; I'll be waiting out front," Davis said, giving Miss Sadie a hug, a smile, and a wink on his way out of the kitchen door.

"It's not up for discussion. Get going," she told Rhys when he moved to unload more bags for her.

"I'm good, Miss Sadie. I don't want to be gone when Maree wakes up."

"Nonsense," she balked. "I've nursed that girl back to health on several occasions, and you need to get out from under this roof for a few minutes. Go catch up to Daniel, and that's an order."

Feeling appropriately chastised for insinuating she couldn't take care of Maree — which was exactly what he'd been bristling about after his conversation with Max — he tucked tail and did as he was told. A mile or so would do him some good, and he could probably be back before she woke up.

"Only if you promise to share a few good stories on *Daniel* that I can use when I need some juicy blackmail material," Rhys relented with a sly smile, which Sadie acknowledged by batting a hand to wave him out of the kitchen.

After he'd changed into shorts and tennis shoes and grabbed his cell phone, he stopped by the couch, crouching next to Maree.

"Hey, beautiful," he caressed her cheek and whispered softly to wake her just enough so she could hear him. "Sadie's here and shooing me out so that she can sit with you for a while. I'm going to go with Davis for a quick run. I've got my phone if you need me for anything, and I'll be back before long."

"Have fun," she said sleepily and closed her eyes again. He kissed her softly, ducked his head back in the kitchen to point out Maree's next dose of pain meds, and left to find Davis.

"Run or walk?" Davis asked as Rhys walked out of the house.

"Run! Why would we walk?" Rhys asked, as if Davis had grown an extra head.

"In case you wanted to talk," he offered, a little on the defensive side. "I was trying to be a good friend," he muttered.

"You *are* a good friend," Rhys assured him with a hand on his shoulder. "Now let's run!" he challenged and took off down the street.

Sadie had been right; Rhys needed this chance to work out the worry and fright and stress of the last few days. He knew he was going at a punishing pace. But Davis didn't complain, so Rhys didn't hold back. When they made it around the park and back to the split where Davis's house was one way and Rhys's was the other, they slowed down and came to a stop.

"Thanks, man," Rhys said after taking a minute or two to catch his breath. He hoped that Davis could hear in his tone just how much he really did appreciate him.

"Anytime, my friend," Davis said with a knowing look and

nod, lifting his hand to Rhys's for a fist bump and then jogging off toward his house.

Rhys started running — at a much easier pace — in the other direction. He was surprised when he found himself at the impound and salvage yard without realizing that he'd been headed that way. He flashed the firefighter's badge in his wallet to the lady working the office. She logged his visit into her computer, entered a code to open the gate, and he was allowed onto the lot.

It wasn't difficult to locate Maree's car and the one that had hit her; they were the freshest pieces of junk in there, front and center.

It took Rhys a minute to come to terms with the fact that the pile of rubble in front of him was an automobile, much less Maree's car. This was all that had been protecting her when the crash occurred. He circled it several times, deciphering the chain of events by how the wreckage had settled in the end.

The more he looked, the faster his heart raced. His skin was crawling. His breathing was shallow; he couldn't gasp enough oxygen to fully fill his lungs. He was dripping sweat, but not from physical exertion.

He reached out to touch the crinkled metal, only to realize that it was coated with her dried blood, and pulled his hand back. The buzzing in his head became unbearable; he had to get out of there.

He took off from the gate, running blind, as fast as he could force his legs to go. He might have gone a fourth of a mile or he might have gone four miles; he had no idea how long he'd run. But when his lungs and his legs finally gave out, he was just outside of town. He fell to his knees and began throwing up. His body convulsed, but he couldn't stop. He was choking, tears streaming down his face, and still, he vomited more.

Davis was right: she should be dead.

When his body stopped betraying him, he walked back to town, stopping at a gas station to borrow a bathroom to clean up and buy a sports drink. By the time he got back to his house, his nerves were under control. But the image of the car, the mangled and distorted interior, and what she'd lived through remained firmly in his mind.

He passed through the front door and went directly to where Maree was leaning against the wall under the open archway to the kitchen, the crutch they'd brought home from the hospital under her right arm to help her balance. She was talking to Miss Sadie, who was tinkering and fussing and chatting away. He brought both hands to the sides of her face, guiding her lips to his, and just started kissing.

Her good hand came up to grab a handful of his sweaty t-shirt, and she kissed him right back. He fully appreciated that while she couldn't know what this kiss was all about, she was definitely on board for it. He tried to pull away once, pressing his forehead to hers as he gulped air, but it wasn't enough, and he went right back to kissing her mouth.

Sadie harrumphed, crossed her arms, and leaned against the countertop to settle in for the show. Rhys had lost conscious thought and forgotten that they had an audience.

He just kept kissing. He would try to stop, fail, and come back for more. At some point, Sadie clearing her throat for the umpteenth time registered, and he slowed down to a mild frenzy. Then he released Maree's lips but kept his face close as he petted the unbruised side of her face, tracing it with his thumb, and sprinkling pecks of kisses on her lips, her eyelid, back to her mouth, and lastly, her forehead as he tucked her into his chest, resting his lips on the top of her head, and hugged her to him as much as he dared without putting pressure on her collarbone and shoulder.

———

*M*aree felt his heart racing against her ear; he had been a bit crazed when he walked into the house. She didn't know what had prompted it, but she did love his display of affection. She loved that he was letting down the guard around his heart. She loved that she could evoke that deep of a passion in this man whom she had fallen for in every way possible.

"Well, are y'all done now?" Sadie asked with an incredulous lift of one eyebrow. She shook her head to dismiss their foolishness and went back to her tasks at hand.

"I hope not," Maree answered, her voice dreamy and muffled in Rhys's chest, but also sounding very much like the cat that just ate the canary. She'd been good and thoroughly kissed, and she was feeling very satisfied.

Slowly, he extricated himself, making sure Maree was balanced on the crutch and her good leg. He leaned down, placing one more kiss — this time gentle and calm — on her mouth. "I've got to shower," he whispered, and walked away.

22

One cannot think well, love well, sleep well,
if one has not dined well.
Virginia Woolf

A cold shower did wonders to restore the control that Rhys had lost.

He came back to the kitchen his usual calm self. He was wearing another pair of well-worn jeans, a Texas Rangers t-shirt to nettle Maree about her Houston Astros (who'd gone on to win while she slept earlier), and nothing on his feet. His dark blond hair was damp, and the waves seemed to beg for her touch. When he stopped in front of her for a chaste kiss and a wink, she grinned into his gaze and reached her hand up for a quick run of her fingers through his hair.

"Here we go again," Sadie muttered with a shake of her head. But when Rhys walked right up to Sadie and planted a kiss on her cheek, too, the older woman blushed like a schoolgirl.

"Miss Sadie, how can I help?" he asked as if nothing odd or unusual had occurred.

"Set the table, please," she instructed, reclaiming her composure. Just as he was grinning and winking at Maree once more, Sadie added. "And set it for four; I told Daniel to come back for supper."

Rhys rolled his eyes in pretend exasperation. "Who's Daniel?" Maree asked, which caused Rhys to laugh outright. The laughter proved to be almost as therapeutic as the running and the kissing, not to mention the retching that was tossed in there, too. The tears — the first ones he'd shed in over ten years — had still not registered. Yet.

The four of them were still laughing when Davis arrived a few minutes later.

Dinner was incredible. Not counting the few meals that Maree had cooked for Rhys and Max, it was the first "normal" family-style dinner that Rhys had experienced since before the fire. Sadie had made an incredible tray of sour cream beef enchiladas with homemade tamales on the side, chips and queso, a fabulous taco salad, and sopapilla cheesecake for dessert. They talked and teased and laughed throughout the meal, although all three noninjured persons in the party kept a vigilant watch over Maree to make sure she was up to the occasion.

When Rhys had returned from his shower earlier, he'd noticed that she was leaning heavily on the kitchen counter rather than standing on her good leg. She was trying to put on a brave, strong front for Sadie, but he could tell she was getting tired.

When Sadie cut dessert for everyone, Rhys suggested that he carry Maree back to the living room so they could prop her leg up better. Maree didn't argue, and everyone knew she was worn out.

"Sadie, why don't you take two cups of tea in there with your cake, and y'all can visit while *Daniel* and I clean up?" He kept a teasing tone to his voice, using Davis's first name again to keep everything light and jovial for Maree's sake.

"I never look a gift horse in the mouth," Sadie replied, which must've meant it was a good idea, because for once she did exactly as someone else asked.

"You boys get after it!"

23

Even miracles take a little time.
Cinderella's Fairy Godmother

The boys were finishing the dishwashing when the doorbell sounded; both doctors had arrived at the same time. Rhys tossed Davis the cup towel he'd been using to dry dishes, a veil of concern falling over his face.

He opened the door, reintroduced himself, and invited the guests to come in. He led them to the living room and helped Maree get better situated for the doctors' visits. His heart was racing, but he did a decently good job of hiding that fact from the rest of the room.

Please let this go well, he pleaded in his head. *Please let her be okay*.

Miss Sadie introduced herself to the doctors. She gave Maree a hug and a kiss with instructions to call to let her know the doctors' findings. Then she instructed Davis to grab his leftovers and see her out to her car. Davis nodded in obedience, said his goodbyes, and happily did as he was told. Rhys followed them to the door, again thanking Sadie for dinner, and closing it behind them with a quiet click.

When he turned back to the room, the orthopedic surgeon was setting up a portable X-ray lamp to explain Maree's X-rays from the hospital, and the second doctor was beginning her exam with the help of a nurse who had accompanied her. She was taking Maree's pulse, temperature, and blood pressure. Rhys knew taking vitals was part of the normal assessment, but he was still a nervous wreck. He felt fidgety and confined. He stood to pace on the other side of the room.

"Please stay," Maree called to him, reaching her good hand out to hold his, so instead of wearing a path in the rug, he sat in the recliner next to her spot on the couch and offered his hand, which amounted to next to no good, but it was all he had to give.

The doctors and nurse poked and prodded. Maree answered questions, he answered questions, the medical professionals hmmm'ed and mmhhmm'ed. A few times they did something that caused Maree's face to go white with pain. Rhys felt as though he was sitting in a torture chamber, helpless to do a thing.

The orthopedic surgeon showed them the X-rays and MRI photos that had been printed for Maree to keep. He explained the operation she needed. It was complicated and involved. He said that he'd like to do it soon, as soon as next Monday, which made her blanch a little more. The longer they stayed, the quieter she got and the colder her fingers became in his hand.

When he thought she'd had all she could take, he decided that was enough.

"If that's good for tonight, maybe we can pick up from here tomorrow?" he suggested with a not-so-subtle expression. That got the attention of all those wearing scrubs in the room. They took better notice of Maree the person rather than

Maree the patient; they saw her weakening pallor, the quietness of her voice, and the shake in her hand.

"Of course," the nurse said on behalf of the medical group. "I'll be back tomorrow afternoon to check vitals and see how you're feeling, Maree. I'll bring the pre-op instructions and paperwork for Monday's surgery then, too."

"Thank you," Maree and Rhys both answered at the same time, which broke the tension a little and caused them to look at one another and smile, albeit faintly. He could swear all was right with his world when she smiled.

"Rhys, could you help me to the back while they pack up, please?" Maree asked. It was the first time she had asked him to carry her, or really do anything besides getting her purse last night. That spoke volumes to him.

"Of course," he said, scooping her up into his arms effortlessly. "I'll be right back to see y'all out," he said to their guests, and carried her to the bedroom.

"Where to?" he asked when they entered the room.

"Bathroom, please," she said, although she was looking longingly at the big soft bed.

He set her down in the bathroom, handed her the crutch, and made sure she had her balance. Then he went back to the living room to ask the question that was concerning him the most.

"There is one more thing, but I didn't want to worry Maree," he began as they walked to the door. "Maree is sleeping excessively. She can hardly stay awake — I'm talking an hour, maybe two max, at a time. She's been up for longer tonight, and you can clearly see the toll it's taking on her. Is this something we should be concerned about?" He asked, his voice was tight. He held his breath awaiting their answer. He was scared. Very scared.

But all three put his mind at ease when the general physician answered for them. "No worries at all. The CT scan looked great; no bleeds, no bruising, no fluids. Her body does still show signs of shock, which is completely normal. Her body is exhausted from all that she's been through, and the pain medication adds to that sense of lethargy. She's doing great. Just be patient with the healing process."

"Here's the thing," Rhys said, leveling with them with a grave tone. "She should be dead. Go see the car, read the report. No one should have survived that wreckage, so we've got to do everything possible to ensure that this miracle is not fleeting. Do you understand?"

"She's going to be just fine, Mr. Larsen," the nurse reassured him. Her eyes were kind and understanding. She reached out a hand to rest on his forearm to relay her message while looking him straight in the eye. "Even miracles take a little time."

24

Mirror, mirror…
The Evil Queen in Snow White

The nurse's guarantees didn't do much to make Rhys feel better. Finding Maree standing stock-still, staring at her reflection in the bathroom mirror, made him feel much, much worse.

She had on only her bra and panties and was studying the myriad of bruises, which were all the deepest colors of the rainbow. The entire left side of her body was starting to turn colors, with additional bruises popping up in random spots. She was taking in the bloody scrapes and ragged scabs forming on her skin, examining the puffy and swollen spots. She counted the nineteen angry stitches along her hairline, across her left eyebrow, accentuating the apple of her cheekbone, and just above her jaw.

He knew that the effort it had taken for her to step into the tub and soak in the hot water for her bath had sapped every ounce of her strength. It was understandable that she hadn't thought to look in the mirror or work too hard to cleanse around her injuries yesterday. Now she was seeing it — truly seeing it — all for the first time. Silent tears streamed unchecked down her face.

Rhys didn't say a word. He didn't want to brush aside this emotional pain that seemed to have crept up on her after the doctors' visit. Nor would he dismiss the physical pain she was bound to be in.

He reached in front of her and turned on the faucet, tossing a washcloth under the stream of hot water. He walked to his closet and grabbed an extra-large plaid flannel. He'd worn it no less than five hundred times; it would be easiest to get on her shoulder while avoiding jostling her collarbone. Plus, it was the softest thing he owned and would keep her warm.

Coming back to her, he stepped around her and turned her ninety degrees so that her back was to the door, and her front was to him. The shower was to her right, and the alienating mirror was to her left. He'd done it on purpose so that the eye that was swollen shut effectively blocked her view.

The first thing he did was grab her leg brace off the bathroom floor where she had let it fall. It boggled his mind that she could stand without it, even with her crutch and the cabinet top for support. He was impressed with Maree's balance on her good leg, yet he knew that she could only do that for so long. He couldn't imagine the pain and discomfort she was experiencing.

He opened the Velcro straps, kneeled in front of her, and refastened the brace in place to prevent her leg from bending and to protect her shattered kneecap.

He stood up, set her crutch to the side, and draped the flannel shirt on her shoulders like a cape. "Lean on me if you need to," he told her. Rhys buttoned just a couple of buttons to keep the flannel in place.

Trying to hide how his hands shook, he reached around to unhook the back strap of her bra, making sure she remained covered. He'd dreamed of the day he would see her unclothed, a day he could worship her. While he looked forward to that day with all his heart, he would not let this dark cloud hang over what he wanted to be a perfect moment for her. Today was not that day, and he made absolutely sure she knew — and that she felt — she was completely safe in his care.

He walked behind her and then reached around her to unbutton the top two buttons he'd fastened before. In one smooth motion, he managed to move the shoulder strap of her bra to the side and lift her left arm so that it wouldn't pull on her shoulder. He held it in place with one hand while sliding the bra off and the shirt sleeve on and up her arm. Wrapping the shirt around behind her, he did the same to her right side. Holding the two sides of the flannel together, he came back around to face her. Then he buttoned the shirt from top to bottom and replaced the sling that she had discarded.

A fine sheen of sweat heated his brow, and he gritted his teeth with the effort he was taking to minimize her pain and discomfort, knowing all the while that it was impossible to completely avoid hurting her in the process of getting her dressed. Nor was it lost on him that she was as white as a sheet. She was past the point of sheer exhaustion. Physically, mentally, and emotionally, she was depleted.

"You okay?" he asked, looking into her eyes, which were still streaming with tears. Standing mere inches from her, he could sense her emotional distance, like she was in a dark tunnel and he had to pull her through to help her find her way back into light and coherence.

Her eyes refocused, and she nodded with a tiny gesture. His heart knew that was far from the truth.

"Tell me when you need to sit down," he said as he reached into the sink, wringing out the now-warm washcloth. He continued to hold her gaze, waiting for an affirmative response. His eyebrows lifted, prompting one more nod.

He started by wiping away tears, running the soothing cloth across her unscathed right cheek first, dabbing carefully along her left cheek, and then swiping down the column of her throat. The soft, delicate skin was terribly abused and scarred. He understood her tears. It was hard to take in, hard to see something so perfect and so beautiful marred with such devastation.

He smoothed the rag over her right eye and repeated the motions carefully on the swelling around her left eye. He rinsed the cloth again, dried blood turning the stream of water pink.

That made him angry. He was angry that the other driver had walked away with only minor injuries while she was facing a long road of recovery. He was angry that she had a significant challenge ahead of her when her upcoming weeks and months should be spent laughing with Hank, cheering for Max, and working on her shop and fabric designs.

He was especially angry that he had let her leave the grocery store when she had, putting her in harm's way. Why hadn't he spent more time with her? He'd meant to when he first saw her. He'd wanted to talk just a little longer, to cherish the sound of her voice.

But Maree had been so polite, even aloof. Like he was no more than an acquaintance. So, he hadn't pushed. Instead, he'd let her walk away and straight into suffering. If only he had stalled her by twenty seconds, she'd have been safe. Mere seconds mattered. Damn it, he knew that better than anyone!

These were the anger-inciting thoughts he had to tamp down so that she wouldn't pick up on his frustration. Not only would that *not* help her calm down, but she might assume that his irritation was aimed at her instead of himself. He took a deep breath and willed his body to relax as the water began to run clear again.

Leaving a little more moisture in the rag than before, he dabbed her hairline. The hospital staff had cleaned her wounds well, removing debris and metal shards. Maree had also tried to clean them a little in the bath; yet, just like with the cuts and scrapes, there was still more blood. More pieces of skin. More water tinged with her trauma.

After rinsing it one more time, he wrung the water out completely, lifted her hair, and laid the warm cloth on the back of her neck in hopes it would ease the tense muscles. His fingers massaged the base of her head, gently. So gently.

Despite the high doses of pain medication, he knew she hurt. He was an empathetic man and yet, before this ordeal, he'd never have guessed how much her pain would gut him.

Keeping his right hand behind her neck to hold the warm washcloth in place, his left hand came up to cup her cheek. His thumb slid across her bottom lip, and he let it linger on the corner of her mouth. Then he stroked toward her jaw, feeling the soft patch of unharmed skin under her cheekbone. His eyes never left the places he traced.

Taking a step closer — so close that his words were hardly more than spoken caresses on her lips — he began, "You are beautiful, Maree." He felt her sob and watched her eyes close, but he kept on.

"These bruises will fade, the cuts will heal, and although you'll have at least one badass scar from the stitches, these sexy-as-hell curls will hide the worst of it." Rhys lifted a handful of her thick, wavy hair, bringing it to his face to feel its softness, then letting it fall before running his hand down her temple and tucking a strand back behind her ear.

Her eyelids opened again, slightly. He looked back into her eyes, with a hint of a smile.

Then his gaze resettled on her mouth. With the merest touch, he traced his thumb over the soft skin just below her bottom lip. She didn't move or respond. Her heartbeat sped up against his chest; her pulse was racing. Her breath was coming in short wisps.

He touched his lips to hers. Too briefly.

"I wish I was honorable enough to say that your injuries make me want you less"— another nip at her lips —"but that would be a lie."

Another kiss.

"It's all I can do to keep my hands off you."

Kiss.

"And I'm failing miserably at even that."

Two kisses.

"When I hold you, my only worry with your wounds — my only hesitation — is that I'll cause you pain. These cuts and bruises don't deter me one bit."

Kiss.

"When I look at you, I see my grocery girl, my dancing partner at Scooter's, and my drop-dead-gorgeous date to the ball."

A longer kiss.

"And when I am kissing you, I can't think at all."

And then the mother of all kisses.

———

*S*he could no longer think, either. She'd stopped crying when he had started the kissing. Now she only wanted to get closer and closer. She wanted to melt into him. She wanted this feeling to last indefinitely, infinitely, forever.

Thank heavens he continued to support her neck; otherwise, she would have crumpled when his lips made their way to her jaw and the sensitive skin just under it. She thought he continued to murmur soft promises, but her mind was whirling and she couldn't be sure. Maybe this whole thing was just a dream. She'd had so many of him. Of them. Talking, sharing, laughing, teasing, kissing, and cuddling. But she knew this was not a dream. Because this felt far better than she'd known how to imagine in her dreams.

"I could do this endlessly," he pledged in her ear, just before nibbling his way back to her lips. He never stopped kissing as he removed the washcloth and dropped it toward the sink, reached beneath her legs, and lifted her to his chest. He just kept on kissing her as he walked to his side of the bed, kneeling on it with her still in his arms, and finally lowered them together, all the while being mindful of the cumbersome brace that he'd put back on her leg.

He continued the sweet exploration of kisses as he laid her down, tucked a pillow behind her sling and two beneath her leg, and leaned over her to brace his own weight.

Maree guessed that he intended to kiss her senseless just to be sure that he'd chased the sadness away. She appreciated that he was *not* skimping on the job.

How had she never known that a person could kiss like this? Drawing her need to the surface, and then soothing her when she couldn't take any more. Caressing and nibbling and nipping and pecking and comforting and exciting and pleasing in so many delicious ways.

When, after a wonderfully long time, he brought them back to brief touches and light pecks, he eased her toward him and tucked her into his chest, showering baby kisses over her hair. When he finally stilled, he continued to hold her tight.

Maree filled her lungs with a deep, cleansing breath, and after her chest gave a little shudder, she exhaled and drifted off to sleep.

25

Of all the liars in the world,
sometimes the worst are our own fears.
Rudyard Kipling

ying still, holding her as she slept, Rhys finally released the hold he'd had on himself. He gave himself permission to play the "what if" game for just a minute…What if they'd not arrived in time to extinguish the sparks… What if the jagged metal shards had pierced her heart or lungs… What if the impact had ejected her from the car… What if she'd not regained consciousness… What if she had not made it through?

He recognized the bitter taste that filled his mouth and the violent roil of his stomach.

Rhys continued to hold her tight. He allowed himself to admit just how much she meant to him. And he came to terms with what her death would have done to him.

He could not keep heading down that road. He forced his mind back to the present, ran a hand through the length of her hair, placed a few more soft kisses on the top of her head, engulfed her again in his embrace, and allowed himself to join her in sleep.

Rhys slept soundly the whole night through, but somehow he still felt out of sorts the next day.

––––––

*M*aree had *definitely* overdone it with visitors and dinner and doctors and emotions the evening before. She was trying to put on her game face and trudge through, but exhaustion was spoiling her efforts.

As was Rhys's less-than-cheerful mood.

Maree was drooping and dragging, nodding off to sleep every few minutes. She wanted to help with meals, but she could hardly stay upright. She wanted to talk and spend time with Rhys, knowing he'd be back at work the next day. She wanted to encourage some more of his TLC, but she simply didn't have the energy to do any of those things. They all sounded great in theory but were not easily executed in reality.

Rhys was kind and attentive, but he was obviously agonizing over something. Maree knew that on top of her sheer exhaustion, she looked even worse today than yesterday. She chalked his worrying up to these sad facts because she didn't have the wherewithal to think any deeper than that.

The day continued on: Maree napping and Rhys brooding.

But as afternoon flowed into the evening, Maree's gut told her something was off. But in her mind, she could not conceive that anything could be amiss after his loving affection last night.

Unfortunately, her gut proved to be the better instrument for measuring the situation.

When the nurse from yesterday stopped by to take vitals and check on Maree, Rhys sat on the opposite side of the room and did little more than nod his head when asked a question.

For dinner, Rhys heated up another casserole that Miss Sadie had left labeled in the fridge. As hard as Maree tried to engage him in conversation while they ate, he was distant and had little to say.

After dinner, Maree tried to help clean up the kitchen, but Rhys wouldn't hear of it, settling her on the couch and handing her a book, the remote, and her sketchbook... anything to entertain her so that he could hide out in the kitchen.

---

*M*eanwhile, Rhys continued to wear himself out with a mental ping-pong match of thoughts that volleyed between *"I love her"* and *"I can't protect her,"* complete with spikes of *"she loves you"* and *"you don't deserve her"* and detrimental aces that screamed, *"she's better off without you."* He was lying to himself, one way or the other, but he didn't know which message was the truth.

By the time they called it a night, Rhys was a bundle of energy and doubt. He sensed that Maree was thoroughly confused by his change of heart. He knew that both of them were staring off into the dark while pretending to be asleep.

Thursday was Rhys's first day back on shift. While he was worried about not being there in case Maree needed him, he was equally glad to escape to the firehouse.

Just as he was about to leave for work, the thunk of Maree's crutch signaled her making her way down the hall. She met him at the back door with a resolute look on her face.

"You didn't have to get up to tell me bye." Rhys shuffled his backpack on his shoulder and fidgeted to look engaged, but his eyes were downcast at the hardwood floor.

"I did, Rhys." Something in her tone caught his attention, and his gaze lifted to hers. "I hope it's a very boring shift," she teased in reference to her accident taking place during his last shift.

"Me too." He forced a smile and even stepped forward to give her a hug before leaving.

"You're the only person I've ever met who can be in two places at once," she told him in a patient voice.

"What does that mean?"

"At the exact moment you are here giving me this amazing hug, you are also a million miles away."

"I'm so sorry, Maree. I—"

"I don't want to make you sorry, Rhys," she interrupted.

He didn't know what to say to that. Instead of speaking, he just tightened his hold, hugging her to him a little closer.

———

*D*id he also sense that this was more than just a simple hug before a routine day?

Sometime during the night, Maree had acknowledged to herself that he was sliding back into his default mode, the one that convinced him that it was his fault when bad things happened to the people he loved.

She'd decided that this time she would be the one to take a step back.

She'd convinced herself that this was the best way to guard her heart until he was able to release the guilt and remorse that he felt for tragedies that were beyond his control, until he was ready to live a full life, facing whatever may come. Good and bad. Together.

She'd learned to maneuver pretty well with the crutch and leg immobilizer. She'd even mastered the mechanics to make her way up and down stairs…good leg up first, bad leg down first. She told herself that she would enjoy being in her own space, alone for the weekend before her surgery on Monday, so as soon as Rhys left for work, Maree called Landry for a ride to her studio.

Twenty-four hours later, Rhys returned home from work, only to find an empty house and a note that read, *"Thank you, Rhys — for everything! You have my heart. Always. —Maree"*

26

When it rains, it pours.
Proverb

*T*he arsonist was stepping up his game, Maree was gone, his world was crumbling, and he couldn't seem to stop the avalanche from coming. He sat on the couch in the dark, silent room, not knowing how to move forward.

A few hours later, his cell phone startled him awake. Rhys was needed back at the firehouse.

It was technically his day off, but the station was stretched thin, so he'd put his name on a call list in hopes that a little extra time out of the house would clear his thoughts.

He'd never expected her to be gone when he returned, but now that she had left, he was extra glad to be called in. The house was too quiet; it felt dull. Without her there, the air was lifeless. She'd taken all the positive energy with her, and his home now felt like a prison cell.

As he walked back out to his truck, he texted Maree.

- Headed back to work. Another possible arson fire. Looks like the same guy. Again. You OK?

- I'm good. Thank you for checking on me.

- I left the door unlocked for you.

- That's okay — I'm all set here.

Rhys didn't know what to type next. He froze like a deer in the headlights, knowing that three dots flashed on her screen, indicating that he was there but silent. She was waiting for him. He was still staring at the blinking cursor on his own screen when she sent one more message.

- Be safe, Rhys.

When he pulled into the station, all hands were on deck.

He parked, grabbed his backpack, and hustled in for a quick briefing.

"Our bug has upped the ante," the fire chief briefed those coming in voluntarily to help out. "We've got two crews out on fires that mimic what we believe to be an arsonist in the county. But these two calls both came from in town. We appreciate—"

Before he could thank the extra workers for giving up their day off, the sirens went off again.

"Ten-forty-one, code one. Multiple parties reporting smoke from structures in the alley along the 100 block of Main Street, directly across from the courthouse," the dispatcher announced over the speaker system.

Upped the ante, indeed. Their arsonist had just set fire to occupied structures. Structures that were on the same block as Maree's shop.

There was no time to think. For that, Rhys was thankful.

I have had worse partings, but none that so
Gnaws at my mind still. Perhaps it is roughly
Saying what God alone could perfectly show—
How selfhood begins with a walking away,
And love is proved in the letting go.
"Walking Away" by Cecil Day-Lewis

"Maree, are you at home?"

"Hi, Mrs. Dawsey. How are you?" Maree was surprised to receive a call from the dear woman who owned the candy shop on the corner of her block.

"Oh, well, I'm a little worried. There is a strange-looking fellow in our alley. Have you noticed? He seemed disoriented at first, stumbling and such. I thought maybe he'd been drinking or maybe was on some drug or something. Then he began sorting through the trash bins," she relayed.

It wasn't at all what she'd expected to hear; Maree was startled to attention.

"No, ma'am, I didn't notice. That does sound strange. You stay put in your shop, and I'll go out on the balcony to see if he's still there. Maybe lock your doors if you're there alone without any customers right now, okay?" Maree didn't want to alarm her, but Mrs. Dawsey knew every person in Green Hills. If she didn't recognize someone rifling through the alley, there was a definite cause for concern.

"Maree! Maree, can you still hear me?" Mrs. Dawsey started calling out to her. "Maree, he just started a fire in the big dumpster!" Her tone was both anxious and flustered.

"Okay, Mrs. Dawsey, listen closely. I'm going to hang up and call 911. Please go out your front door right now. I'll meet you across the street by the courthouse."

"Oh no, he's started another one on the pile of wood crates behind the pub."

"Go now, Mrs. Dawsey," Maree instructed, trying to sound firm without being too harsh.

She hung up the phone and dialed emergency response as she grabbed her purse and crutch and began the arduous chore of hobbling down the stairs that led to the shop. If someone was in the alley setting fires, she didn't think it was a good idea to join them. Instead, she would go out the glass door of her storefront and find Mrs. Dawsey to be sure she was okay as well.

By the time she one-footed it down the stairs and made her way across the street, the fire engines were already pulling into the alley — one of the benefits to a small town: everything was only a few minutes away from everything else.

There was quite a commotion on the lawn of the courthouse.

Being early afternoon, the stores along the block were fairly empty, so the business owners and the few customers they'd been helping were all lined up, staring at the front of the buildings, conjecturing about exactly what was going on in the alley.

"Mrs. Dawsey, are you okay?" Maree asked, making her way to the elderly woman, who was standing beside one of the reading benches. Maree plopped down onto it after wearing herself out on the stairs and trek over.

"Yes, dear, I'm fine, fine. But are you? I didn't expect to find you home after your accident. I'm so glad I called. Oh, just think of what could have happened!"

Her kind neighbor and friend was shaking with worry, so Maree reached her left hand out to rest on top of Mrs. Dawsey's wrist. Maree knew firsthand that a gentle, reassuring touch could be very calming; she also knew exactly how helpful human contact could be.

"Let's not go down that path," she said, redirecting Mrs. Dawsey's panic. "It looks like everyone got out unharmed, and the fire station responded very quickly. I bet they've already got it under control."

Just then, three firefighters walked around the end of the buildings and toward the waiting crowd. Maree recognized the fire chief from when they'd met at the Fireman's Ball.

The second firefighter was Harleigh Steele, who Rhys had mentioned was a fabulous cook. Maree recognized her from speaking to her in passing at the local yoga studio out by the lake, but she had never learned her name to connect the dots of who Harleigh was.

Maree was reminded how connected the folks of Green Hills were, how lives and relationships overlapped here, and how good that felt.

The third firefighter was Rhys.

He was headed straight for her, and he did not look happy.

The warm, neighborly feeling she'd had at realizing his coworker was her casual acquaintance dissipated at the icy look in his eyes. She oomphed her way to standing; she did not want to be sitting down or looking frail as he approached.

"Did y'all catch him?" Maree asked with a degree of hope and belief. By the tense set of Rhys's jaw, she guessed that he was not sharing her optimism.

"No, but we did put out the two small starters he'd placed in the dumpster and the woodpile. Both were intended to slow burn, producing more smoke than flames, but that doesn't make them any less dangerous. Especially in an area of compact buildings that are all connected like the storefronts. Are you okay?" He was still riled up, but she saw him calming by degrees as they spoke.

"Yes, thank you. Rhys, this is Mrs. Evelyn Dawsey, she owns the candy shop there on the corner." She tried to pull Mrs. Dawsey into the conversation, and she wasn't too proud to admit that she was positioning the sweet woman to be a buffer for her agitated boyfriend. Or whatever he was. "She's the one who saw the man in the alley and noticed the smoke. She called me to see if I was home, and I called 911."

"It's very nice to meet you, Mrs. Dawsey," he said and nodded in greeting. "You did a great job when you saw something suspicious. Next time, be sure to call 911 first, okay? And thank you — I sure appreciate your quick thinking to check on Maree."

"Is it safe to return to my candy store?" Mrs. Dawsey asked, beaming under his praise.

"Yes, ma'am. I'll walk you and Maree back over," he decided for everyone.

Mrs. Dawsey chattered like a magpie, telling Rhys everything she had noticed about the man in the alley. Rhys didn't get too far away from her, but Maree was grateful that they went on ahead of her, since she was rather slow on the crutch. By the time she made it to the front door of her quilt studio, he had already seen Mrs. Dawsey to her store and even walked through it to make her feel safe and comfortable.

The short walk from her shop to Maree's turned out to be plenty of time for Rhys's anger to resurface.

"Why didn't you call me, Maree?" For a guy who liked to look down when he was unsure of what to say, he had no problem directing his stern gaze right through her eyes and into her heart.

Why must I love him so much?

"I called 911, Rhys. That's what we all learned to do back in kindergarten, remember?" She was suddenly feeling a little testy herself.

"You just left," he said, switching gears on her in a heartbeat.

"Yes, I—" She blinked a few times to catch up, but he stopped her before she could explain herself.

"I can't protect you if you're gone."

"Rhys, you've taken the very best care of me this week. I can't tell you how much that has mea—"

"Then let me take care of you now," he interrupted again, obviously still antsy and agitated.

"No," she replied.

"Because I can't keep you safe." His words were flat and defeated, said as both a question and a statement of fact.

"No, you can't, Rhys."

His body flinched, as though she had physically struck him. Pain rippled through his eyes; he visibly fought for a breath.

With a nod, he made a move to walk out.

"Rhys!" She grabbed his arm as he stormed by. "You aren't supposed to keep me safe."

He was dumbfounded by her words.

"You are this incredible superhero — you literally rescue people on a daily basis. But, Rhys, I don't need you to be my savior. I've walked away from three car accidents in my life. Major ones. The first one killed my parents. The second one diverted my future to this amazing little town. And by everything that I can tell from all the hushed whispers that no one wants me to hear, I should not have survived this third one. You had nothing to do with any of those. Not the losses and not the blessings that have come from those tragedies. You are not personally responsible for guaranteeing my safety. In fact, you can't. Not because you are not able, but because that is not your role in my life. When bad things happen, it's not a direct result of your doing — or *not* doing — anything." Maree was on a roll, but she paused for a moment to tamp down her temper. And to let all she had just said sink in.

"Rhys, I love that you can be a role model for little kids, a guardian angel to those you help," she went on. "But I'm not looking for a hero. I'm looking for a partner. A man to love me and experience life with me. A champion to celebrate my wins, but also an anchor, someone who is there to hold me and grieve through the losses."

He was speechless, his head hanging in defeat.

"Rhys, look at me. Please," she asked. "Rhys, I love you. I have for a long time now. And I know that you love me, too. But we can't work if I'm merely a damsel in distress who you feel compelled to protect. I can't live on a pedestal under a glass dome that you can watch over to keep me safe. Life is messy. It's scary and it's hard and it's painful. And every bit of it is worth the risk because love is so much more than any one of those difficult emotions. It's more than all of them put together. That kind of love makes every day a little brighter. It makes colors more brilliant and laughter more contagious. It's wonderful. It's all-encompassing. And it's a gift."

She stepped closer, placing her right hand over his heart.

"Rhys, that's the kind of love I want. That's the kind of love we can have. Together."

You learn eventually that, while there are no villains,
there are no heroes either.
And until you make the final discovery
that there are only human beings,
who are therefore all the more fascinating,
you are liable to miss something.
Paul Gallico

*M*aree leaned into Rhys, grasping his uniform and pulling him down to brush a slow kiss on his cheek. She paused for a split second, as if savoring the moment, before turning away. Using that crutch and her determination, she made her way into her office and closed the door.

Feeling effectively dismissed, he stayed planted in place for a long breath and then left.

By then, most of the spectators on the courthouse lawn had scattered, so Rhys walked back around to the alley. Since he was not on a shift, he wanted to see where he could be most helpful, either here pitching in with cleanup or back at the station on standby for another call.

"Larsen, that was good work. If you hadn't noticed that tinderbox smoking under Mrs. Dawsey's awning, the building might've caught." The chief clapped him on the back as he joined the investigative crew.

"I was thinking he might have set it first, up close to the building where she couldn't see him from her windows upstairs. Once she noticed him rummaging through the trash, I'm certain she didn't take her eyes off of him. At least until Maree told her to leave through the front," Rhys shared.

"Good news is that she gave us a detailed description. Now we know we are looking for a male, medium to large build. She suspected him to be older, maybe by the way he moved or his posture," Davis added.

"What about cameras? Anything here in the alley?" Rhys asked.

"Nah." Davis shook his head.

"Green Hills is known for being quaint and quiet," the chief explained. "People say it has a sense of magic about it, that it exists in an invisible cloak of kindness. The townsfolk are very supportive of one another; it would never occur to them to install security devices to monitor their friends. Hell, they rarely even lock doors around here, just in case someone needs to get inside while they're away."

"Makes it a great place to live," Rhys nodded, "but it doesn't help catch criminals."

"Very true," the chief agreed. "Let's get back to the station to write up the reports. Rhys, you can ride with me."

Rhys and Davis exchanged looks. The chief had something on his mind, and that something was focused on Rhys.

Rhys gathered equipment, replacing things where they went on the engine and in the chief's truck. Then he took one last walk around the alley, cataloging where everything was placed, imagining the steps their arsonist had taken.

"Hop in," his boss instructed.

"Yes, sir." Rhys was glad the drive back to the station was less than four minutes.

But Chief Everett didn't put the truck into gear.

"How's your girl?" he asked Rhys. "She's sure been through a lot."

"Maree is…" Rhys paused, not sure how to answer. "She's unbelievable. She has to be in pain, and I know she's nervous about the knee surgery scheduled for Monday. But she just keeps moving forward. She is so strong, stronger than I knew a person could be. No matter what happens to her, she keeps going. And always with that damn smile. But it doesn't appear that she's *my* girl."

"I can see where the smile could be a problem for you." He grinned at Rhys. "She really lights up a room. My wife loves her work. Green Hills is quite a quilting community; Maree fits in really well here. Lots of ladies love to spend time in that studio Maree's always working on, checking out new fabric and visiting with her. They say she's wonderful — welcoming and kind. A real treasure."

"Well, she just kicked me out of that welcoming quilting studio. Said she doesn't want a hero, that she doesn't need a savior," Rhys said, looking out his side window. His voice was low, flat, and grim.

"Hmm." The older man thought for a second. "Did she tell you what she does want? And what she needs?"

"She wants it all, Chief," he said, looking over at his mentor. Rhys was perplexed, and the pain he felt was palpable. "Big love, a full life, every bit of the fairy tale."

"So, give it to her," the chief answered, turning the key to start the truck's engine.

Rhys grunted. If only it were that easy.

"You love her?" the chief assumed.

Rhys nodded his head without hesitation, then looked down at the floorboard.

"Then grab on to what she's offering, son. Those blessings are precious and not to be ignored."

"But what if something happens to her? My family—"

"I know, son." Rhys's head popped up. "I did my due diligence before offering you a job. I know what happened to your brothers. I know what it did to your folks. I know what it has done to you."

Rhys felt empty, like a fragile shell trying to balance a huge weight without cracking.

"That loss was devastating. It was huge. Something that immense shapes you. It has made you the man sitting right here: a brilliant firefighter; an honorable person; a strong, devout friend. That type of tragedy changes you, for sure. But it doesn't curse you, Rhys." He paused again. It allowed time for Rhys to truly hear his words. "Think about that, son. You are not bad luck. You are not a detriment to the people who love you." He put the truck into gear. "So let her love you. Love her back. And cherish every single moment you have together." With that, he pulled out of the alley and drove to the firehouse without saying another word.

29

Good things come to us just when we need them the
most, like an angel throwing us a life-preserver before
we go under the waters of despair.
Bryant McGill

He'd felt lost, floating through time. The hours between arriving home after the incident downtown Saturday afternoon and leaving for the hospital Monday morning were agonizing.

Rhys had worked Sunday. It had been a slow day, which was both good and bad. Good in that there had not been any fire calls. Bad in that he had a hard time keeping his mind off his worries when there wasn't anything that needed to be done. He was a pro at switching off personal thoughts and worries when a call came in, but even Rhys felt challenged to keep his mind right during those twenty-four hours.

He'd stayed in touch with Max. He had wanted to check on Maree every minute of the weekend; he needed to know that someone was with her leading up to the surgery.

He couldn't go to her, yet he couldn't keep her away. She

was on his mind and in his thoughts continuously. He replayed their conversation in her shop and the chief's advice, over and over and *over* again. It was true that he'd felt cursed. He felt like there was something wrong with him, something that caused the people he loved to leave. Not just leave, but suffer. He was the common thread, so he'd determined long ago that it must be his fault.

He understood that bad things happen to good people from time to time. But every single person he'd loved had died a tragic death. Accepting that those things could not be avoided felt like the coward's way out, like not owning up to his role and responsibility in the world. It was why he'd worked so hard — never ceasing to get better, never relenting to *be* better — to be there when others needed help. Needed saving. Needed a hero. If that was not who he was supposed to be, then what — *who* — was he?

He didn't have the answer. But he also didn't have the emotional strength to stay home, recycling these questions, mentally beating himself to a pulp.

On Monday, he was at the hospital, his head hanging in his hands, sitting in a chair by the admission area when Max and M'Kenzee brought Maree in midmorning. He'd come straight from work when his shift ended, just waiting in that chair since 8 a.m.

————

*R*hys might've drifted off to sleep; he must not have heard them arrive. He was as still as a statue, and looked as bleak and desolate as frozen tundra.

Max leaned down to beg in Maree's ear as they entered through the sliding doors. "M, please, for the sake of all men everywhere, toss him a lifeline."

She looked over at Rhys with a small — even forgiving — smile.

M'Kenzee grunted a harumph, not interested in a formal introduction, and looking at him with a very *un*forgiving frown.

Max and M'Kenzee left Maree balanced with her crutch, standing in front of him while they walked on to the admissions counter to get her checked in. She reached out a hand to touch his hair, ever so lightly.

Rhys dropped his hands from his face and sat up straighter, but he left his eyes shut. He took a deep breath to soak up her touch. "Thank you for being here, Rhys," she said softly. "Come on back with us."

Without a word, he opened his eyes, stood, and moved to walk beside her.

30

The future belongs to those
who believe in the beauty of their dreams.
Eleanor Roosevelt

*A*s predicted, the procedure took several hours and included a partial knee replacement, a prosthetic kneecap, and the reattachment of two ligaments. The surgeon also cleaned out torn fragments of meniscus, cartilage, and bone. Rhys refused to leave, no matter how much M'Kenzee tried to push him out the door.

Seeing Maree in the hospital, watching her go through this surgery and the post-op and the recovery was — and would continue to be — torture. The only thing worse would have been not seeing her at all. He wouldn't leave.

The surgeon told them that Maree had to stay a night or two for them to monitor her vitals and manage pain, so the nurses brought a pillow and blankets for the couch in the private hospital room that Max had arranged. They camped out there, waiting for her to be returned to them.

While Max watched game film on his tablet and M'Kenzee

edited photos on her computer, Rhys rested his eyes for a minute. He was still sitting on the couch, dozing — conked out, actually — when they brought Maree to the room after being in recovery for about an hour.

———

"*T*here she is," Max said when they rolled her in. M'Kenzee had never heard his voice so soft and gentle; it was laced with gratitude for the successful operation. Maree was still very groggy and half-asleep.

"Hmm," was all she managed in response.

"That's okay, honey," M'Kenzee told her as she set her laptop to the side and stepped forward to help straighten Maree's hospital gown and smooth out the heated blankets piled upon her gurney. "You go on back to sleep." M'Kenzee continued to tuck her in, thinking that Maree had followed her instructions.

"So pretty," Maree mumbled.

M'Kenzee smiled at her nonsense, smoothed out her hair, and let the nurse reconnect her electrodes and set the in-room monitors. Maree was still whispering something, but M'Kenzee couldn't make out the words.

"Honey, you need to rest; I know it's confusing right now, but once the anesthesia runs its course, you'll be right as rain," M'Kenzee soothed.

"No," Maree blurted out, sounding panicked and causing everyone to jump, including Rhys, who had been startled out of his sleep. In an instant, he was standing beside her bed.

Maree's face was turned toward M'Kenzee, so she tried to smile and look reassuring, just in case Maree opened her eyes. But when Rhys started to reach out toward Maree, as if to stroke her face and hair, M'Kenzee glared in his direction until he dropped his hand back to his side.

"Go back to sleep, M," Max interjected.

"This is a dream... If I wake up, I'll lose him again; it hurts so bad... I can't sleep; please don't make me, Max, it's too hard. It hurts so bad," Maree moaned and mumbled, opening her eyes to look directly at her big sister. "Please; I love him, Kenz... So pretty; he loves me... Don't wake me up... Please let me dream. Please." Tears escaped her eyes, in turn making tears escape M'Kenzee's, too. "The dream," she added. "He's so pretty." Closing her eyes, she drifted into sleep.

The doctor walked in at that moment, saving everyone from sorting through the litany of confusion that had them frozen stock-still.

———

*M*ax and M'Kenzee stepped up to face the doctor; Rhys moved to take Maree's right hand. His left hand went to the top of her forehead, smoothing back her curls. The gentle touch woke her just enough to turn her head his way. She smiled up at him, her expression quite dreamy as she was still heavily under the influence of the drugs. He simply smiled right back.

"As I mentioned at our last visit, Maree will be in the hospital for a day, maybe two, but I am really pleased with how we put everything back together. It's a long recovery, but she's young, in great shape, and very strong. I expect her to be as good as new."

"Thanks, Doc," Max pumped the doctor's hand with emotion and took the lead on receiving the post-op orders. "What do we need to do?"

"Well, this first month will be very uneventful. I see you have planned for someone to stay in the room with her tonight; that's good in case she wakes up disoriented. Once she's home, she will stay there for four weeks. A nurse will stop by each day, the physical therapist will come by three times a week, and I'll be by about every ten to twelve days. The collarbone will continue to heal itself, so while it's cumbersome, it won't negatively affect her progress. In four weeks, she can begin to get out as she feels well enough. She'll be busy with physical therapy, and by the four-month mark, she'll be released to do whatever she wants…run, swim, dance, tennis, basketball, whatever. It will continue to heal and restrengthen for another twelve to fourteen months. Within eighteen months, I expect she will have a perfect knee and enjoy a normal, active life."

"Wow!" M'Kenzee exhaled. Tears streamed down her face; Rhys figured that this time the tears were in joy instead of sadness.

The doctor smiled broadly at the group and their happiness. "So, who's staying tonight?"

A bold "me!" boomeranged at him from all three of them in unison.

Max and M'Kenzee both turned to look directly at Rhys.

The doctor looked from person to person. "Well, whoever stays, just keep an eye on her when she wakes, which might be on and off throughout the night and next day. She will be pretty out of it for the rest of today. We don't want her to try and shift her weight, and certainly not stand without trained assistance, until we know that the nerve block has completely worn off. If she gets too agitated, we can attach tether straps to the bed to keep her still, but that's a last resort. Call the nurse for anything and everything, and they'll be by regularly to check on you. They have orders to call me with any questions or concerns, no matter the time."

"I'll keep her safe," Rhys said from where he still gazed into her eyes, holding her hand and her head at her bedside.

31

Older siblings...
The only people who will pick on you
for their own entertainment and
beat up anyone else who tries.
Author unknown

"*R*hys, can we speak to you in the hall for a sec?" Max asked between clenched teeth once the surgeon had left Maree's room. The strain of Max's voice broke through Rhys's trance. He looked up at Max, then M'Kenzee, and saw the steam coming off them both.

He was officially in trouble.

Looking back down at Maree, her eyes now closed and sleeping softly, he brushed his lips over her forehead and pushed away from her bed railing to follow them out of the room.

"You don't get to do this again," M'Kenzee spat at Rhys.

"It's time," Max commanded at the same moment. M'Kenzee turned on her big brother with daggers in her eyes.

"No!" she argued emphatically. "You don't get to be on his

side, Max. He has trampled all over her for weeks and weeks. He plays like she matters—"

"She *does* matter," Rhys interjected with his own dose of anger.

But M'Kenzee wasn't to be deterred.

"...and then pushes her away. Over and over. Leaving a broken shell of our incredible little sister. He does NOT get to do that again." She was a picture of defiance, hands fisted at her sides, chest lifted in strength, eyes shooting darts at both men despite the fact that they towered over her tiny, five-foot-nothing self.

"She's right about that, Rhys. It's one thing for you to be here for the surgery, lending support. But it's something else to entrust you with her care again. I know you love her. I see it, I feel it, and I know you do, too. I'm not sure what has you so spooked; Maree says it's none of my business, and that you're worth waiting for, no matter how long it takes you to get *un*-spooked. Rhys, it's time. Now."

Rhys gave one nod of agreement.

M'Kenzee huffed back into Maree's room with a dramatic "*grrrr.*" Max took a deep breath. He closed his eyes for an extra split second while Rhys waited without moving a muscle. The he exhaled and gestured for Rhys to go first as they followed M'Kenzee. Rhys thanked God that the confrontation was over.

Rhys understood their concerns. He'd dropped the ball a few times. Even when he had wanted to be all that she needed and deserved, he'd fumbled. And in all likelihood, there would be times in their lives together that he would fall short again. But he'd never left the field. He knew now that he never would. He never could.

The moment Maree had smoothed his hair back in the admissions lobby, the moment he'd felt her touch, something had finally clicked into place.

He'd known that the next few hours, the next few days, and

the next few months would be hard. She was in for a fight, and he would be the one to help her through. Not fix it for her. Not remove the pain and challenges. He would be the person to cheer her through the challenges, to take her mind off the pain. Not a hero, not a savior. Her partner, just like she wanted.

He'd looked in her eyes before her surgery and seen their life together. After that, he couldn't envision the world any other way.

That had not been the time for declarations. She'd had enough on her mind going into the surgery, and honestly, he wouldn't have expected her to believe him. Over the past couple of days, his actions had spoken louder than his words could in the few minutes they'd had before she was taken to anesthesia. But he'd felt it, the shift.

He'd never fully recover from losing his family, especially from losing his little brothers in that fire. He'd never stop worrying that the people he loved could be hurt in some way, never stop feeling responsible for their safety, but his talk with Chief Everett had helped.

Rhys had not known that the chief hired him already knowing about his failure to save his brothers, his failure to help his parents. The department had recommended Rhys, and the city of Green Hills had approved him to be a fire-fighter, someone they trusted and depended upon in the worst of emergencies, in the most dire of situations. Surely, if he was cursed — a bad omen — they wouldn't have taken a chance on him. The chief and Davis and his fellow firefighters would not have welcomed him if he was a detriment to their lives. They believed in him.

And so did Maree. He'd never doubted that, only himself. His worth and his abilities.

Being at the hospital during her surgery had helped, too. He'd had no control over what was done in that operating room. He'd had to have faith that Maree would be okay, that the doctors and nurses would take care of her. He'd even prayed that she would have a successful surgery and the smoothest possible recovery afterwards.

He'd been a little dumbfounded to acknowledge that after he'd thought that prayer, he'd had a sense that it was being answered. A wave of peace had washed over him — so much so that he'd even relaxed enough during the hours she was gone to rest and catch up on some desperately needed sleep. He'd closed his eyes with assurance that it was all going to be okay.

The foundation holding the walls up around his heart was crumbling. The walls were coming down. She'd done that for him.

He was honest enough to concede that after ten years of fear and anger and disbelief, he had a lot of work to do to slay his demons. For the first time, though, he clearly saw that he could — and would — defeat them.

He'd ask Chief Everett for guidance; his mentor was a smart man, and Rhys was suddenly eager to grow, to put this chapter of pain behind him. Not to forget it — he would never forget — but to move past it, as Maree had been able to do after the tragedy of losing her parents.

He'd open up to Max, who had also lost a great deal and figured out how to be a leader for his family without shutting out the world. He'd continue to build his friendship with Davis; Rhys letting his guard down around him had been monumental and a balm to his emotional scars.

Best of all, Rhys would lean on Maree. Not just protect her and keep her safe, but be there for her during the peaks and the valleys of life. And he would allow her — rely on her — to do the same for him. He was too human to never mess up, so he knew he'd blunder and make mistakes. He'd likely still drive her crazy with safety precautions and checking on her when he wasn't needed. Accepting that truth took the weight of perfection off his shoulders; it was a smothering burden lifted.

He figured it — this new mindset and approach to life — would be a process, a transition that would take time. But he knew with all certainty that whatever time they had together was worth *whatever* the future held. That certainty was like a breath of fresh air, filling his lungs after suffocating in stale smoke for too long. Even the room felt brighter and more vibrant, as if a veil or a barrier to the world had been lifted.

Would the future be easy? Would life always be safe? No.

The only guarantee was that they'd love one another every single second.

For Rhys, it was settled. From here until forever.

32

The greatest gift is a portion of thyself.
Ralph Waldo Emerson

"A lot of stars tonight?" she asked quietly.

He whipped around from where he was standing between her bed and the window; he'd been looking out into the night sky. His eyes searched her face for signs of strain or pain. Seeing none, his eyes traveled over her from head to foot. He was relieved to see that she hadn't tried to move while he was stargazing, thinking of her. Of them.

"Let me get the nurse," he offered. "A lady named Rachel is on shift for the night, and you've got her all to yourself. She stopped in about twenty minutes ago, but I talked her out of waking you up just yet. She said it's important that we stay ahead of the pain; are you in pain?"

"Rhys, take a breath," she consoled him. "I'm okay."

"Okay," he breathed with a nod.

"I was afraid you weren't really here. That I'd dreamed you again."

Rhys didn't know what to say in return.

He was once again saved from the awkward moment by medical staff. There was a light knock on the door as it opened, and Rachel came in with a cart and a clipboard and a big bright smile. "I could tell by your monitors that you had woken up," she chatted. "How and what do you feel? Fuzzy, confused? Nausea, hunger? Thirsty? Soreness, pain? I'm Rachel, your nurse for the night; it's a pleasure to meet you, and I'll do my best to get you out of this fancy resort as quickly as possible." She ended her rambling stream with a wink as she tweaked machines, read printouts, and moved around the room like a frenzied wood ant.

Rhys stepped back to stay out of the way.

"Keep backing out, good-looking," she bossed him kindly. "She's mine for the next thirty or so minutes. Take this time to shower down in the family lounge, grab dinner in the cafeteria, or jog the halls to work off steam. Whatever floats your boat; just don't come back in this room until you see the door wide open to welcome you."

"Yes, ma'am," he answered, trying to get close enough to Maree to tell her bye.

"She'll still be here when you return; get going, handsome," she said as she put a hand to his shoulder, gently pushing him out of the room and closing the door behind him.

Once out the door, he wasn't sure what to do with himself.

He was still in his jeans and the GHFD t-shirt that he'd thrown on after his shift that morning in a rush to get to the hospital, too afraid to miss her before surgery to tarry long enough to shower at the station.

Home it was. If he hurried, he could shower, grab a Dopp kit for the night, and still hit Green Hills' version of fast food: a fabulous hole-in-the-wall restaurant called The Three-Toed Turtle that served greasy fried foods right next to organic veggies and green smoothies. He'd call ahead to make the stop as speedy as possible. He didn't even have to go in to pick it up;

instead, he'd pull up to the drive-in where waitstaff still delivered orders wearing rollerblades and old-fashioned skates. A cheeseburger and fries for himself and a strawberry shake to share with Maree sounded just about perfect.

Max called his cell while he was driving back to the hospital. "Hello?"

"Damn it, Rhys, why does it sound like you're driving instead of sitting next to Maree? I believed in you! What the hell are you doing?"

"Rachel, the night nurse, kicked me out for thirty minutes. She said I wasn't allowed. I guess she's helping Maree to get cleaned up, use the restroom, that kind of stuff. I just picked up a milkshake for Maree, and I'm pulling into the hospital parking lot as we speak."

"So, she's awake? She's good?" Max asked, shifting gears on a dime.

"Yes. I think," Rhys tried to answer. "She'd just woken up when the nurse burst in, shoving me out the door within two minutes. But, yeah, she seemed pretty great when she woke up," he finished with deep praise in his voice.

"Did you get her a strawberry shake from Triple T's?"

"Of course," Rhys answered. That had felt like a test — had he passed?

"You still want to take the night shift?"

"I'm taking *every* shift, Max. I've already called the chief, and he approved my leave for as long as we need it, a full month off, if necessary."

"I want this for y'all, Rhys. I really do, man, but if you need me — or anyone — for some support, for a break, for anything, you gotta call. You hear me?"

Concern filled Max's voice, and Rhys appreciated the belief that Max was showing in him.

"Of course, Max," Rhys reassured him. "We'll stay in touch every day, I promise."

After a pause, and remembering his vow to open up more to the important people in his life, Rhys added, "Thank you, for trusting me with the most precious gift I've ever known."

"Just be sure to treasure it," Max demanded. Rhys wasn't sure which gift Max thought he meant — for allowing him to be there for Maree, for giving him another chance, or for Maree, herself — but Rhys understood that ultimately Max was demanding that he cherish all three.

"I will." Rhys's tone was emphatic.

"Well, since you're good, I'm going to take off for Kansas City tonight. I'll call Maree once I'm on the road. Just so you know, M'Kenzee is not as inclined to trust you as I am, so I would expect her to be around, doubting you, and driving you crazy. Maree will love it. You will not."

"I get it. I've got some work to do there."

"Well, if you're lucky, she'll get an assignment and be off to far-off regions of the world snapping her photos," Max laughed.

"Either way, I've got this. I'm good."

Even Rhys could hear a new level of confidence and certainty in his voice, one that brought a measure of peace — and a measure of happiness — he'd never known.

33

Life is a balance of holding on and letting go.
Rumi

$\mathcal{R}$hys was standing guard outside Maree's door when it finally opened, and Rachel emerged. "She's asleep, but she made me promise that you'd let her know when I let you back in."

"How is she?" he asked, clearly worried about her patient.

"Exactly how we'd expect after having her leg surgically put back together today, with a few shiny new metal parts thrown in for good measure," she confirmed.

"Can you be a little more specific? Is she in pain?"

"Yes, some." She was direct with her answer, and Rhys appreciated it. "I have increased the drip on her pain meds for the night. We'll try to back that off again in the morning. Our goal is to wean her off the IV pain medication and switch to pills by early afternoon. She was able to get up and out of bed, which is important for circulation and recovery, but it also wore her out — again, to be expected. We got her bathed, which goes a long way to feeling better, but it also reminds her of how dependent she will be for the foreseeable future. That's a tough prognosis for any young person used to doing for oneself. I've only spent thirty" —she paused, looking at her watch to be precise— "actually forty-four minutes with her, but I can see that she is strong and determined; she's going to be just fine," she concluded with a smile and a friendly wink, then walked away without waiting for Rhys to respond.

Oh, thank God. A wave of nerves trembled through his body. He had to wait just a second. *Just breathe*, he reminded himself. The nurse had given him such a great update. But all of a sudden, he was shaking. Just standing in her doorway, watching her sleep, and shaking. *Damn adrenaline.* Usually, he controlled it. It made him stronger, faster, and better in a crisis. Right then, it was backfiring.

Rachel must've seen his back and shoulders rise and fall in rapid succession. She made her way from the nurses' station back to Maree's room. "It's okay to let it out now," she assured him with a gentle hand on his back. "I understand she's been through a lot. It's okay to let it all sink in now that you know she's going to be just fine."

Something tickled his cheek. He raised a hand to it, his fingers coming away wet. Tears were leaking from both eyes — the second time now.

"Come on." Rachel coaxed him into the room, pulling a chair right up to Maree's bed. "Malt or milkshake?" She indicated the forgotten jumbo-sized cup in his hand. "Yum — strawberry from the Turtle. Good choice! I'll put it in the freezer until she's ready for it."

She took the ice cream, pushing him into the chair and lifting his now-empty hand to Maree's. "Let her know you're here; she's going to be fuzzy and a little loopy, but I promised." With that, she left the room, closing the door softly behind her.

"Hey, gorgeous," Rhys whispered, half-afraid to wake her, but also desperate to see her open her eyes. His fingers were stroking hers, his left hand going back to brush the curls from her forehead. "Maree, I'm here."

"A dream?" she murmured, not yet opening her eyes.

"Not a dream," he answered. "I'm here, and I'm not leaving this room until you do. I promise."

"Hold me?" she stammered. "Please," she added when he hesitated.

"I don't want to hurt you, Maree," he cringed, hating to say no to anything she asked.

"Mmm," she mumbled, "please?"

"Okay, just until we get caught, and I get in trouble," he gave in, oh-so-gently lowering his weight onto the mattress along her right side and far, far away from the splinted and bandaged left leg.

He was holding himself rigid to be sure that he didn't cause her any pain at all, but she immediately snuggled into his chest.

He remained still — stiff as a board — and his body was starting to cramp when Rachel came in to check vitals and machines a while later. "You're not going to hurt her, honey. Just relax and be close to your girl."

My girl, he thought.

That was all it took.

Rhys exhaled, letting his muscles release. His left arm was now pillowing her neck, and his right hand reached up to envelop hers. That was how M'Kenzee, Miss Sadie, Landry, Janie Lyn, and Davis found them the next morning.

34

Breakfast is everything.
The beginning, the first thing.
It is the mouthful that is the commitment
to a new day, a continuing life.
A. A. Gill

"*J* do *not* want to like him," M'Kenzee professed. She was still peeved and defensive.

"If it's not worth fighting for, it's not worth having," Sadie observed.

"Hmph," M'Kenzee rebutted.

"Hey, guys," Maree whispered, eyes open and face smiling.

"Hi, sweetie," M'Kenzee said, matching Maree's smile with an even larger one. And effectively ignoring Rhys. "We brought breakfast from the outside," she said in a stage whisper.

"And your favorite quilt to make it feel like home," Janie Lyn added, unfolding the quilt hanging over her arm, the one Sadie had given her as a housewarming present when Maree moved into the apartment above her design studio. It was the quilt that Sadie had made while taking care of Sam, the same one that had comforted Maree again and again over the past two years.

"Is that food I smell?" Rachel came bursting in, tsking.

"Busted," Davis laughed.

"All right, Romeo, give me my patient, and take all these visitors right down to the family lounge," Rachel ordered Rhys, who was blinking himself into awareness of the suddenly chaotic room.

"I—" he tried to argue, holding fast to Maree. To no avail.

"Do as you're told. This angel deserves a little privacy to start her day. I'll bring her to you in ten minutes." With that she shooed them all out (with the exception of Landry who, as a doctor-in-training at this hospital, had talked her way into staying to help).

"I sure do like that nurse," Sadie acknowledged as they walked down the hall.

This time it was Rhys's turn to answer with a "hmph."

Secretly, M'Kenzee smiled, pleased to see Rhys disgruntled.

Once in the family lounge, Rhys headed for the restroom, Davis pushed three small tables together and scattered chairs around them, and M'Kenzee and Sadie began setting out the pastries, scrambled eggs, bacon, and fruit that Sadie had packaged straight from her kitchen before Landry drove her to town that morning.

———

True to her word, Rachel rolled Maree to them in nine minutes; Rhys was counting. Rachel parked her at the end of the table with the left leg of the wheelchair lifted and ice bags packed along the brace that protected her knee. Then she handed Maree an extra blanket and gladly accepted the homemade blueberry muffin that Sadie extended to her with a conspiratorial grin.

Rhys immediately crouched in front of her to be at eye level, raising a hand to brush a finger across her cheek and leaning in to brush a kiss across her lips. "Hi." His voice caressed over her. "You okay?"

Maree answered with glistening eyes and an exuberant nod. He winked at her and stood up to grab a cup of coffee.

———

*J*t did not go unnoticed when Rhys walked right back to her with his cup of coffee as well as a cup of hot tea prepared just the way she loved it. M'Kenzee was willing to give him credit for that.

Nor was it lost on the group that he didn't move beyond Maree's reach, keeping a hand on her at all times…fixing her plate, resting a hand on her right arm or leg, holding her hand, and shaking out the blanket to tuck around her when she shivered involuntarily.

"I think my breakfast is coming back up," M'Kenzee grumbled when Rhys tucked a strand of Maree's hair behind her ear as if they were the only two people in the building.

"Ah, let 'em be," Sadie shushed her, earning the group yet one more *humph* and an unmistakable glower as M'Kenzee tugged on one of her own curls.

Landry was the one to break the spell over Rhys and Maree when she escorted Maree's surgeon into the lounge.

"You've got quite a fan club, Maree," he joked. "Oh wow, thank you," he said as he graciously accepted a muffin and a cup of orange juice.

"The best," she concurred.

"Well, I'm a fan myself, and I'm thrilled to see you up and out of that hospital bed."

"Does that mean I can go home today?"

"Possibly. Even probably, but I can't make any promises until we visit over afternoon rounds. I start those at three o'clock. We will make a decision then."

"Anything particular you want her doing – or not doing – until then?" Rhys asked.

"A little bit of mobility to keep the blood pumping, with a nurse's assistance, of course, plenty of liquids and as much of this delicious food as your stomach can tolerate. Lots of rest. Doctor's orders," he prescribed on his way toward the hallway. "And thanks for the breakfast!"

"You heard him," Sadie said, sending an unspoken message to Rhys who was already gathering up Maree's hot tea, piling some fruit on a paper plate, and grabbing two water bottles.

"Yep," Rhys chimed in, "back to bed." M'Kenzee had noticed that Maree's energy was starting to wane and that her color was not quite as peachy as it had been. Time to break up the party.

――――

*B*y the time they each gave gentle hugs and said their goodbyes, Maree was practically asleep in her wheelchair.

The day nurse, Suzanne, met them at the door to introduce herself and help Maree get back into bed. Maree's eyelids were just too heavy to hold up any longer; she was dozing peacefully before Suzanne had finished her tinkering and charting.

Rhys pulled up a chair next to Maree's bed, laid a hand just above her good knee, and picked up the television remote to find a game to watch on mute. Automatically, Maree's hand covered his, then she took a deep breath and settled deeper into sleep.

Her nap lasted a good two hours. Rhys had noticed that she was starting to grimace a bit as she stirred. Worried that she was in pain, he'd just reached to push the call button when Suzanne entered on her own.

"Maree, can you wake up a little for me?" she asked, efficiently moving IV lines and monitor cords from here to there. "Let's see if you can swallow these pain pills." The nurse rolled the tall tray over the bed. "Water or juice?" she asked as Maree's eyes fluttered open.

————

"*H*mm? Oh, um, juice, I guess," Maree tried to answer through the fogginess in her head.

"Great! Apple, orange, or cranberry?"

"Ummm, let's see." She was still trying to catch up. "Cranberry, please?"

Suzanne was all business. By the time the nurse was finished with her dizzying whirlwind of activity, Maree was fully awake; she'd taken a dose of pain pills, been carted to the bathroom and back, moved to a recliner to sit up for a while, and handed a bowl of red gelatin and a granola bar to snack on.

"Wow," Rhys commented.

"Wow is right," Maree agreed, a little shell-shocked by all the activity.

Then, because neither could hold it in any longer, they both burst out giggling.

35

Humble yourselves, therefore,
under the mighty hand of God
so that at the proper time he may exalt you,
casting all your anxieties on him,
because he cares for you.
I Peter 5:6-7

*I*t felt so good to laugh together. And yet, Maree was understandably cautious. She didn't know what Rhys had figured out since she'd walked away from him at the studio. She didn't realize that he'd had an epiphany, or the power of it.

"Rhys, I think we need to talk," she started.

He nodded his head in agreement and stood up to pace the few steps across the room.

"I appreciate your being here so much, Rhys; it means the world to me."

"There's not anywhere else I want to be."

"But for how long?"

"When you get dismissed — today, tomorrow, whenever — I'd like for you to come back to my house."

"That's not an answer, Rhys," she pointed out.

And she wasn't wrong.

And she deserved more. She deserved all of him.

"Since the moment I saw you, I've been bewitched. You're like a magnet that I'm drawn to by a force of nature. My North Star. But all along, I wasn't sure I could do this, Maree."

———

*T*he worry in his voice was startling to her.

"Do what?"

"This. Us."

"What does that mean, Rhys?" she asked, trying to be patient as he obviously fought and picked his way through this explanation, this landmine. For this — whatever it was to be — to last, he had to get to where she was on his own.

She loved him, and they both knew it.

He loved her, and they both knew it.

For them to continue on together, he had to find a way to be okay with all that knowledge.

This was their moment of truth. This was his opportunity to not only share his fears, but to share his readiness to overcome them, his chance to share in Maree's belief that they would be — were meant to be — together. Maree felt sure that if he could get through this, they could have it all.

"I want to. I want to do this. With you. So much," he strained. "For the last ten years, I have believed that everything I touch — everything I care about — suffers and is eventually broken."

"We've been through this — I simply don't subscribe to that. You're a fireman, Rhys; you save people's loved ones and important pets and meaningful things every single day. Sometimes they can't be saved, and that's a tragedy, but you never stop trying."

He'd stopped pacing, but he was silent, looking down at his hands for so long that she feared that maybe this really was more than he could accept.

"Everything I've ever loved has been destroyed." His voice broke, raw with emotion. "I just keep coming back to the idea that I can't survive that again. Not with you."

"Rhys?" Sympathy filled Maree as Rhys ran his hand through his hair; it looked like something, some fear, was eating him alive from the inside out. But this time he wasn't running. He wasn't hiding from his fear. He was standing here ready to face it together.

"Rhys, look at me. Please?" She sat up taller in the recliner and waited until he lifted his eyes to hers.

"I love you, too," she declared, picking up on the most important part of what he had said and managing to smile through the words.

She paused to let that sink in.

———

*H*e knew that she did. She didn't have an ounce of guile. Her emotions had been clear and present for all to see since the first day they'd seen one another in the produce department.

But making a mental decision to let go of his fear and belief that he brought harm to those he loved was different from actually accomplishing the feat. He'd promised himself he could do it; he'd talked himself through the process. He'd even come up with tangible ways to move forward with Maree and his growing group of friends. Now he had to cross that bridge.

He wanted to believe, but what if…

What if something happened to her?

He searched her eyes, looking for answers. His heart was saying, "Yes, this is the way forward" even as his past was telling him, "No, don't risk her safety." All the while she offered a continuous look of reassurance.

"And I'm right here," she added, stressing each individual word.

Maree lifted her hand toward him in a gesture for him to come closer. He answered her unspoken request by taking her hand in both of his as he kneeled in front of her chair.

He was still looking down at the floor. She moved her hand under his chin and gently but firmly lifted his gaze to hers. She forced him to meet her eye-to-eye.

"I will always be right here, Rhys. Always!"

A tear slipped down her cheek, and that was his breaking point.

Half pulling her into his arms and half falling into hers, he held on for dear life. A sob wracked his body.

"I love you," she whispered again and again, emphasizing every word until his wall finally crumbled.

Tears streamed down both of their faces. They held on tight.

The grief he'd held onto for so long found its way out.

"I couldn't get to them," he relived, just as he'd relived it on repeat for ten full years. "I couldn't get to them," he cried over and over again. It was a mantra he had never been able to escape.

"I know," she empathized. "I know," she kept repeating.

"I couldn't get to them." His torrent of despair was losing its force.

"That's true, Rhys, but not because you failed them. You simply could not reach what the fire had consumed. You are not to blame."

"I couldn't get to them. I tried so hard, but I couldn't get to them. I couldn't get to them," he said again, but this time with the finality and the understanding that he truly had not been able to get to them. It wasn't a lack of effort. It wasn't his fault that they had died. He physically could not have reached them to get them out of the fire.

"No, Rhys, you couldn't," Maree agreed, cradling his face with her hand and smoothing away his tears with her thumb as she caressed his cheek.

"Oh, God," he said, closing his eyes on a prayer for peace and praise for lifting this burden.

36

My destination is no longer a place,
rather a new way of seeing.
Marcel Proust

ike clockwork, Maree's surgeon arrived at three o'clock on the dot. He entered her room to find Maree and Rhys cuddled on her bed, heads huddled together, and a baseball game muted on the TV. Suzanne was hot on his trail with a tray of medical materials in hand.

"Ready to remove that IV and start the arduous process of getting out of here?" he asked, immediately piquing their interest.

"Absolutely," Maree replied, all smiles.

"Remember, homebound for a month. Anyone you need has to come to you, understood?"

"Yes, sir," she agreed.

"You'll also need lots of help these first few weeks, someone twenty-four-seven for several days. Have you made arrangements?"

"Yes," Maree and Rhys answered at the same time, eyes meeting, cheeks blushing, and both voices sounding a little shy.

"Good, good. And where will you be recuperating?"

"Together," they answered in unison.

————

For what it's worth:
it's never too late or, in my case,
too early to be whoever you want to be.
There's no time limit, stop whenever you want.
You can change or stay the same,
there are no rules to this thing.
We can make the best or the worst of it.
I hope you make the best of it.
The Curious Case of Benjamin Button
by F. Scott Fitzgerald

————

he End.

But not for long. Please enjoy this sneak peek into Book 2…

IN THE TRENCHES

*What if everything you see is more than what
you see—
the person next to you is a warrior
and the space that appears empty
is a secret door to another world?
What if something appears that shouldn't?
You either dismiss it,
or you accept that there is much
more to the world than you think.
Perhaps it is really a doorway,
and if you choose to go inside,
you'll find many unexpected things.
Shigeru Miyamoto*

Max Davenport was running.

Away from the press.

Away from social media.

Away from Mary Beth.

Max Davenport was running home.

The drive from Kansas City usually took five hours; today he'd made it in just over four. Four hours and fourteen minutes to be precise.

Usually, Max took his time to enjoy the trip. It was a gorgeous route along the western edge of the Ozarks, down into Tulsa's green country, and finally into the thick, lush terrain that gave Green Hills, Oklahoma, its name.

Today, however, he simply wanted to get there. To a place of peace and tranquility, where photographers didn't chase him, and where he could enjoy the slow pace of a small town and an empty house.

He loved his life in Kansas City — he really did.

From as far back as he could remember, he'd fantasized about playing professional football. Now he was living the dream. He was the starting tight end for one of the most successful teams in the NFL. They'd won two of the last three Super Bowls, they had a talented team with great camaraderie, and they'd managed to retain a fabulous coaching staff through the boom.

It was fun, and it was fast-paced. It was also hard work, long hours, and very intense.

On top of football practices, strength and conditioning workouts, mobility and yoga sessions, film study, game prep, and meetings, there were community service projects, media engagements, and more interviews than he could keep up with.

And there was Mary Beth.

Both being rather famous in Kansas City and both being rather active in the local social scene, Max and Mary Beth had each been aware of the other, but they'd never been introduced before. In fact, they'd never even spoken in passing.

Mary Beth was a renowned restaurateur in Kansas City, and the night they'd first *officially* met, Max had been asked to represent the Chiefs' organization by appearing at a fundraiser.

The event was being held at one of Mary Beth's incredibly popular restaurants.

Truth be told, "restaurant" was a bit of a misnomer for this particular establishment. Josephine's was a Prohibition-style supper club that featured big band music, jazz, singing, dancing, and phenomenal, American cuisine. It was a lively, happening lounge with a rich, soulful ambiance. It had great energy.

Max and Mary Beth had been seated side by side at the head table, and they'd spent the evening talking and laughing throughout an amazing seven-course meal. He was one of the best-known bachelors in town. She was young, successful, and stunningly beautiful. People noticed.

With a plethora of photographers, journalists, and gossip-mongers present, several photos were taken — both posed and candid. Whispers and speculations were running amuck by the time coffee and desserts were served.

The final piece of the night's program was a celebrity date auction.

Max avoided these things like the plague, but tonight's event was raising money and increasing education to end Alzheimer's disease, a cause near and dear to his family. Their beloved friend and pseudo-grandmother, Miss Sadie Jones, had been widowed by the fatal disease, and one of her boarders at her home, the Marshall Mansion, had made it her mission in life to serve families living with ALZ. Janie Lyn was close friends with his sister, Maree, and when he'd told them about this opportunity, they'd begged him to do it. Of course, he'd agreed.

The celebrities were being auctioned off for an evening of dinner and dancing here at Josephine's. Max was one of a handful of candidates — professional athletes, a few local news anchors, the two most popular local radio deejays, one famous author, and a half-dozen A-list actors and singers who lived in Missouri and Kansas, all eager to see to whom they would go.

The whispers about Max and Mary Beth became roars when he stepped on stage and the bidding began. With a calculating look in her eye, it was clearly evident that she intended to win. A few other ladies in the crowd jumped into the fray, raising their bidding cards for one thousand, two thousand, four thousand dollars. Then, seemingly tired of playing the game, Mary Beth stood, raised her card high in the air, and announced, "Twenty-five thousand dollars."

The room went silent. A statement had been made.

Max clapped and cheered, all the while fighting an urge to tug on his collar.

"Wow," he said, sitting back down at their table. "You've already done so much to make tonight a huge success — that was a very gracious donation."

"All for a good cause," she responded. "Besides, I feel certain you're worth it."

Again, his fingers itched to loosen the top button of his shirt. He needed air.

One of the administrators from the local Alzheimer's Association came to thank Mary Beth and congratulate Max, which allowed for an easy escape from the table. He circulated around the room, visiting with teammates and friends, dancing with a few of the players' and coaches' wives, and smiling for lots of pictures.

When the band announced their final set, Max scanned the room, looking for Mary Beth. No reason to put off the inevitable. He wasn't even sure why he was resisting.

Mary Beth was amazing. Tall, lean, and lithe, she looked like the college track star she'd been at Kansas State. Her eyes were the deepest, darkest brown, and her skin was like caramel velvet. Tonight, she had her hair out, and it was something to behold. With her shoulders back confidently and her smile dazzling the room, she resembled a royal African princess adored by all her subjects.

He could admit that while he was a little intimidated, he was also a little smitten. She was smart, accomplished, and kind. The auction date would be fun; in fact, he knew that the auction results could have turned out much, much worse.

He was actually looking forward to making plans with her when they exchanged phone numbers.

Their date had taken place that week, and they'd had a wonderful time.

The food was again fantastic, the Duke Ellington tribute band playing that evening was incredible, and their conversation had flowed easily and naturally. He'd been worried for no reason at all. Mary Beth wasn't looking for anything more than Max was wanting out of a new friendship. And that was all it needed to be: a friendship.

When he'd taken her home after their "date," Max had been relieved that there wasn't an awkward moment. Mary Beth was relaxed when she reached out to give him a brief hug and brushed a slight kiss on his cheek, thanking him for a fun date. He'd genuinely enjoyed himself and had offered to meet her for lunch whenever she had a day off. She'd said that sounded good, and he'd said, "Good night."

Max had felt great.

He'd driven to his townhouse, changed out of his suit, and let his dog, Hank, out in the back courtyard to do his thing. Everything was great.

Until he'd opened his phone.

It was lit up like the Fourth of July. He'd been tagged in numerous posts, tweets, and photos of his evening with Mary Beth. They were being touted as a "power couple" and "the face of new love." *What??*

Max felt sick.

He'd been so careful through the years, making *absolutely*

sure that he didn't — even accidentally — lead on the girls he dated. He wasn't looking for a long-term relationship. He didn't want to be half of a couple; nor did he want to be the face of any kind of love. He wanted to play football, spend time with his dog, and hang out with his family.

But the internet wasn't having any part of that.

Within a couple of days, more photos from the fundraiser surfaced. One photo gave the impression Max was whispering sweet nothings into Mary Beth's ear, when in reality, he'd turned his head around to answer a question from the waiter standing behind them. Another zoomed in to his hand on her lower back, *above* the low V of her open-back dress, while he was leading her to the table after the auction. The caption read, "A lover's touch, as soft as silk."

With each new "report," Max felt more and more hunted, exposed for something that wasn't even real.

He and Mary Beth met for that lunch. Max had hoped they could nip this thing in the bud, but it had all backfired when Mary Beth had confessed that she agreed with the paparazzi; she thought they looked great together, had fun together, and should give it a shot.

He sat dumbfounded as she chattered on about attending a tennis match together on Saturday morning, another fundraiser they should be seen at Saturday night, and brunch at Josephine's on Sunday.

"We've never even had a real date," he stammered.

"Oh, Max, we fit like a glove," she said, waving away his objection.

She was caught up in the limelight, and he couldn't breathe.

He had to get out of there.

He had to go home.

"*I never should have done that auction,*" he repeated to himself over and over as he sped toward Green Hills.

But that had not been an option. Maree might have been disappointed, and he definitely couldn't have let Janie Lyn down. The quiet, mysterious girl had been quite an asset to him since she'd arrived at Miss Sadie's last year. Besides placing her deep accent in the South, Maree didn't know where she'd come from, or even how old she was, but his sister liked and respected Janie Lyn very much.

Through her volunteer work at the local memory care facility, Janie Lyn had proven herself to be a champion of those who could no longer speak for themselves. She might look eighteen years old in her braids and thrift-shop overalls, but she had a keen mind for logistics. She'd organized several Alzheimer's awareness events in town, helped Maree with a fundraising quilt collection, and started hosting support group meetings for community members faced with the struggles of caregiving.

Not only had she made a huge impact on Green Hills, but she'd also been integral to the completion of the remodel work of Max's house there. It was a 1930s Craftsman-style home with three bedrooms, three full baths, a huge wraparound porch, a brick porte cochere, and a carriage house that would someday be turned into a detached garage with an apartment over it.

When Max had found it a few years ago, the entire property had been in bad shape. The floors had to be refinished, the masonry needed new mortar, all the appliances required replacing, and the wall coverings were atrocious. Worst of all, the hand-carved trim throughout the house — the intricate designs formed by hours and hours of skilled labor — was covered in coat after coat of thick paint, which muted its beauty and the craftsmanship that made the structure so unique.

Max did as much of the work as he could during the off-season. He loved researching a technique, learning about how the house would have originally been built, and then pairing the best of the history with all that modern life had to offer.

After stepping in to assist Maree one time when the painters needed access to the house, Janie Lyn had essentially become his project manager. No one had ever given her that title; they'd never even officially discussed that she'd take over the scheduling and tracking of contractors. It had happened organically, and Max no longer knew how he'd managed without her help.

No, he hadn't had an option. He owed Janie Lyn way too much to disappoint her by declining an opportunity to raise money for the cause she was so passionate about. He'd had no choice, and now things were totally out of control.

Hence the reason he'd run.

Max pulled into the drive, parked under the porte cochere, turned off the ignition to his truck, and let out a deep exhale. It felt good to be home.

He grabbed his bag from the back seat, unlocked the side door of the house, and opened the fridge, looking for a drink. His day turned up another notch when he saw that someone had been at the house and left an almost-full pitcher of sweet tea. He grabbed an insulated cup, filled it with ice, and poured tea to the rim. He took a long, deep drink, then refilled the tumbler and set the lid in place.

He planned to hop through the shower, grab some swim trunks, and hit his new pool. He'd helped design it last winter, but he'd not yet seen the project finished. Janie Lyn was still working with a landscape architect to finish the green spaces, but the pool was ready, and he could not wait to jump in.

Feeling refreshed from his shower, he put on the shorts, grabbed his tea and his sunglasses, and walked toward the wall of glass windows and doors looking from his living room into the backyard.

He was shocked to find someone already out there. Not just some*one*, but some woman.

She was standing on the edge of the pool with her back to the house. The one-piece swimsuit was a deep shade of orange that reminded Max of the poppies planted in the front flower beds. It looked like something straight out of an Esther Williams movie that he still remembered watching with his mom, many years ago. It was strapless and gathered and showed off a pair of strong legs, muscular shoulders, and a perfect tan. Thick dark hair hung in cascading waves down her back.

When she dove in, Max slid open the door and walked toward the pool, stunned but very interested.

She swam to the back wall and performed a precise kick turn without breaking stride. She swam to her starting point, reached for the edge of the rock coping, and hoisted herself up to the deck in one smooth motion.

"Janie Lyn?" Max was astonished. This was not the young girl who wore nothing but old t-shirts, overalls, and Chuck Taylor Converse. She was voluptuous. Grown-up. And gorgeous.

"Oh!" Her head snapped up in surprise. "Maxwell," she breathed his full name. "You're home."

ABOUT THE AUTHOR

Ashli Montgomery is a wife, a momma, and an author whose passion is sharing love stories, books, quilts, yoga, recipes, and all of her favorite things in life. She is quilting to mend the mind by spearheading a community of quilters through Quilt 2 End ALZ, Inc., a 501(c)(3) nonprofit she launched to use her quilting hobby as a platform to advocate for an end to Alzheimer's disease.

Ashli writes under the pen name Virginia'dele Smith to honor Syble Virginia Tidwell, Adele Gertrude Baylin, and Etta Jean Smith. These three cherished grandmothers were beautiful role models, teaching Ashli to love without judgment and to always put family first. Through Grandma Syble's journals and appetite for books, through Momadele's priceless cards and handwritten letters, and through many, many hours of visiting over fabric at Mema's kitchen island, Ashli also learned to treasure words.

You are invited to join Ashli in Green Hills and learn more about Virginia'dele Smith by subscribing to Ashli's newsletter, The Gazette, at AshliMontgomery.com.